LUKAS KRUEGER FICTION PRESENTS

The Ghost Ninja of HONG KONG Island

A Novel By:

LUKAS KRUEGER

For Elsie

CONTENTS

The Ghost ninja of Hong Kong Island
Copyright © Lukas Krueger 2021
Copyright © Lukaskruegerfiction 2021
lukaskruegerfiction.com

Cover Design: Stranger Than Fiction Studios
Editor: Kisa Whipkey
Interior Book Formatting: authorTree

Independently published.

CHAPTER 1

Pain awakened him.

Benny Lau had been twitching in fits for an hour, weaving in and out of consciousness as a warm, wet fluid oozed out of his nostrils.

He licked at his swollen lips, sampling the taste, wondering if the sensation of beaten flesh around his head was a figment of his imagination. In another moment, he remembered it all.

He erupted into a fit of panic when the horrific ordeal crept up on him, returning to pay visit behind his eyes.

By the time Benny Lau had arrived at the Zhang Industries warehouse, he had reached the end of the line, strategically pursued into the dead end by a tightly knit gang of psychopaths, men and women who relished the scent of death.

He peeled open a swollen eye to discover what he presumed to be his home, but he couldn't be sure. The concrete jungle and filtered neon billboards arrived in his eye as though it were a dream, softly glowing behind the tiny woven holes of the burlap sack that had been draped over his head like a sock.

Benny wanted to cry out as the neon lights of Hong Kong disappeared, his view masked suddenly by a huge, hook-shaped shadow that was headed for his face.

As the sack was removed from his head, Benny appraised the silhouette of a man standing on the deck of what appeared to be a fishing trawler of some kind. Someone who was the height of a child, yet robust, solidly built from the ground up like an immovable chunk of dense concrete.

"Dozer," he whispered to himself, recalling the man behind the brutal onslaught of feet and fists inside the Zhang Industries warehouse.

Dozer reeled the burlap sack into the shadows with a fishing pole and stowed it in a cradle.

As his senses caught up with the rest of him, Benny rolled his bloodshot eye skyward to discover he was dangling from the boom of the fishing trawler, hanging mid-air over the ocean like a piece of shark bait, his torso tightly wrapped in snakes of thick rigging rope.

"How's that water view treating ya, Benny?" asked Mr. Kile as he emerged from the shadows. He brushed aside his hair with his hand to reveal his vampire-white complexion.

"Please don't hurt me anymore," Benny moaned.

He tried to cover his face with his hands as Mr. Kile unbuttoned his coat and presented a marshalling of throwing knives strapped around his waist like bullets in a gun belt.

Dozer flicked a switch, sparking to life a network of tiny amber lights scattered throughout the framework of the trawler.

Blinking dazedly, Benny took in more of his new surroundings and found two more arrive in the twinkling lights. He gulped when the giggling voices of Mia and Kelly Kwon arrived in his ears. Together, they arrived on the starboard side and joined forces with Dozer and Mr. Kile.

"He looks like a bloodied piñata," laughed Mia Kwon.

The identical twins ran their hot pink fingernails to their lips to shield their laughter.

"Knock it off," a man ordered from the trawler galley in Cantonese.

Benny aimed his defeated eye toward the galley door as it creaked open, the new voice unmistakable to his ears.

He found none other than the concrete jungle's top mob boss on board the trawler, the Cantonese Godfather of Asia's world city, the cunning and ruthless Johnathan Zhang.

Dozer, Mr. Kile, and the Kwon sisters parted like the sea, respectfully clearing a path for Zhang, as if making way for a king.

Benny's heart hammered against the walls of his chest as Zhang cruised his way along the starboard side, his face sliced in half by the moonlight, his thinly cut eyes cold and calculating.

It suddenly dawned on Benny why he hadn't been gagged. It didn't require much thought; he knew exactly why. Zhang and his tightly knit gang of psychopaths had taken him out to sea so no one would hear his tortured screams. The way Benny saw it, he had but one option left: talk his way out.

"Oh Mr. Zhang, I was hoping that was you. There has been a terrible misunderstanding."

Saying nothing, Zhang clicked his fingers in the air and proceeded to draw a thick cigar from his jacket pocket. Dozer reacted to the clicking with lightning speed, sending a timber crate skimming across the trawler deck with the stab of a foot.

He stood on the timber and repositioned the fur coat on his boss's shoulders, flipping the collar to mask the cold.

"You know," said Zhang, pausing momentarily to light his cigar, "in ancient times, those who were announced thieves would suffer one of what was known as 'The Five Punishments.'"

The Kwon sisters giggled, cupping their hands over their mouths as Zhang continued.

"Apart from the death penalty, the remaining four punishments for thieves and slaves were designed to inflict immense pain. Sometimes, their bodies would be marked for life. Sliced off noses, lobbed off hands, tattoos, lashings, and my personal favourite: the amputation of legs."

Benny groggily glanced over to find Dozer arriving at a baiting tub. He rolled up the sleeves of his shirt and drove his iron fists into a farm of live maggots, worms, and expired fish carcases.

He started shovelling the bait overboard, flinging dead guts and blood-covered maggots into the sea beneath Benny's feet.

Benny sucked in a breath when something disturbed the water, clearly answering the summons.

"Mr. Zhang, please! I just need more time."

Zhang plucked his cigar from his teeth and pointed the fiery tip at Benny.

"You were given that money in good faith, Mr. Lau, and today, we intercept you at Hong Kong International Airport, passport in one hand and a suitcase full of our money in the other."

Benny watched Mia and Kelly Kwon proudly share matching smiles, gratified by their apprehension.

"Drop him in the sea," ordered Zhang.

Mr. Kile drew one of his throwing blades form his knife belt and cocked it behind his head.

"No, wait!" pleaded Benny. "Mr. Zhang, I have what you asked for. It is finished!"

Zhang shot his hand in the air, signalling for Mr. Kile to stand down.

Benny gulped as Zhang crept forward and snarled in the moonlight.

"There is only one way back to dry land, Mr. Lau. Where is my fucking plate?"

Benny spoke quickly, stumbling on his words as the arrival of dorsal fins sliced through the water's surface beneath his feet.

"The plate is in Stanley, Mr. Zhang, Stanley Bay."

"Where in Stanley Bay?"

Benny cringed in his straight jacket of rope, knowing all too well that if he gave Zhang everything, he would never set foot on dry land again.

Zhang impatiently tore his cigar from his mouth.

"Dozer, I want to believe him. Make me proud."

The Cantonese micromachine started to wind the winch of the trawler boom by hand, the gear teeth chinking and grinding as the pulley slowly lowered Benny toward the thrashing seawater.

Benny started up his legs, kicking wildly, as if he were riding a bike in mid-air.

"A few more turns of that winch, Mr. Lau, and tomorrow, you'll be picking out your first wheelchair."

"Stanley Market. Stanley Market!" cried Benny.

Zhang flipped up his hand for Dozer to chock the winch.

Benny jolted to stop about a meter above the water's surface, his legs tightly tucked into a ball around his chest.

Zhang cupped his hand around his ear and leaned over the starboard side.

"Did I hear Stanley Market, Mr. Lau?"

Benny sent his words racing again.

"Yes, Mr. Zhang, my uncle—he has a store there. Yuen's Engravings. Yuen's Engravings."

Zhang pulled his cigar from his teeth with a sigh.

"Imagine what happens, Mr. Lau, if the plate isn't where you say it is. Think very carefully about all we will do to you."

"It's there, Mr. Zhang. I promise. In the back of the store. He keeps all his valuable pieces in a safe that's housed in the floor. Only he knows the combination, but it's there."

"A safe in the floor, you say?"

"Yes, yes, Mr. Zhang. In the floor. In the floor."

Zhang shook his head, appearing to be at a loss.

"What am I going to do with you, Benny?"

He adjusted the fur coat on his shoulders and flicked his spent cigar in the drink.

"Can you be trusted to tell the truth now? Will you be honest and loyal from this day forward?"

Benny nodded rapidly in reply, his wide eye loaded with promise, Zhang's words providing him with a glimmer of hope that he would live to die another day.

"Oh yes, Mr. Zhang, I swear. I swear."

Mr. Kile and Dozer smiled in commentary, amused by Benny's tears and childlike whimper.

Zhang drew a fresh cigar from his jacket and clicked his fingers.

Mr. Kile flicked opened a chrome-plated gas lighter and mashed his thumb on the ignition switch.

"Dozer," said Zhang as he casually brought his new cigar to life, acting as if he had all the time in the world. He pulled the stogie from his teeth and glared at Benny through the haze of smoke.

"On second thought, I think it's time for Mr. Lau's swimming lesson."

"No, Mr. Zhang. Please!" cried Benny.

Dozer retuned to the winch and started to wind, sending the rope running through the pulley of the trawler boom.

Benny Lau kicked the South China Sea upon entry, his crazed legs sending the sharks into a bloodthirsty frenzy.

"Mr. Kile," ordered Zhang as the first set of shark jaws locked onto Benny's lower half, taxing bloodcurdling screams from his body.

Dozer choked the winch and Benny jolted to a stop suddenly, his lower half served to the ocean.

"Day after tomorrow, we head to Stanley Bay, see if we can find this uncle of his."

Mr. Kile silently nodded in salute.

He hauled the curtain of hair from his face and slid the blade back into his knife belt.

Zhang, Dozer, Mr. Kile, and the Kwon sisters all merged into a huddle, as if they were a tight-knit, loving family. Together, they stood off the shores of Hong Kong Island, witnessing Benny Lau's final agonising moments of life, equally unfazed by the blood, piss, sweat, and tears that oozed out of him.

CHAPTER 2

I f it were a film, a cinematic crossfade would have hooked us
from the disturbed, smoke-hued eyes of Johnathan Zhang,
then sent us on a journey four thousand miles east: crossing over
the South China Sea, passing through the volcanic islands of
Indonesia and into the suburb of Randwick, Sydney, Australia.
That's where Brandon Willis was when his drug dealer
found him.

He propped himself up on the steps of Trinity Community
College and discreetly eyed a sea of young men barrelling down a
hallway.

He hid himself behind a concrete pillar, his face neatly sliced
in half by the brickwork, using one eye to analyse the impeccable
pairings of blazers and ties as they headed for class.

To these private school brats, Brandon Willis was deemed
inadequate, his half-Australian, half-Cantonese bloodline met by
a wall of rejection. As far as the Brat Pack were concerned,
Brandon Willis was a ghost, a lost and battered soul rejected by
the living, aimlessly wandering the outer limits of Trinity
Community College alone.

A face in the crowd spotted Brandon hugging the brickwork.
They locked eyes and shared a nod. Brandon put on his backpack
and slipped into the student-filled corridor, moving against the
stream of oncoming students while they took turns deliberately
clipping him with their shoulders.

Brandon bobbed and weaved, staying low, slipping into the
gaps of young men as they became available, brushing off the
tirade of cowardly racial slurs, words he'd heard before, words he
chose to ignore, words that hurt.

He moved into position and plucked a fifty-dollar note from his pocket, then folded it neatly into his hand. The fifty found a new home when the hands connected at high speed to make the exchange, as did a small bag of snow-white powder.

Brandon sharply exited the corridor and found exile in an empty bathroom.

Gulping with anticipation, he opened his hand to find a saddy bag, along with a piece of folded paper he didn't feel in the exchange.

He unfolded it and read the words written in thick black text: "*Don't shoot it!*"

Undeterred, Brandon raced for a cubicle, smirking at the author's instruction, his lungs barely able to keep up with his racing breath as he locked the door.

He folded down the toilet seat and dove into his bag, pulling out his pencil case, rummaging inside like a madman, sifting through the rubble until he found it: the thin, clear shaft of a syringe.

"Hello there, my little friend," said Brandon.

He pulled an empty soda can from his bag and stabbed it with a pair of scissors, dissecting it like an aluminium frog, hacking it to pieces.

He opened the mouth of the saddy bag and strategically tapped his drug into the concaved base of the can, substituting it for the belly of a spoon.

This would be Brandon's third time running the gauntlet with the street drug known as heroin.

He had flirted with it twice before and managed to come out unscathed.

The first time, Brandon found himself on his knees, hanging on for dear life, shaking uncontrollably while he hurled chunks into a trash bin.

Throughout the sequel, Brandon was hit by an incomprehensible wave of warmth, unaware he was capable of ever feeling that much joy. In fact, he'd felt so much that he started to feel nothing at all, and that's precisely why he perused it.

For Brandon Willis, heroin was like finding that special someone who was missing from his life: a loving girl, a best friend, or perhaps a counsellor with calming motherly instincts who could soothe his aching heart.

He had found his shoulder to cry on, someone who would listen to his problems, someone who could cut out the pain with surgical precision and wrap him dearly in their arms.

Brandon gently sat the half can of snow on his trouser leg.

He pulled the orange cap from the syringe with his teeth and stabbed the needle tip into a minute cartridge of sterile water, flooding the shaft.

The water found its way into the base of the can as Brandon's trembling hand drove the plunger forward.

The calculated mixture of heroin and water started to bubble and simmer before he removed the lighter from underneath the jagged edges of the can.

Brandon took his time, strategically drawing the toxic mixture into the needle shaft, his fingertips gently retracting the plunger backward as it sucked on the vile concoction, until the needle tip made an abrupt slurping sound, like a straw draining the bottom of a milkshake.

For Brandon, that moment couldn't come fast enough.

He rolled up his sleeve, eagerly teared at the packet of an alcohol wipe with his teeth and pulled his red-and-blue striped Trinity tie from around his neck.

Brandon fed his arm inside and choked it with the Windsor knot, restricting blood flow as the needle tip hunted for a thirsty vein.

Brandon savoured the calming wave of euphoria he had expected, smiling blissfully into the tiled lines on the floor that were now overlapping, criss-crossing one another.

A new sensation arrived by way of sound. The distant echo of heeled shoes clapping on bathroom tiles met his ears, instantly snatching the blissful grin from Brandon's cheeks with a sigh. He knew who it was.

CHAPTER 3

Mr. Johnson, or "Johnno" as the students called him, had been known to stalk the bathroom walls of Trinity, soon after the bell had gone, hoping to sniff out the straggling cigarette smokers of the private all-boys College.

Johnno took to the row of cubicles, barking at an audience he wasn't sure was there, kicking white melamine doors open one by one.

"I had better not find anybody in here, gentlemen. You all know the law."

Johnno caught a glimpse of himself in the bathroom mirror, so he smiled and stopped for inspection. He smiled like a man who was proud of what he saw, a man admiring what he'd describe as perfection.

Brandon peered through the gap in the door, spying on the ex-police sergeant turned school teacher, observing his wrestler-sized framework, one that came with bulging biceps and rounded shoulders.

Johnno leaned on the basin, eyeing his chiselled features in the mirror, turning his ripped jawline left and right, admiring his clear olive skin while he whispered, "That's one damn good-looking man right there. Yes, indeed."

He caressed the sculptured lines in his short black hair and winked at himself in the glass.

Unbeknownst to Johnno, Brandon was quietly stashing away his drug paraphernalia, lifting the ceramic tile from the plumbing tank of the toilet and dropping his pencil case inside, drowning the evidence from investigative eyes.

Johnno gave himself a *"gotcha"* smile in the mirror when he heard the toilet flush behind him.

He spun around on the spot, eyes beaming in realisation when the lock on the door snapped.

Brandon quickly darted out of the cubicle, head down, attempting to leave Johnno in his wake.

"Sorry, sir," he blurted, racing for the door.

Mr. Johnson shot his arm out in front of Brandon, using it as a blockade.

"Hold it right there, Mister. You know the law."

Johnno scanned the cubicle with investigative eyes, sniffing at the air, searching for anything that felt out of place.

"What's the big hurry, eh?" he asked, turning back to Brandon.

Brandon failed to answer. Instead, opting to study the tiled floor in silence, eager to conceal the evidence of drugs in his eyes.

Johnno snarled at the silence, crossing his arms and leaning in. "Answer me, half-breed!"

"I'm late for class, sir."

"No fucking shit, you're late for class."

Johnno took his time, scanning Brandon, circling him on the spot like a shark.

"Look at me, son!"

Brandon's eyes remained low while he lethargically licked at a dried spot on his lips and fell backward.

Johnno caught him mid-flight, snatching him by the jaw, viciously redirecting his face toward his.

Johnno could easily recognise the tell-tale signs of intoxication from his days on the force; for him, it was like riding a bike, second nature.

"What are you high on, Willis? Huh, what are you on?"

Brandon remained silent, the drugs muffling Johnno's words of interrogation, as if he were talking underwater.

Johnno snapped his fingers in the air and drove a finger toward the ground. "Backpack, now. Off your shoulders, young man. On the floor. Do it now!"

Brandon carelessly slipped his bag off his shoulder and dumped it on the tiles.

Johnno crouched down and went to work, rummaging inside Brandon's pack.

"I don't know who you think you are, Mr. Willis, but the same rules apply to everyone. You know the law."

Johnno sighed when his search came up empty. He raced the zipper closed and returned to his favoured position: towering over the five-foot-eight students of Trinity, belittling and intimidating whenever he saw fit.

He analysed Brandon further, coming up with creative ways to antagonise.

"You think you can make up your own rules, huh?" Johnno started to walk Brandon backward into the wall. "Huh? Mr. Badass!"

He eyed Brandon's unkempt presentation and ordered him to address it.

"Straighten up that tie."

Brandon reluctantly did as he was told. He pinched his Windsor knot and drove it toward his Adam's apple, working overtime to conceal his anger inside.

Johnno waited until Brandon's hands returned to his sides before giving the next order: "Shirt, too."

Brandon blew out a breath, then tucked in his shirt while Johnno continued. "You think you're special?"

Brandon shrugged in reply.

It wasn't that he was intimidated by Johnno, he was just sick to death of hearing the annoying voice that was fucking with his high.

"I asked you a question, zipper head!" Johnno pressed his palm on the tiled wall and got in Brandon's face. The racial slur failed to have the desired effect he'd hoped for, so he dug a little deeper.

"What, you think that because you recently lost a loved one, it's gonna get you a fucking free lunch around here or something?"

Brandon slowly turned his head toward Johnson and delivered a voiceless message with his eyes: "*Fuck off.*"

He watched Johnno smile cunningly, taunting to spark a physical conflict. "You can drop the thousand-yard stare. I've seen it all before, tough guy. This whole fuck-the-world act doesn't get my dick hard, Willis."

Brandon let out the built-up tension in his chest, failing to realise he'd stopped breathing a few words ago, or that his hand had curled into a fist all by itself.

Johnno smirked as he studied the anger on Brandon's face, captivated by his infuriation.

"Maybe I'll get your mum over to my place tonight to work me over. I bet she's real lonely, given that your old man has checked out." He licked his lips at Brandon, his eyebrows jumping with joy. "You know I just can't get enough of those one-eight-hundred Asian whores."

Before Brandon knew what had happened, he had grabbed onto Johnno's cotton vest and delivered a headbutt to the bridge of his nose.

Johnno stumbled backward, his face in his hands as Brandon gave chase.

He pushed off the wall and made a lightning-fast shoot for Johnno's legs, performing a takedown, using his explosive rage to upend the much bigger Johnno and spear him head first into the tiled floor of the bathroom.

The pair crashed to the ground as one before Brandon went to work.

He scrambled on top of Johnno and bombarded his face with a series of left- and right-hand punches and hooks until he lost consciousness.

CHAPTER 4

B randon found himself on a wooden chair outside Headmaster Jones's office, heroin still lingering in his blood, regretfully examining the bruises across the bridge of his bloodied knuckles.

He stretched out his hand, looking at the speckled dots of Johnno's blood when the floor started to shift, breaking apart without warning and releasing broken chunks of concrete into a non-existing atmosphere, as if some distant platform hoisted high in the sky was on the brink of collapse.

A door fired open at the end of the corridor, the individual almost tearing the door from its hinges, the tremendous crash of timber and wall hauling Brandon from his dream-like state, delivering him back to the here and now.

Great. Here we go again. Brandon sighed.

He squeezed his eyes shut and shied away, anticipating a venomous, cursing tirade in Cantonese, one that would go unchecked from the Western ears inside the Trinity Administration building.

He feared Lena Willis would arrive in anger, eager to play the role of a furious educator on top of outraged mother after receiving word mid-lecture.

Brandon took a sideways glance, watching as she stalked down the hall. Something inside the professor changed during her long, angry strides. He watched as the fierce anger in her eyes subsided, the sight of blood on his Trinity blazer obviously more than enough to dump the furious educator/mum and turn her into just a concerned mother.

Brandon sighed, slumping in shame as Lena slowed to a stop

and leaned down to tenderly wipe a speckle of blood from his chin.

"Jesus, Brandon," she whispered.

He closed his eyes, welcoming the tender feel of her hand as an office door opened in front of them.

Headmaster Jones closed the buttons on his jacket and stood in the doorway, almost filling it up.

"Please stay in your seat, Brandon. Your mother and I need to talk."

Jones nodded in appreciation when one of the Trinity nurses arrived with a warm smile, delivering a damp cloth to Brandon for the speckled blood that was stuck to his skin like paint.

"I'm sorry, Lena," Jones apologised as he closed his office door. "Feels like I'm dragging you down here every five minutes of late."

He retrieved an inch-thick manila folder from a filing cabinet and positioned it on his desk. "Please have a seat."

Lena took the chair opposite and eyed Brandon through the slits in the office blinds, watching him strategically wipe blood from his battered hands.

"This is unbelievable," sighed Lena, shaking her head.

Jones interlocked his fingers on Brandon's folder and spoke softly.

"Third time this month I've had him in here for fighting."

Lena regretfully nodded as she concurred with the statistic.

"His temper is way out of control," said Jones. "I think it's obvious he's still having trouble adjusting since . . ."

Jones trailed off, reluctant to complete his sentence.

Lena did it for him. "Since his father passed?"

Jones bunched his lips together and eyed his desk with a remorseful nod.

"It's okay, Jonesy. You can say it. It's been nine months."

Lena plucked a tissue from the box on the desk, preparing for the gathering of tears she expected to arrive, but didn't. "Who was the lucky recipient this time?" asked Lena, referring to Brandon's latest bout.

"Mr. Johnson."

Lena shook her head in disbelief and closed her eyes. *The rearranging of students must have grown old*, she thought. *He's decided to move on to teachers to spice things up.*

"Is he all, right?" she asked.

Jones flipped the lid of Brandon's folder and read Johnno's medical assessment.

"He shattered Johnson's left cheekbone, dislocated his nose, and gave him a nasty row of stitches under his right eye." The tissue Lena had hoped to toss in the bin unused found a misty eye as Jones continued. "It took Mr. Stonecipher, along with three other students, to pry him from Mr. Johnson."

Jones frowned, appearing to be at a loss.

"He's on a dangerous path, Lena, and next time, the recipient might not be so lucky."

Lena dabbed at one of her eyes as Jones took his turn eyeing Brandon through the blinds.

"Lena do respect my judgement?"

"Yes, of course."

Jones moved around his desk, crouching by Lena's side.

"Your son is harbouring an awful lot of rage at the moment, and his anger is dangerously fused with his fighting ability." Jones shook his head, alarmed concern in his eyes. "It's a lethal combination, and it could easily become a deadly one."

"He's just a boy, without a father."

Jones offered Lena the box of tissues from his desk and she took another.

"Are you sure you still want to go through with your plans?" he asked.

"We leave tomorrow."

"Are you sure it's a good idea? A new country, along with everything else? Are you sure he's—"

Lena interjected. "Jonesy, he's been through hell these past nine months. He needs a fresh start. We both do."

"I understand," Jones said, nodding. He stood and returned to his seat. He closed the folder and placed his hands on top, as if burying a secret.

"Well, there is no need to worry about any legal implications," he said, returning to the business at hand. "We have spoken to Mr. Johnson about the delicate nature of Brandon's situation and he has agreed to allow us to manage this in-house. New South Wales Police won't be involved in any way, shape, or form for now. We consider this to be a private matter, a Trinity matter."

Lena sat back in her chair, relieved beyond words. "Thank you, Jones."

He drummed his fingers on the folder, then leaned forward to whisper. "Quite frankly, Johnno has been pushing a lot of buttons around here for far too long. Perhaps he received what was well overdue."

Before Jones could finish, a bitter laugh escaped Lena's lips.

"The school nurse said she'd never seen a grown man cry like that before." Jones laughed.

"Student: one, cowardly narcissist: nil." He pushed out his chair, buttoned his jacket, and headed for Lena with open arms.

"One final laugh for the road, Mrs. Willis?"

Lena wiped her eyes and stood with a warm smile.

"Thanks for everything, Jonesy."

"Don't mention it. The Australian International College of Hong Kong will be lucky to have you. Good luck, Lena."

CHAPTER 5

T he entrance doors of the Trinity Administration building blasted open like they had been kicked.

"Jesus Christ, Brandon," shouted Lena over a college bell. "Talk about going out in style! When are you going to learn that you can't solve every problem with your fists?"

Brandon shifted gears in an attempt to keep up with his mother's quickening pace.

"We'll be lucky if Johnson doesn't try to sue," said Lena as Brandon arrived by her side.

"Are you serious? Fuck that prick!"

"Mind your tongue!" scowled Lena in Cantonese.

"Okay, listen. Trust me, Mum. If you were there, you would have reacted exactly the same way."

"Really? Hmmm, let me think about that. I would have executed a UFC style takedown on one of my colleagues, driven them head-first into a tiled floor, and punched them senseless until they lost consciousness?" Lena raised her eyebrows and flashed Brandon a look a scepticism. "I don't think so, Brandon."

She pulled the keys to her Mercedes Kompressor from her purse and stabbed at the button until its lights blinked.

"Consider yourself lucky you're not spending the next year in juvenile detention."

Brandon groaned. He didn't want to admit it, but he knew she was right. She usually was.

He looked skyward, blew out a breath, and pulled on the passenger-side door handle. He rubbed at his hands in the passenger seat, observing the black and blue evidence that had started to form under the skin. Lena inconspicuously glanced over and examined the bruising across her son's knuckles as she wheeled the Kompressor out of the Trinity carpark. Somewhere between the outskirts of Randwick and the central CDB, she felt her anger subside.

They had left Trinity College in their rear-view mirror and were now drafting their next chapter as mother and son. There was no need to hold on to what would soon be lost to the past. She eyed the road ahead, able now to think clearly, calmly putting all the pieces together.

She remembered what Jonesy had said regarding the rearrangement of Mr. Johnson's face, and how it may have been overdue. She revisited the times in her mind when she herself had encountered Johnson and his toxic, bullying nature. Those memories made her realise that for Brandon to react the way he did, he must have felt truly threatened. Despite his recent outbursts, he'd never been the one to initiate, only to defend.

Lena glanced over to find Brandon frowning at the shark-shaped fins of the Sydney Opera house.

"Stop looking at me," he said.

Lena sighed, already regretting the verbal spray she'd given her son.

She gripped the steering wheel and smiled as it dawned on her how to lighten the mood.

"The nurse at Trinity said Johnno cried like a little bitch after you served him one of your signature punch combinations."

Brandon snapped his eyes to Lena to find her lips bunched together, working overtime to seal an outburst of laughter. "Made his arse pucker up to the size of a decimal point," she said.

Brandon's glare faded away when he found laughter in his mother's eyes.

"Of course, he did!" said Brandon. "Everyone knows the insides of bullying narcissists are made of nothing but mush, the cowards."

The afternoon sun flickered on Brandon and Lena's faces as

the Kompressor skimmed past the steel arches of Sydney Harbour Bridge.

"Brandon, I know this year has been more than a little tough, but things will get better." Lena reached across and affectionately ran her fingers through the back of Brandon's blonde hair.

"Tomorrow is a new chapter, a fresh start."

Brandon chimed in, playfully rolling his eyes and mimicking the words Lena had had stuck on repeat for over a month now.

"A new beginning for us both," they said together.

"Things will turn around, you'll see. I'll be teaching part time at this new school. It's a good place for you to complete your final year, and I get to spend more time with my favourite guy."

Brandon may have pretended to smile woefully, but deep down, he was glad to hear it.

When the Kompressor pulled up at the Willis home, Brandon got out and headed for the door.

"Finish packing please, Brandon," yelled Lena. "I'll get us something yummy for dinner. You cool with pizza? All the dishes are packed."

"Yeah, fine. Whatever," replied Brandon. He weaved through a small army of uniformed removalists who were busy packing the Willis home into assorted boxes.

He leaped up the stairs and arrived at the entrance of his bedroom, discovering columns of storage boxes that were marked in thick black text: *"Brandon's room."*

Brandon peeled his backpack from his shoulder and observed a removalist approaching a timber shelf that was littered with framed family pictures. He reached out to collect one.

"It's okay," said Brandon "Leave those to me."

The removalist lowered his arm mid-flight, dropped a box on the floor, and then left the room.

Brandon approached the shelf and reached for one of the frames, taking his time, hesitant to touch it.

He found his own reflection in the glass before adjusting his eyes to find the sixteen-year-old version of himself in the picture, standing arm-in-arm with his father, Eric Willis.

"One, two, one-two. Harder! Faster!" Eric ordered.

Brandon's bare feet quickly carried him around the dojo mat, thundering his fists into the punching pads held by his father.

He worked his fingers to the bone, ignoring the pain, his arms as heavy as lead.

"Ten seconds, Brandon. Harder, faster!"

Despite the exhaustion, Brandon spent the final ten seconds delivering freakishly accurate combos to his father's hands. Hook, hook, hook, uppercut, overhand right, straight-hand right, finishing with a lightning-fast roundhouse kick.

"Time," Eric shouted as a buzzer sounded.

Brandon hoisted his gloves on top of his head to open his lungs, heaving in breath, drenched in sweat.

Eric laughed in approval, wondered by Brandon's lightning speed and raw strength.

"Wow, check out that power, hey?" Eric tore his hands from the pads and shook the stinging sensation from his palms.

"You think I'm ready to be graded?" asked Brandon as he straightened his gee and tightened his brown belt.

"Absolutely."

Brandon's eyes beamed in surprise. "Seriously?"

"Yeah, no doubt." Eric shook his hands again, playfully pretending to be in torturous pain.

"Got a little a snap in those punches, haven't ya?"

Eric put his arm around Brandon and guided him toward the end of the mat.

"Better watch your back, old man."

Brandon dropped toward the ground and tried to take his father's legs from under him.

Eric blocked Brandon's playful attack and placed him in a headlock with ease.

"You're going to be a great one, kiddo."

Brandon felt the triggering demons of grief and despair return. As he placed the frame back on the shelf, he suddenly found himself calculating a return to Trinity, envisioning himself scaling the front gates of the school under the dark of night, skimming along the empty corridor walls, using its shadows to evade late-night eyes.

He'd slip into the toilet cubicle and flip the tank tile where he'd hidden his *friend*, the one who would welcome him with open arms and soothe his heavy heart.

Lena's words inexpediently echoed through his head as he fantasised about the blanketing warmth of heroin wrapping around him.

"Tomorrow is a new beginning . . ."

Brandon leaned against his bedroom wall and recalled the tragic tales of heroin users, how their reason to live had become their reason to die.

He pondered how he was still inside what was known as the flirting phase: a recreational taste-test with a get-out clause, someone who'd still be able to walk away before the drug dug it hooks in.

Brandon's dreamlike gaze faded from his eyes and travelled back to the picture frame on the shelf. He looked deep into his father's eyes and sighed as a sensation of disgust and guilt over-whelmed his desire for heroin.

Brandon respectfully repositioned the frame and looked at Eric.

"You were the great one."

CHAPTER 6

T he kangaroo-decaled airliner drifted through the clouds of the South China Sea, hauling rows upon rows of passengers who sat transfixed by tiny screens housed in the backs of headrests.

Lena sipped on a vodka lime soda as she watched a giant cyborg covered in living tissue stab a blade into its arm.

The machine-like man drew a straight line with the tip of the blade from its elbow to its wrist, opening up the skin. A terrified husband and wife watched on in horror, desperately clinging to one another as the mammoth cyborg tore a glove of living tissue from its forearm without pain.

The cyborg casually worked the functions of its endoskeleton limb, slowly opening and closing its silver fingers before curling them into a fist.

The sight of blood-stained metal was enough to haul Lena's eyes away from the screen. She veered off momentarily and found Brandon finger-picking at the fibreglass wall that held his passenger window.

She raked her headphones from her ears and noticed the blank screen in front of his face.

"Nothing good on?"

Brandon shrugged. "Meh. I've seen everything they've got."

Lena watched Brandon investigate the drifting clouds through the oval of Perspex when she suddenly remembered her purchase from the Airport Newsagency.

She flicked the buckle on her seat belt, rose up toward the overhead compartment, and unzipped her backpack.

Brandon turned toward Lena's rummaging and found a book coming his way.

"A book?" Brandon said, surprised.

"Yeah." She placed the book in Brandon's hands and returned to her seat.

"You guys have your heads buried in way too much technology nowadays. I thought you might dig it."

Brandon found a young Cantonese woman on the cover, dressed in a scarlet-coloured satin robe with white-laced, frog button fasteners. He made the assumption that she might be a Tai Chi practitioner, until he found the book title beneath her feet: *"The Six Forms of Wing Chun."*

Brandon gasped at the woman's beauty, admiring her olive skin and deep amber eyes that instantly sparked an attraction. But upon closer inspection, he found something even more powerful, something more worthwhile.

He absorbed the raw intensity and focus in the young woman's eyes. He could feel the power and ferocity oozing from her threatening fighting stance.

He opened the cover and ran his fingertips over chapter titles that were written in calligraphy in both English and Cantonese.

Lena observed Brandon's infatuation with the book and smiled, easily spotting how captivated he was by the artistic swirls in the text, along with the strength of the Wing Chun practitioner on the cover.

"Wing Chun is one of the youngest and most contemporary styles of Kung Fu," said Lena.

She crossed her legs and leaned over as Brandon turned the pages.

"This isn't going to turn into one of your harrowing history lectures, is it, mum?"

Lena smiled. "It might," she said.

Brandon groaned, but she could tell he was interested. Happy for the opportunity to connect with her son, Lena took the bait.

"Over 300 years of existence, founded during the Qing Dynasty around 1700 by a Buddhist nun."

"A nun?" Brandon looked up in surprise. "As in a girl, right?"

Lena nodded. "Ng Mui. One of the top five fighters of her time."

Brandon ran his eyes over the pages of drawn sketches, following a series of hand- and foot-fighting techniques as Lena continued.

"Legend has it, she found her inspiration after witnessing a fight between a stork and a large rodent." Brandon smiled awkwardly as Lena used her hands in front of her face to mimic the confrontation.

"The stork was able to repel the rodent's attacks by using its wings and legs to both attack and defend. Ng Mui named her new style: Wing Chun. Translated as 'everlasting springtime.'"

Lena handed her empty cup to a passing flight attendant, then drove her chair back with a yawn. She pulled a blanket up to her neck and flicked off her overhead light.

Brandon found a photograph of Bruce Lee in the middle pages of the book, his trademark frame slim and shredded, as if his body had been carved from a block of stone.

In the photo, Bruce was clenching his fists so tightly it was as if his knuckles were about to burst through the skin of his hands.

"Mum, Bruce Lee was Cantonese like you, yeah?"

"Yes. Like you, too."

Brandon thought about his response and eyed Bruce's filmography in the wings on the page.

"Was it his Wing Chun ability that made him such a big deal in Hong Kong?"

Lena's eyes softly drifted open, more than fine with resisting the urge to sleep to make sure she gave an answer that did Bruce justice.

"Bruce was a legend for the people of Hong Kong. Sure, he was an actor, director, and martial artist. But I remember him as someone who fused the cultures between the East and West."

Brandon turned the page and found another photo of Bruce,

this one with a painted dragon woven around him as he stood in a fighting stance. Underneath, was an inscription: *"Founder of Jeet Kune Do."*

"What's Jeet Kune Do?" He looked at Lena, eager for her to elaborate.

"It's the martial art style created by Bruce Lee," replied Lena with a tired, raspy voice.

"What's it like, though?"

Lena closed her eyes and adjusted the blanket around her neck. "Maybe in the morning, we'll learn about it together."

Lena softy tapped at the pages of the book with her fingertips and then rolled her head away in the headrest.

Brandon's eyes retuned to the pages. He recited one of the many passages under the photo of Bruce.

"'A fighting system developed by fusing different aspects of other systems together'?" Brandon's questioning eyes retuned to Lena. "That sounds strange."

Lena's eyes drifted open again.

"Jeet Kune Do showed people it was okay to break the rules and walk outside the lines, that the art was all that mattered. It was that type of free-thinking philosophy that bought your father and I together. If it wasn't for people like Bruce, we may never have met."

Brandon's eyes fell into a dreamlike state and suddenly, he felt a great sense of calm. For the first time, he felt free of the cruel, cowardly racial slurs of Trinity's corridors and considered himself unique.

He slipped his boarding pass into the book, using it as a bookmark, and turned it over to find the author info on the back.

It was the same Cantonese practitioner from the cover, but this time, she was standing at the gates of a Wing Chun school. *"White Crane Wing Chun."* He studied the oblong-shaped sign filled with Cantonese characters and spotted a circular drawing of a defending crane doing battle with an attacking snake—the trademark symbol of White Crane Wing Chun.

He ran his finger across the woman's name in the photo and whispered it aloud: "Elizabeth Chan."

Sunlight from the South China Sea flickered in Brandon's eyes through his passenger window.

He peered outside to find the sun stabbing its rays through clusters of fluffy white clouds.

There, he envisioned a giant-sized version of Elizabeth Chan drifting in slow motion, gracefully showcasing her hand- and foot-fighting techniques through the clouds, bobbing and weaving, pretending the drifting clouds were striking attackers.

Brandon may have been drawn in by her beauty, but he found himself captivated by her undeniable spirit and beating heart.

CHAPTER 7

Police Inspector Kaiden Chan screwed up his face at the morning sun when it found him hiding behind a 7-Eleven convenient store. He turned his back on the beacon of light, flipped the collar of his beer-stained trench coat and contentedly swigged on a piss-warm bottle of Heineken.

He set off, stumbling and staggering his way through a wave of drunken tourists, listening to the clinking of beer glasses and fast thump of Rock 'n' Roll that was Lockhart Road, not that he knew where he was.

Kaiden sat his bottled beer on an electricity meter box and retrieved a tattered soft pack of Chesterfields from his coat. He patted down his pockets in search of his lighter, but failed to find one.

He fed a bent smoke to his lips and shot out his arm at the speed of light, plucking a lit cigarette from a passing tourist's hand.

The tourist stood dumbfounded; his hand frozen in action in front his lips as he watched the swaying stranger use the smoke to light his own.

The tourist silently grimaced and stepped back when he observed the unkempt state of the man who resembled anything but a police inspector. To the stranger's eyes, he looked more like a homeless man that had just crawled out of a dumpster to beg for change.

The tourist snatched back his smoke from Kaiden's hand. He swore under his breath and shook his head in disgust before going about his day.

A suggestion of sleep bled into Kaiden's beer-soaked mind

when the Chesterfield taxed the tiny pockets of oxygen meant for his brain. His tired eyes began to flicker and drift to a close when the erratic tinkering sound from a nearby pedestrian crossing jolted him awake.

He lifted his sleepy head to find steam jetting from a noodle stand behind a steady flow of identical red-and-white striped taxis, and with that visual, he suddenly knew where he was: Wan Chai, the red-light district of Hong Kong Island. Listening to the sounds of his stomach, Kaiden made his way toward the stand, forcing the taxis to screech to a halt as he stepped off the curb and staggered through the intersection.

"Here," said the noodle chef as the inspector fell onto a barstool at the stand. He poured Kaiden a much-needed cup of coffee and snatched the bottle of beer from his mouth mid-sip, tossing it in the trash.

"There's enough caffeine in this brew to kill an elephant. You look like you need it."

The chef tossed a tea towel over his shoulder and silently observed Kaiden's struggle to raise the cup to his lips. "Late night again, Inspector Chan?"

"Busy night at the precinct."

The chef laughed. "At the precinct? Tell me, when did Hong Kong Police start running operations from all-night bars of Wan Chai?"

The chef twisted a tiny mountain of wheat noodles into a bowl and stabbed two
chop-sticks inside.

"Order up."

Kaiden plucked the chopsticks from his noodles as a tinkling sound emanated from his clothing. Annoyed, he jerked his dated flip phone from his coat and flicked it open.

"Kaiden Chan."

The voice on the other end failed to identify itself, but after the first few words, Kaiden knew who it was: fellow police inspector, Lindsey Chow.

"Call came over the radio over an hour ago Kaiden. Superintendent is going to have a litter of kittens if you don't respond soon! Where the hell are you this time?"

Kaiden slurped on his noodles and blew out a cloud of steam from his mouth. "I'll give you two guesses, but you'll only need one."

Kaiden smiled, picturing Chow shaking his head on the other end of the line.

"Yeah, well, I guessed right. Wan Chai! So, I took the liberty of arranging some transport for you."

Kaiden paused during the next load of noodles as he felt a presence arrive behind him. He spun on his stool to find two uniformed officers silently standing to attention, their hands neatly pinned behind their backs as if they belonged to a military unit.

Unfazed, Kaiden sipped on his coffee, then spun back toward the stand.

Its possible Chow may well have been shaking his head on the other end of the line, just as Kaiden had envisioned, and if that were true, then there was now a good chance he was smiling from ear to ear.

"We found the remains of someone that comes in two parts now," said Chow. "Your little friend Benny was found on a fishing trawler that ran aground early this morning inside Junk Bay."

Kaiden breathed voicelessly into the mouth piece, then used a napkin to wipe his mouth.

"Benny Lau?"

"Yeah, and unfortunately for Benny, someone thought he'd be better off without the use of his legs." Kaiden heard Chow gasp before he spoke again. "You gotta see this, partner."

Without warning, Kaiden stabbed the chopsticks into his half-eaten noodles. He folded a fifty-dollar bill in his hand and slid it under the bowl. "See you in twenty."

Kaiden clapped his phone shut and left the noodle stand, the uniformed cops hot on his tail.

CHAPTER 8

The wheels of the Airbus A330 scorched the tarmac and puffed clouds of grey smoke as it landed, pulling in to its assigned terminal at Hong Kong International Airport.

Lena and Brandon collected their carry-ons from their overhead compartment and began the dreaded journey toward the endless lines of Immigration.

They pocketed their passports and arrival cards, then found themselves at carousel number seven, waiting beside a train of moving bags.

Lena turned toward Brandon and observed a yawn escaping his mouth.

"Tired?"

"Wrecked."

"Maybe a little market shopping will cheer you up?"

Brandon rolled his eyes, then lunged at their moving bags.

"Hey, come on," begged Lena as they exited the airport terminal. "Stanley Market is perfect place to unwind after a long trip."

"Sounds boring, and you sound like one of those cheesy tourism commercials. Forget it."

They pushed their luggage carts toward an ailing red-and-white Toyota Crown that sat curb side with its trunk gaping open, its Hong Kong skin witness to lengthy bouts of traffic wear and tear.

"Shoes, jewellery, gadgets," said Lena. "Right on the beach, breathtaking views."

"Shotgun."

Brandon quickly slipped into the front passenger seat and closed the door to place Lena on mute.

Lena hopped in the back just as quick, sitting directly behind him, vowing to not give up without a fight.

Brandon studied the Fu Manchu moustache and satin bucket hat of the taxi driver as he took a hold of the wheel and pecked at the meter.

"So, where to?" he asked, his thin, friendly eyes running together as he smiled.

"We're going to—" Brandon started, but Lena raced forward, propping up her elbows on the bench seat to interject.

"If we go shopping at Stanley, I'll let you have a beer with lunch."

Brandon turned back to Lena, her suggestion almost ripping his eyes from their moorings.

"We're in Hong Kong now," assured Lena with a wink. "It's a little more relaxed over here."

Brandon turned to the driver and found him smiling even wider now, nodding rapidly in agreement with his mother.

Brandon uttered two words, finishing his earlier statement: "Stanley Market."

CHAPTER 9

Inspector Chan moved with purpose, flicking away the butt of a spent Chesterfield as he entered the galley of the Police Harbour Vessel.

He approached the mammoth dashboard control panel and parked himself beside the uniformed officer who was steering the boat with one hand, eyeing the scene ahead through a pair of binoculars with the other. Kaiden plucked the binoculars from the driver's grasp and ran the lenses to his eyes.

He made out a dozen or so uniformed officers making their way through a cluster of police vehicles, carrying forensics kits and sealing off the wharf entry point with yellow banner tape.

Kaiden panned the lenses like a movie camera and found the fishing trawler run aground, tilted on its side, its bow nestled on a bed of rock with her stern dipped in the waters of Junk Bay.

The uniformed cops on board the trawler watched on as the Police Harbour Vessel approached. Handing the binoculars back to the irritated officer, Kaiden exited the galley and took position on the starboard side rail, while the engines gurgled seawater and hauled the vessel to a stop.

When they were close enough, Kaiden leaped through the air, landing on the deck of the fishing trawler with a *thud*. Calm and commanding, he walked the deck, ignoring the eyes that followed him, leaving little doubt who was in charge of this scene.

"Glad you could join us," said Lindsey Chow.

"Yeah, traffic was hell."

Kaiden drew a fresh Chesterfield from his soft pack and stuck it in his mouth.

"Man, I thought I looked bad," said Kaiden. He inspected the reddened glaze in Chow's eyes.

"Been up with your kid all night again?"

"Yeah." Chow stretched out his back and turned sideways. "Feels like I'm destined to spend the rest of my days sleeping in hospital visiting chairs, but I wouldn't have it any other way. At least I get to be there with him."

Kaiden watched Chow as he sat on the starboard railing of the trawler and rubbed at his eyes.

"What do the doctor's say?"

Chow let out a breath and stared at Kaiden for a handful of seconds.

"The cancer is back."

Gutted for his partner, Kaiden closed his eyes and rubbed at his forehead. He pictured the sweet, smiling face of Lei Chow, then silently cursed the name of God.

He looked around Junk Bay, struggling to put together a collection of words that would be of comfort. At a loss, he decided the best course was to change the station, eager to curb the sorrow in Chow's mind.

"Come on, partner," he said suddenly. He took Chow's arm and bought him back to his feet. "Let's get back on the clock. Time to go to work."

They made their way across the deck while Kaiden observed the men and women of the forensics team, housed in snow-white hazmat suits, dusting the time-worn timbers of the trawler for prints and shooting the scene with huge forensic camera lenses.

Kaiden eyed the trawler boom overhead that was sticking out from the starboard side. He studied its rusted, dilapidated framework all the way to the tip, where he found a frayed piece of rope dangling from a pulley.

Chow cleared his throat in a bid for Kaiden's attention.

"In a minute," replied Kaiden with a wave of his hand. "I'm thinking"

He thought about lighting his Chesterfield when he found Chow squatting on the deck beside a blue tarp covering something—or perhaps, someone.

Kaiden reneged mid-light and pinned the Chesterfield behind his ear.

"Wanna do the honours?" asked Kaiden. He lowered toward the tarp and hung his wrists over his knees.

Chow peeled back the tarp and unveiled Benny's pasty, blood-splattered face.

The officers scoffed in sync and ran their gloved hands to their mouths when two tiny mud crabs raced out of Benny's gaping mouth, scurrying across his dead cheeks.

Chow kept going. He rolled the tarp down further and revealed the space where Benny's legs used to be, the visual bringing one uniformed officer to his knees, crash landing on all fours to shower the deck with his vomit.

"Can someone get this virgin off the crime scene, please?" ordered Chow.

An unfazed Kaiden kept his eyes on the prize, analysing Benny's paper-white skin, along with the remains of his torn legs.

"Well, that's Benny all right. I wonder what the little pest did this time to find himself in this much trouble?"

"Gambling debt?" asked Chow as he hauled his tie to his mouth to mask the smell of blood, fish, and piss.

Kaiden reached across and lifted Chow's pen from his jacket pocket without invitation. He rifled through the legs of Benny's torn silk trousers with the tip of the pen, investigating the wounds.

"Forensics say the wounds are unmistakably consistent with shark bites," said Chow. "Turned Benny into a Cantonese Lieutenant Dan."

Kaiden hauled the tarp back up, covering Benny, and proceeded to scan the deck, searching for clues, his eyes fiercely focused.

He plucked a pair of forensics gloves from the back pocket of a uniformed cop without request and moved toward a small pocket of water that formed a puddle in the corner of the trawler deck.

He tapped on the bobbing, obliterated remains of a tobacco stalk and realised it was the butt of a cigar.

He immediately flicked through a series of identities inside his mind, attempting to attach a name or street profile to a possible owner, no matter how slim the possibility of establishing a connection.

"This all seems a little excessive for our little pal Benny, don't you think?" said Kaiden.

Chow looked around the deck. He shrugged and drove his questioning eyes back to Kaiden. "Yeah, maybe a little."

"I'm guessing the trawler was stolen?"

Chow flipped the lid to his notepad and ran his eyes over his notes. "Trawler was boosted from Aberdeen Harbour two days ago, belongs to Red Dragon Fisheries."

"So, who would go to the trouble to steal a fishing trawler, have a gang of sharks tear Benny Lau's legs from his body, and then run it aground for the world to see?"

Chow tucked his notepad away and placed his hands on his hips.

"Okay, partner, I'll bite. Who?"

Kaiden flicked away the soaked remains of torn tobacco leaves and wiped a thick residue from the faded emblem on the cigar butt. It read: *"Punch Cigars."*

He quickly turned to Chow, his eyes beaming in realisation.

"Someone who wanted to send a message." Kaiden tore an evidence bag from the hands of a forensics officer and dropped the cigar butt inside. He sealed it, handed the bag to Chow, and pulled the stashed Chesterfield from behind his ear. "Johnathan Zhang."

Kaiden rested on the portside rail and peeled off his gloves to light his smoke.

"You don't go through all this trouble unless it serves a purpose," said Kaiden as cigarette smoke trailed from his nostrils. "Not unless you want to send a message. A very public and brutal message."

"Okay, so what kind of message?"

Kaiden didn't answer. He studied the cherry of his burning cigarette as the idea of sleep derailed his train of thought.

"Ah, Superintendent said it's up to us to notify the next of kin," said Chow.

Chow waved his hands in front of Kaiden's sleepy eyes to see if he wanted the gig. "Earth to Kaiden. Come in, Kaiden."

He come too with a shake of the head. "I know Benny's uncle. He has a small market stall at Stanley Bay. I'll drop the bombshell."

"Okay, you give him the good news, and I'll finish up here."

Kaiden flicked his half-smoked stick of tobacco overboard as he disembarked the trawler, finding the concrete wharf under his feet.

"Wait—hey, Kaiden. Suppose this was Johnathan Zhang."

"It was," Kaiden replied immediately.

"Okay, it was then. What was his message?"

Kaiden trudged up the wharf as the wind flapped the tail of his trench coat.

He replied without turning back. "Steal and you'll be disfigured."

Kaiden jumped in driver's seat of an idling squad car that wasn't his. He closed the door, threw it in gear, and left clouds of dust and gravel in his wake.

CHAPTER 10

As far as road vehicles were concerned, Zhang's 1958 Fleetwood Cadillac was fit for a Bond villain: a merciless, threatening sight, with pitch-black paint, obscured windows, and custom chrome, cylinder-shaped exhausts that looked like flamethrowers.

Mr. Kile steered the charging beast through the hills of Hong Kong Island, its V8 engine roaring and weaving through the dawdling traffic, Johnathan Zhang riding shotgun. Dozer, Mia, and Kelly Kwon were in the backseat.

Zhang flipped the lid of his alligator-skin cigar box and selected one of the many torpedo-shaped beauties inside. He ran the tobacco-leafed curvatures under his nose and nodded in approval, savouring the strong aroma of rum and wine.

When the car's cigarette lighter popped, he placed the butt between his teeth and let Mr. Kile press the searing coil into the tip of the cigar, enabling him to puff it to life.

Mr. Kile thought about who was in the back seat as he changed lanes, glancing in the rear-view mirror to find a long-faced Dozer tightly wedged between the Kwon sisters, who were busily popping bubbles of chewing gum.

Mr. Kile smiled as he observed the trio in the back seat, thinking that if not for Dozer's thin black moustache and shaved receding hairline, a stranger's eye may have mistaken the Cantonese micromachine for the twins' adopted dwarf or some special needs man child that was in Mia and Kelly Kwon's care for the weekend.

Amused, he twisted the nob of the old-school Fleetwood radio and surfed the airways, hoping to find a certain kind of sound that would heighten Dozer's agonising experience and coax the twins into performing one of their torturous signature duets.

"This one's for you, Dozer," said Mr. Kile as he turned the volume knob clockwise, sending the sound of thumping Congo drums pounding through the Fleetwood speakers.

The Kwon sisters' eyes beamed at the music. They immediately turned to one another in sync, easily recognising the intro to "Barbie Girl," by AQUA.

Dozer used his fat, stubby fingertips to plug his ears as the interior of the '58 Fleetwood started to sound more like a boozy karaoke bar.

Mia and Kelly Kwon broke out in song, riffing off each other, screeching horribly out of key while they nudged at Dozer, forcing him to join in.

Dozer reluctantly found himself nodding in time to the beat of the timeless '90s classic. He unexpectedly got in the groove, swaying in sync from right to left with the Kwon sisters.

"Remind me to have that radio removed," said Zhang as he opened the glovebox, eager to haul his eyes and ears from the horror show unfolding in the back.

He unravelled a copy of the South China Morning Telegraph as cigar smoke drifted past his eyes.

He read the headline, screaming tabloid-style with mammoth block letters that looked like they had been applied with a stamp:

SECOND ARMS FACILITY RAIDED FROM NORTH KOREAN BUNKER!

Zhang smiled at the article, seemingly thrilled by the news that thousands of rounds of ammunition had suddenly disappeared, along with shipping containers filled with small arms, submachine guns, and God only knows what else.

"Mr. Zhang," said Mr. Kile. Zhang lifted his eyes to find Mr. Kile pointing at the road ahead.

Zhang read the sign in English: "*Stanley Bay.*"

He wiped the grin from his face and bellowed above the music in Cantonese: "Ten minutes. Game faces on."

In the blink of an eye, the Fleetwood karaoke bar shut up shop and gave birth to a crew of stone-faced killers, one that would've rivalled any special forces army unit or cartel hit squad.

Zhang peered into the back seat, marvelling at who he considered to be his children of war.

He smiled when the Kwon sisters wriggled up their skirts, revealing holstered Walther PPKs strapped to their muscular thighs. The girls plucked their custom-built pistols from their holsters, gripping the ruby-pink gun grips, confirming their minute clips were stuffed with tiny brass-tipped bullets.

While the Kwon sisters where busy fussing over their 007 classics, Zhang paid attention to the middle, watching Dozer feed armour-piercing slugs into the chute of a stub-nose .38 revolver, the size a child would select if given the chance. He spun the wheel and flicked it closed with a nod.

Zhang turned back in his seat, eyeing the road as he hauled out his pride and joy from his fur coat: a Heckler and Koch P7M13. He screwed on the suppressor and yanked on the barrel, taking a moment to admire the brushed silver finish and blackened hand grip, reflecting on why he'd killed someone for it all the way back in 1994.

The first time he'd laid eyes on the pistol was during a cinematic experience in a downtown Kowloon movie theatre. A terrorist was giving a Japanese business man an ultimatum: give up the computer code to his vault or die. The terrorist counted to three, but the Japanese man—Tacargi was his name—chose to do it the hard way. Zhang remembered it vividly: the gun went bang, a brilliant starburst of fire driving the bullet into the middle of Tacargi's forehead, showering his brain matter over a pane of frosted glass behind him.

Zhang smiled, replaying the scene in his mind, enjoying the mass explosion of brain fragments as though he were back in the movie theatre, shovelling popcorn in his mouth while other moviegoers turned from the screen.

The feel of the Heckler and Koch in his hands was the only thing Zhang loved more than his Punch cigars, especially when he was about to perform what he vulgarly referred to as a "Tacargi."

He lowered the pistol when he caught sight of one of Hong Kong's 20,000-something iconic red-and-white taxis roll into his peripheral.

In the front passenger seat, he found the tired eyes of a young man who was using the framework of the passenger door to nap. In the back seat, he found a Cantonese woman who could have been the boy's mother, aimlessly skimming through the pages of a magazine.

He went on to study the driver, spotting his Fu Manchu moustache and tiny dome hat as Mr. Kile hit the indicator, steering the Fleetwood toward Stanley Bay, side by side with the taxi.

CHAPTER 11

L ena went on and on in the taxi like a broken record about how Stanley Bay was one of the must-go places for any tourist when visiting Hong Kong. Tomorrow, they would move into their residential apartment in Kowloon city and become locals, but for now, they were those pesky, sightseeing tourists they'd grow to despise inside of six months.

The morning was just about as beautiful a day as you could expect at Stanley Bay in the winter, the sky a crisp and frosty blue, the sun a blinding beacon showering the ocean with sunlight.

"See, what did I tell ya?" said Lena as they entered what appeared to be an endless corridor of market stalls.

"Are we sure we can trust that cabby to take our bags to the motel?" asked Brandon as he weaved under the humming blades of a remote-controlled army helicopter.

"He had an honest face."

Lena ducked with Brandon to escape the chopper's path.

"Bandon, oh my god!"

Lena towed him toward a loaded stall full of silk garments, Chinese costume jewellery, and souvenirs that lit up her eyes like it was Christmas.

She dropped him like a bad habit when she arrived at a Chinese silk evening dress that took her breath away.

"My mother used to wear these when I was a little girl."

She plucked the dress from its hanger and turned it over to study the picturesque floral arrangement made of trumpet flowers and sweeping birds.

"Yeah, great," groaned Brandon as the stall's owner arrived to whisper words of negotiation and price in Lena's ear.

Before Brandon knew what had happened, Lena had stowed her backpack on his shoulder without invitation and was making her way toward the changing room for a fitting.

"Yeah, okay, no worries," yelled Brandon over the market crowd. "I'll just wait here, then, shall I?"

He shook his head and repositioned the two backpacks on his shoulders.

"Holy shit," he blurted when a tiny long-tailed macaque bolted through the gap of his legs.

Brandon watched the tree monkey as it bounced from stall to stall, ricocheting off market walls like a stray bullet. It landed on the ground, knocked over a stall sign, and skimmed through the thin gap of a roller door.

Brandon curiously approached the aluminium tinwork. He bent down on one knee and looked through the gap to get eyes on the freakish speedster.

"Hello?"

When no one answered, he called through the gap again, patiently waiting for a reply that wouldn't be returned.

He dropped the backpacks on the market floor and scooped up the stall sign, reading it aloud: "Yuen's Engravings."

He repositioned the sign against the wall and quietly hoisted up the roller door to find the stall's interior loaded with Chinese calligraphy scrolls, beautifully coloured paintings, and dozens of canvases that were well on their way to becoming stunning works of art.

Brandon approached a scroll on the wall that was filled with traditional Chinese characters he didn't recognise. He took a moment to appreciate the skill, the time, the patience and dedication that would have been required to create such artwork.

He reached out to flip the price tag when the long-tailed macaque returned out of nowhere.

The monkey dropped down on top of Brandon's head,

slapped him with his miniature-sized hand, and leapt back up onto a row of bamboo monkey bars like a circus acrobat.

"Hello! Welcome to Yuen's Engravings," a voice shouted from the back of the store.

Brandon lowered his defensive monkey-attack guard to find a tiny old man with long silver hair drifting through a curtain of beaded bamboo, aided by a timber walking stick.

Brandon found a striking resemblance in the old man, as though he were a miniature-sized version of someone who went by the name of Pai Mei, the cruel yet unbelievably powerful Kung Fu master from a film title that somehow escaped him.

Brandon looked on in astonishment as the elderly five-foot-nothing Cantonese man tossed his long stringy beard to the side of his face and cackled.

"I'm very sorry. Heart bigger than brain." The old man pointed the tip of his walking stick at the macaque, who was now dangling crazily overhead.

"Sometimes, he thinks he is a big strong mall security guard like Hulk Hogan, with the hard, chiselled abs of Mark Wahlberg and lightning-fast hands of Jackie Chan."

Brandon smiled in amusement as he observed the monkey dangling wildly from the bamboo overhead.

"Cool monkey."

"His name is Franco, and I am Yuen. And you are?"

"Brandon."

"Ahhhh, your accent, it is New Zealand? You kiwi?"

"Nah, I'm Aussie. Well, Cantonese-Australian actually."

"Ahhhh, g'day there, mate," joked Yuen in his best version of an Australian accent. He snatched the strings of his beard and tossed them aside while Brandon worked to contain his laughter.

"Did you do all these?" Brandon pointed toward one of the many magnificent scrolls that were pinned to the wall.

"Yes, yes, I am artist," Yuen said proudly. "Everything you see in here is handmade: drawn, written, or painted by me."

"They're really cool."

"Thank you, thank you."

"Man, I wish I had your talent."

"Come, come, you try." Yuen latched onto Brandon's arm and towed him toward a tiny timber desk that was littered with jars of used brushes.

"You try, very easy. Come, come."

"Ah no," laughed Brandon.

Yuen pulled a blank canvas from a drawer and slid it on the desk face.

"Trust me, I don't have a creative side," Brandon waved both his hands in front of his face and pulled away.

"Come, come, how do you know if you've never tried Chinese calligraphy?"

"Trust me, I'll murder that canvas if you let me anywhere near it."

"Clear your head." Yuen followed the lines of a Chinese character on the wall with his finger.

"Study and memorise character, feel its shape and curvature, notice all the beauty in its line, so simple, yet so perfect, you, see?"

Brandon doubtfully shrugged at his shoulders. "Yeah, I guess so."

"Now, close your eyes."

Brandon closed his eyes and awaited Yuen's instruction. He stood on his tippy-toes and whispered into Brandon's ear: "Now draw."

"Are you serious?" said Brandon, his eyes still closed. "I'm gonna suck if my eyes are open, but I'll be useless if I'm blind."

Yuen spoke softly. He moved from side to side behind Brandon, using the calm tone of his voice to ease all doubt.

"The mind must be calm and tranquil, like a still pool, for creativity to unconsciously emerge. Be calm and still, like tranquil pool."

Brandon didn't realise it at first, but he had begun to take a series of breaths that weren't directed. He breathed in softly through his nose and gently blew the air out through his mouth.

He felt a tingling sensation in his fingers and grew goose-bumps on the back of his neck as he flooded his body with oxygen. Yuen continued as he studied the relaxation slowly arriving in Brandon's expressionless face.

"Breath in, breath out. Calm your mind. Consciousness of breath is everything." Yuen paused momentarily and turned to the canvas. "Now draw."

Brandon slowly reached out and pulled a brush from one of the jars with his eyes closed.

He dipped its bushy head into a cartridge of black paint and gently wiped its edges.

Yuen folded his arms and smiled in admiration as Brandon effortlessly guided the brush to the canvas unassisted.

Brandon drew the lines perfectly, running the brush tip sideways, then up and down on the canvas. He made the final stroke and flicked the tip of the brush head on the edge of the canvas as if he had done it a thousand times before.

He had drawn the Chinese character for strength.

He knew he had finished it, knew he had completed it perfectly, but still he held his eyes closed.

Brandon hadn't felt this calm and at peace since his father was alive, and for a brief moment, he felt what it would be like if someone plucked out the pain from his heart and replaced it with feelings of joy and happiness, the same feeling he had taken a needle to his arm for in the toilet cubicles of Trinity.

Brandon opened his eyes and looked at the canvas.

"Wow."

He examined the lines of the Chinese character and compared it to the one on Yuen's wall.

"They're almost identical."

"You see? If the mind is calm, clear, and relaxed, it can be free to accomplish whatever it desires."

Franco dropped from the rows of bamboo and landed on Yuen's shoulder. He flashed his teeth, signalling Yuen with an ear-piercing screech as the stall's door came crashing down.

Brandon and Yuen followed the craziness in Franco's beady eyes and found Johnathan Zhang standing proud with his gang of mutants in front of the roller door.

CHAPTER 12

"He's cute," purred Mia Kwon. The Korean nutcase pulled her Walther PPK from her leg holster and ushered Brandon backward with it. She flattened him against the wall and smiled deviously, her hand inappropriately wandering, pink finger nails crawling like spider's legs around his crotch.

"He's clean."

Zhang nodded in approval and casually unbuttoned his fur coat, setting his dark and calculating eyes on Yuen while Franco hissed at him.

"If that baboon makes another one of those god-awful screeching sounds, I'm gonna separate its head from its body."

Zhang brushed what hair he had left, on his head then directed Mr. Kile and Dozer with his eyes, positioning them like chess pieces around Yuen and Franco.

Brandon gulped at the fear inside Yuen's eyes, his warm, accommodating smile now a thing of the past.

"He's not a baboon," said Yuen. "He's a long-tailed macaque! His name is Franco, I am Yuen, and none of you are welcome in my store."

Yuen pulled a small banana from his pocket and drove it toward his shoulder. "Off you tootle, Franco. Out back." The tawny-coloured sidekick plucked the banana from Yuen's hand and went to ground, scurrying across the market floor and shooting through the curtain of bamboo.

"What do you want?" asked Yuen.

Zhang plucked his cigar from his mouth. "I want what your nephew promised me." He blew a cloud of smoke in Yuen's face and stabbed the fiery tip into Brandon's newly created canvas on the desk, using it as an ashtray.

"I don't know what you are talking about."

"You will." Zhang smiled and then frowned at the scattered artwork on the walls of Yuen's store.

"Your nephew took a great deal of money from me to arrange the creation of a specialised counterfeiting plate. I know he utilised the skills of a very talented artist. I also know it was someone close to him." Zhang redirected his taunting eyes at Yuen. "He confided in me before I took away his legs."

Brandon watched as the Kwon sisters joined forces with Dozer and Mr. Kile, the quartet laughing at Benny's cruel demise.

"I don't believe you." Yuen shook his finger and folded his arms in protest.

Mr. Kile plucked a black-and-white polaroid from his jacket pocket and flicked it in his hand like a speedy card dealer at a casino. He stuck it in Yuen's face with a smile.

Brandon frowned as Yuen studied the photo, the image sending his shoulders slumping toward the floor and forcing tears into the corners of his eyes.

"Lieutenant Dan," laughed Kelly Kwon.

Mia laughed in Brandon's face, then cocked the hammer of the PPK when he wriggled against her grasp. Brandon felt his moral standards dwindling as the idea of breaking Mia Kwon's face suddenly appealed to him. He had never envisioned striking a woman—despised it, in fact—but today was a new day.

He was close enough to witness the corrosive edges of Mia Kwon's soul, peering deep into her cold and troubled eyes, smiling as she pressed her gun to his cheek.

If the opportunity presented itself, he was gonna disarm the bitch.

When the cruel sounds of laughter became unbearable, Yuen flipped his walking stick in a fit of rage and stabbed the end into Zhang's mouth.

Mr. Kile and Dozer quickly countered, rushing forward to restrain Yuen in a chokehold.

Appalled, Zhang took a folded handkerchief from his pocket, dabbing at his mouth, taking his time to study the blood-soaked "*Zhang*" sewn into the border of the handkerchief.

He lifted his hateful eyes from the cotton square and stared at Yuen.

"Put him against the wall."

Mr. Kile obeyed, tossing Yuen across the store like a small child.

Kelly Kwon rushed in. She positioned herself perfectly in fighting stance and shot out a side kick, the sole of her hot pink Converse sneaker connecting with Yuen's larynx. She locked her leg in place, using her power to pin Yuen against the wall like one of his canvased artworks.

Brandon lunged forward in an attempt to break free of Mia Kwon's grip. She drove him back into the wall and pressed the barrel into his cheek again. "Don't move."

"He's just an old man," pleaded Brandon. "Let him go, you fucking cowards!"

Mia pulled down on Brandon's jaw and poked the muzzle of her Walther PPK inside his mouth.

"I want the plate, Yuen," said Zhang as he spat the remainder of the blood from his mouth. "Along with the combination to your safe—the one I'm sure you'll say you don't have."

Zhang pulled his Heckler pistol and yanked on its barrel.

"I don't have a safe," said Yuen.

He ran his hand down the sole of Kelly Kwon's shoe and squeezed it to elevate the crushing of his throat. He looked down the barrel of her bulging leg to find a pair of smiling eyes staring back at him.

Zhang directed Mr. Kile with a wave of the hand, sending him toward the back of the store.

He raced through the curtain of bamboo and began tossing tables and chairs around like a burglar ransacking an apartment. Franco hid behind a ceramic buddha, banana in hand, clutching at its robust belly when the crashing sounds became too much for his tiny ears.

Mr. Kile drew one of the sliver blades from his belt holster and started hacking the floor, dissecting square pieces of carpet to unearth the safe.

"It's here. I've found it."

Dozer parted the bamboo curtain with his tiny hands and found Mr. Kile sitting amongst the carved remains of Yuen's floor, hovering over the safe, assessing the dial combination lock.

Dozer turned back at Zhang to deliver a nod. The safe was theirs.

"The combination, please!" demanded Zhang as he directed the pistol barrel toward Yuen's head.

"There is nothing in floor other than my art. Combination is useless to you."

"Then there's no reason not to give it to me."

Yuen gagged as Kelly Kwon pressed forward with her foot, compressing his airway.

"You have many fine works of art here, Yuen. It would be a shame to ruin them with the icky fragments of your brain."

The Kwon sisters laughed as one, amused by the thought Yuen's mind was about to meet the light of day.

"I'm going to count to three," said Zhang. "Don't ask for a four. Give me the combination."

Zhang teased Yuen with the Heckler's suppressor, rubbing the cold cylinder along the beaded sweat on his forehead.

"One . . . two . . ." Zhang cocked the hammer and took a backwards step, ensuring a starburst of brains wouldn't meet with his designer fur coat. "Three!"

"The combination come to grave with me," said Yuen.

Brandon felt the tension in Mia Kwon's gun hand dissipate, her focus shifting momentarily to watch Yuen's head explode.

"I was hoping you were going to say that," said Zhang as he

fired his gun, instantly sending Yuen to the other side in a starburst of blood.

Brandon slapped away Mia's gun hand and extracted the barrel from his mouth.

He dropped to the floor and attacked Mia's legs, lifting her off the ground and spearing her head first into the concrete floor as though he was back inside the walls of Trinity.

Kelly Kwon let Yuen's dead body fall to the ground and rushed to her sister's aid. She responded with a powerful push kick, driving the sole of her blood-splattered shoe into Brandon's chest, the force driving him through the wall of Yuen's store with a tremendous burst of plaster and wood.

Zhang directed his attention toward the starburst opening in the wall and studied an empty cloud of plaster and dust. He regretfully stuffed his Heckler back inside his coat when he knew there would be no shot, his target suddenly gone, fled on foot inside Stanley Market.

"Mr. Kile, Mr. Dozer, please dispose of that and get what is mine from that safe."

Zhang looked and Mia and Kelly Kwon, then relit his cigar.

"You two, no witnesses. Hunt him down!"

CHAPTER 13

Brandon clutched at the stabbing pains inside his chest, coughing and stumbling backwards into the bustling market-filled corridor.

He propped himself up on a step, heaving in breath, scanning the crowd for Lena, who he found wondering aimlessly, bagged evening dress draped over her arm.

"Shut up and keep moving," ordered Brandon as he intercepted his mother at speed, grabbing her by the arm, hauling her with one thing in mind: *Get as far away from Yuen's store as possible.*

"Where the hell have you been, Brandon? I leave you for five minutes and you—"

Lena's words died on her tongue when she observed Brandon clutching at his chest.

"What's wrong?" She studied the agony in his eyes and assisted with the pain, gently pressing her palm on his chest as they weaved around the flock of marketgoers.

"Some girl back there kicked the shit out of me." He laughed half-heartedly in transit, still trying to race air back into his lungs. "Drove me through the damn wall like a featherweight."

"A girl? Is this a joke, Brandon?"

He shook his head, anxiously peering over shoulder and into the crowd.

"I wish! I've never felt a kick that powerful before. Stop here," he said, pulling Lena to a halt.

He used her shoulder to set himself up on a minute staircase, turning his eyes back towards Yuen's store.

"Shit, we gotta keep moving," said Brandon when he found the roller door starting to rise.

"I don't understand."

"I'll explain later. Come on."

Mia and Kelly weaved under the moving roller door and scanned the crowd with their thin, radar-like eyes. They hoisted themselves up onto a step-in sync and found a cloud of white dust trailing from someone's head—exactly what they'd expect after the explosion through Yuen's shop wall.

"There, up ahead," pointed the twins as they locked onto Brandon, watching him tow a woman though the crowd like a battering ram.

The Kwon sisters returned the soles of their matching Converse sneakers to the market floor, preparing to seep into the crowd and give chase when a rapid zipping noise diverted their attention.

They poked their heads around the corner and peered into a workshop, following the greasy arms of a bike mechanic as he worked on two Ferrari-red Ducati Panigale motorcycles, firing wheel nuts with an air compressor gun as if he was in the pits at a Moto Grand Prix.

The kwon sisters studied the jaw-dropping paintwork of the bikes and slowly turned toward one another. They locked eyes and smiled.

CHAPTER 14

S ensors pinged as Kaiden Chan elbowed open the door, slipping inside the 7-Eleven in Stanley Bay smelling like an abandoned distillery, the dregs of beer, wine, and whisky still seeping through the pores of his skin.

He waved lethargically at the two uniformed clerks behind the counter and headed for the bain-marie, desperately in search of some kind of greasy concoction that would mitigate his hangover.

He parked himself at an oblong-shaped panel of glass and grimaced, his eyes landing on the most pitiful-looking pepperoni pizza the world had ever seen. He made a disgusted noise. *That looks just how I feel*, thought Kaiden: shrivelled, time-worn, and desiccated, aching to be discarded.

Undaunted, he tapped on the glass to signal the clerk.

"One slice," said Kaiden as he slid out a stool at the counter, relenting to the old-man soreness in his back, reliable aches and pains he could set his watch to every time the alcohol wore off.

He shimmied onto the stool and leaned to the left when a customer squeezed by, yanking on the store's refrigerator handle to select a drink.

Kaiden smiled pleasantly, welcoming the arrival of the cool air as it touched his face.

He stared through the chilled panel of glass when it closed, considering the vast assortment of canned beer in front of him that was aching to be consumed.

He licked his lips and looked around the store, noticing the clock, his mind ticking in time with the hands that told him it was only nine a.m.

Pretending he didn't see it, Kaiden hauled the flap of his

trench coat over the charcoal-handled grip of his Glock, then discreetly pulled his badge from his hip and stuffed it in his pocket, intentionally throwing the clerks off the scent that there may have been an on-duty cop in their store, improperly chugging on cans of beer.

He leaned across and opened the fridge door, took out a can, and sat it on the counter when his pizza arrived.

"Put it back," he thought, wrestling with temptation, tossing up paper-thin excuses that would permit consumption. *It's just one drink—stop being such a pussy. It'll numb your back pain.*

Defeated, he snatched the beer off the counter and cracked it open.

Kaiden froze mid-drinking action, turning curiously toward the store's entrance as the terrified screams of a young man drifted inside.

Unconvinced there was cause for alarm, Kaiden Chan chugged on the can of beer and took a bite of his pizza, wiping melted cheese from his mouth when the young man raced past the store, holding on to the arm of a lady, her eyes wide with fear.

Kaiden left his stool and headed for the entrance, remembering what it sounded like in the stands at the 51st Macau Motorcycle Grand Prix two years earlier.

He frowned as the threatening roar of wide-open throttles arrived in the store, worrying sounds that prompted him to grip the handle of his Glock.

CHAPTER 15

I t was an ordinary morning for the staff members at the China Village Restaurant located a few streets over from Stanley Market. Ordinary, that is, until Brandon drove a thundering side kick into the back door of the kitchen and rushed inside.

"Come on."

He reattached himself to Lena's arm, towed her inside, and slammed closed the door.

They quickly manoeuvred through the confused kitchen staff who were frozen at their benchtops, clutching at their cleavers, wondering who the two geniuses were that couldn't tell the restaurant's entrance from its rear.

Brandon arrived in the empty restaurant setting and looked down stupidly as a waitress happily greeted him in Cantonese, offering two menus for his trembling hands. "Table for two?" she asked.

"No, I need a phone." He made the shape of a phone with his hand and put it to his ear. "Phone!"

"Good morning," said the bartender. He lifted the reservation phone from the wall and spoke to it.

Brandon quickly weaved around the waitress, leaped over a banister, and rushed behind the bar to de-phone the bartender.

"He'll call you back!" Brandon said abruptly as he tore the receiver form the bartender's hand.

He stared at the glowing numbers of the keypad, listening to its purring dial tone as he realised, he didn't know the number he wanted to call.

"Shit! What's the number for the police here?"

Brandon studied the confusion in Lena's eyes as she abandoned her reply mid-sentence, stepping to direct her attention toward the escalating humming sound at the rear of the restaurant.

Together, they looked through the kitchen corridor, where they studied the back door and waited, though not for long. Within seconds, they began backpedalling, distressingly aware that something was dangerously approaching on the other side of the door.

"Get out of the kitchen," screamed Brandon. "Move!"

He waved his hand and offered the kitchen staff a parting glance as he pulled Lena toward the entrance of the restaurant and kicked it open.

Kelly Kwon made the valves of her Ducati engine scream as she viciously broke through the kitchen door, tearing it from its hinges, obliterating it.

She raced at warp speed through the guts of the kitchen, sending pots and pans flying as the Ducati miraculously missed out on the opportunity to turn the China Village chefs into road kill.

Lena screamed as Brandon tackled her into the immaculately kept display gardens of the China Village restaurant. The high-pitched whining sound of the Ducati's engine exploded through the glass doors, sending shards of glass through the air, winking like diamonds under the Stanley Bay sun.

Brandon lifted his head to get eyes on the bike, peaking over a row of box hedges until he found the waters of Stanley Bay.

The setting of the China Village Restaurant was positioned in front of breathtaking ocean views, with its very own curved-timber promenade that ran toward the lush green jungle back-drop of Stanley Bay, but Brandon and Lena wouldn't have noticed it; they couldn't have.

What they did notice was Kelly Kwon aggressively choking the brake of her Ducati, making the tyre scream before coming to an abrupt stop.

Brandon reeled Lena to her feet and started to walk her back as Kelly Kwon placed her shoes back on the foot pegs, taunting them with the threatening roar of the blood-red Ducati.

Brandon and Lena's feet found the timber decking boards of the promenade as Mia Kwon arrived, creating a blockade with her Ducati, rolling onto the boardwalk up ahead, the move offering Brandon and Lena only one route for escape.

Brandon studied Mia and Kelly Kwon as they spoke to one another with gunmetal eyes, working the throttles of their Ducati's, imploring Brandon and Lena to make a run for it.

"Let my mother go," Brandon yelled above the duelling Ducati engines. "She didn't see anything!"

Lena hysterically ran into Brandon's arms and squeezed him.

"See what, Brandon? What do they want from us?"

Brandon failed to reply as he observed Mia and Kelly steer their Ducati's into what looked like a side-by-side attack formation, as if they were salivating hunting dogs, itching to sink their teeth into prey.

"Run," screamed Brandon. "Now, run!" Brandon turned with Lena and started to sprint down the promenade, their feet thumping into the timber boardwalk.

Brandon sighted Mia and Kelly Kwon out of the corner of his wide eyes, peering over his shoulder when he heard the Ducati's tyres scream, sending puffs of black smoke pluming from the rear wheels, forcing the tails of the Ducati's to drift from side to side.

He didn't look back again. He ran faster, his heart thumping, his lungs burning.

Brandon squeezed his eyes shut and gritted his teeth, holding on to Lena's arm when the harrowing sound of screaming tyres took her legs from underneath her.

He reeled her upright, screaming in her ear. "Keep moving. We have to make it to the end of the promenade."

The bikes roared side by side, barrelling down the promenade like fierce rivals gunning down a checkered flag on a raceway, mother and son duo in their sights.

Lena Willis took her turn, peering over her shoulder as the bikes neared, realising her son was a split-second away from certain death.

"We're not going to make it," Brandon screamed.

"You are."

Lena drove her shoulder into Brandon, sending him tumbling over the concrete retaining wall of the promenade and into the waters of Stanley Bay.

CHAPTER 16

Kaiden tore the Glock from his hip as he weaved through the totalled entrance doors of the China Village Restaurant. It was there he watched in horror as the blood-red Ducati's ran Lena into the decking boards of the promenade, annihilating her body in a brutal hit and run.

Kaiden winked at his gun's sights as the bikes fled the scene.

"Freeze! Show me your hands," yelled the inspector. He redirected his gun toward a saturated Brandon, who arrived in his peripheral, clambering back over the barrier wall.

Kaiden crunched his way across a bed of broken glass and leaped onto the promenade, realising his demand had gone unheard as the youngster frantically crawled on all fours toward the woman and rolled her lifeless body onto her back, her body plastered in cuts and abrasions.

"Don't touch her. Step away!" the inspector shouted. He took one hand off the falcon grip of his Glock and pulled on Brandon's drenched shirt.

Brandon unconsciously followed the momentum, turning to mail a straight righthand strike and eliminate the unknown threat. The street-wise inspector ducked the blow and countered with the barrel of his Glock, pistol-whipping the youngster across the cheek and sweeping his legs out from under him.

Inspector Chan holstered his weapon, the explosive rage of Brandon Willis forcing him to utilise both hands to pin his arms behind his back.

"Get the fuck off me! That's my mother, asshole," said Brandon as he fought against the inspector's grasp, desperate to get eyes on the rampaging Ducati's that had disappeared.

"Stay still!" yelled Kaiden. He slapped on the cuffs and

rummaged frantically inside his trench coat when Lena's matted mop of blood-soaked hair arrived in his eyes. He reacted quickly, pulling out his phone to punch numbers.

Brandon endured the agonising wait for someone to answer Kaiden's call.

He helplessly rolled on his side and followed the stranger's hands while he investigated Lena's vitals.

"This is Inspector Kaiden Chan," he said quickly. "I need an ambulance. Main Street, Stanley Bay, out front of the China Village Restaurant. Victim is female, mid-forties, with facial lacerations and severe head trauma likely."

Kaiden paused, gently feeling his way around the wet blood on Lena's neck with his fingertips.

"She has a shallow pulse."

Brandon propped himself up on his knees and used his shoulder to wipe the twin trails of blood from his nostrils as the Kwon sisters arrived in his line of sight at the end of the promenade.

"Has that gun got any bullets in it, or is it just for show?" Brandon asked.

Kaiden followed Brandon's line of sight and found Mia and Kelly Kwon circling on their bikes at the end of the promenade, preparing to return for round two.

Kaiden listened to the threatening roar of the Ducati's and rose to his feet, re-drawing the Glock from his hip. The inspector calmly walked into the projected path of the bikes and raised the muzzle of his Glock while the Ducati's' tyres screamed, jetting puffs of black smoke from their rear wheels.

"Hong Kong Police," he screamed as the bikes began their return.

He fired two warning shots into the clouds of Stanley Bay's sky as Brandon wriggled on his belly toward Lena. He rolled on his side, poked both his shoes through the cuffs one by one, and brought his wrists to the front of his body.

Kaiden willingly paced toward the rampaging Ducati's, fearlessly preparing to meet them head-on.

He straightened his arms and randomly selected one of the bikes to place in his sights.

The scent of burnt gunpowder stung Brandon's blood-filled nostrils as a starburst of fire exited the muzzle of Kaiden's Glock, coughing up empty shells onto the promenade.

He followed Kaiden's line of sight and witnessed tiny sparks spouting from the valves of Kelly Kwon's engine, the bullets pinging in ricochet.

Unfazed, the Kwon sisters kept coming, crazily charging toward the starburst of Kaiden's pistol.

Bull's-eye. The explosion of Kelly Kwon's Ducati lifted the tail of the bike off the ground and catapulted her from the seat, as if she had been ejected from the seat of a fighter jet.

Brandon followed Kelly Kwon's lifeless body as it cartwheeled through the air and flopped into the waters of Stanley Bay without movement.

Kaiden robbed the redundant clip from his Glock and slapped in another.

He winked at the gun sights and locked on to the remaining Ducati, panning with it until it abruptly exited the promenade, using a crowd of bystanders to flee the scene.

The inspector turned toward the waters of Stanley Bay as Kelly Kwon's body resurfaced.

She was floating face down.

CHAPTER 17

The shooting at Stanley Bay caught up with the aging inspector back at the precinct.

A cluster of unwanted visuals arrived suddenly in black and white behind his eyes: a sporadic shuffling of mental imagery filled with blood, bullets, and explosions that had gotten the better of him.

He abruptly left his desk, slid into an observation room and closed the door behind him when something arrived in his mouth.

Kaiden Chan unexpectedly broke down against a wall of flickering TV monitors when the smell of sizzling gunpowder and sounds of wailing sirens sent nerve-shredding tension throughout his body.

He clawed at the aluminium framework to remain upright, hung his head, and hurled into a trash bin.

He wiped the vomit from his mouth and appraised the uncontrollable twitch in his hand, swearing out loud at himself, as if he was mad at the shooting, infuriated that it hadn't crossed his path fifteen years and twenty pounds ago, a time when nicotine, alcohol, and the all-night bars of Wan Chai didn't control every aspect of his life.

He closed his eyes and quickly curled his fingers into a fist, fighting until the dregs of aftershock subsided. The inspector took a deep breath, shot out his fingers, and opened his eyes to find his gun hand like it was many years ago: calm and steady.

He winked proudly, as if to himself, rose to his feet and fished out his Chesterfields to celebrate.

"Here it is," said Inspector Chow as he entered the observation room. He waved a manila folder in the air, then kicked the door closed behind him.

"Wow," Chow said suddenly, appraising his fellow inspector's complexion that was white as paper.

"You okay, partner?"

Kaiden cleared his throat and tapped the cigarette on the bridge of his knuckles.

"I'm fine." Kaiden nodded at the folder and lit his smoke "Let's have it."

Chow nodded and flipped the lid.

"Brandon Willis, seventeen years of age, Cantonese-Australian. Mother is Lena Willis, also Cantonese. Husband deceased, died in an auto wreck almost nine months ago."

Kaiden took the cigarette from his mouth and jetted smoke from his nostrils.

"So, what were they doing in Stanley Bay?"

"Mother's occupation is history professor, meant to start at the Australian International College next week. My guess is they popped down to Stanley Market to do a little shopping after their international leg from Australia."

Kaiden took another big drag on his cigarette and studied the ferocity in Brandon's eyes through the one-way glass of the interrogation room.

"What about the kamikaze duo on the promenade?" asked Kaiden.

Chow hesitantly flipped the lid of the folder back open, as if he was revisiting a gruesome chapter in a Thomas Harris novel.

"Hope you haven't eaten," said Chow as he set Kelly Kwon's post-mortem photograph on the table and pushed it Kaiden's way.

Kaiden studied the charred remains of Kelly Kwon's face that was being repositioned by a surgical glove.

Her left side wore the brunt of the explosion, scalding and

melting the skin down her face like she had been hit by canister of napalm.

"Cool," said Kaiden. He stared into the gaping cavity that once housed one of her gorgeous amber eyes and blew smoke at her dead head.

"We had to ID her from dental records. Kelly Maree Kwon, twenty-two, Korean, immigrated with twin sister Mia—"

"Just over twenty years ago," said Kaiden.

"You know them?"

Kaiden tuned away from the glass. He sat in a chair and blew out a dense cloud of cancer.

"Their guardian is a large Cantonese man with thinning hair, fond of fur coats and Punch cigars."

Annoyed, Chow snatched the folder from Kaiden's hands and closed it with a slap.

"You're not letting up on this Johnathan Zhang theory, huh? Somehow, you seem to be the only cop around here that thinks he's some kind of Bond villain. Don't you think that's a little strange?"

Kaiden looked at Chow in disapproval.

"Johnathan Zhang had a fur coat ruined in a Seoul City laundry twenty years ago. Zhang took the owners' twin baby daughters as payment."

Chow stared blankly, struggling to comprehend the cruel nature of Jonathan Zhang. The visual of Zhang tearing away twin babies from a distraught mother suddenly made him feel ill.

"Oh, I almost forgot," said Kaiden, as he rose out of his chair and dove into his trench coat pocket.

"Forensic team found this inside Yuen's Engravings."

Chow eyed a see-through evidence bag in Kaiden's hand and took it.

He used his fingertips to bring the contents closer to his eyes, where he studied the tattered leaves of another cigar stub, identical to the one on Benny's fishing trawler.

"Benny's uncle's store in Stanley Bay?" asked Chow as he viewed the Punch symbol that was looped around the butt of the cigar.

"Yep. We found that, along with a safe in the floor that had its face blown off by some kind of explosive—right after Zhang blew Uncle Yuen's brains out, I suppose."

Kaiden resumed his analysis of Brandon and returned to his position at the one-way interrogation glass. "If we're lucky, the explosive is custom made or exotic. We can trace it."

"Forensics didn't find any of Zhang's prints at Yuen's Engravings," said Chow.

Kaiden shook his head. "Forget the prints. How much do you want to bet that slug inside Yuen Lau's skull matches those of a Heckler and Koch Pistol?"

Chow clapped the folder shut again and stood next to Kaiden, looking at Brandon through the glass.

"You think he saw something?"

"Still not talking yet," replied Kaiden. "But I'll tell you one thing: Zhang didn't unleash his dogs of war on this boy and his mother for no reason. They must have seen something."

Kaiden watched Brandon rub at the butchered rings around his wrists the cuffs had put there. He lifted his vengeful eyes and glared at the glass window, as though he could see people on the other side.

"This kid is harbouring a lot of rage. I practically had to rip his arms out of their sockets just to get the cuffs on today."

"Yeah, well, having your mother driven into the ground by a Ducati at a hundred miles per hour will do that to the best of us."

"No, there's a lot more than that going on here. There's something eating away at this boy. I can feel it." Kaiden cleared his throat and stubbed out his Chesterfield. "What's the prognosis of his mother?"

Kaiden turned to Chow when there was no response.

Chow anxiously stumbled around his reply, pulled the medical report from the folder and handed it to Kaiden.

Kaiden silently mouthed the report as he ran his finger ran across the page, a huge frown settling over his face. He would have to prepare Brandon for bad news.

CHAPTER 18

B randon locked eyes with Inspector Chan as he entered the interrogation room.

"You want your cuffs back?" he asked, maintaining the maddened glare in his eyes.

He offered Kaiden a view of his cuffed hands, lifting the chain in front of his face.

"I'm sorry about the, uh . . ." Kaiden strayed from his apology, lost for words when he found deep bruising stricken across Brandon's face.

"What about the sissy leg sweep? Or the fact you almost ripped my fucking arms off when you cuffed me? You sorry about those too?"

Kaiden remorsefully studied the floor.

He pinned Chow's folder under his arm and cautiously sat on the bench seat next to the seething teenager.

"Fucking police," Brandon whispered. "You're so lucky you're a cop right now."

"I'm sorry?"

Brandon raced upright and squared off with Kaiden, staring fearlessly into his eyes.

"I said, you're lucky you're a cop right now, because if you weren't, I'd smash your fucking face in."

Kaiden quickly motioned toward the one-way glass with his hand, anticipating Chow's arrival through the door, signalling that everything was under control and to let the threat slide.

Brandon's body grew tense to the point of shaking from the outburst, the result of hours spent chained like an animal in silence, locked away in a box where he had endless minutes to kickstart a wave of unwanted scenarios in his mind about Lena.

She's dead. She's alive, but she's a paraplegic, or quadriplegic, an amputee, stuck in a vegetive state like a statue until the end of her days. Either way, it was news he could wait to hear, no matter how bad he wanted it.

Kaiden pulled a tiny key from his trench coat pocket and jerked the lock until Brandon was free.

"Brandon, my name is Inspector Kaiden Chan," he said softly as the cuffs were returned to his hip. "I have some evidence in our report I'd like you to take a look at. Do you feel you'd be up for that?"

Brandon rubbed at his butchered wrists and glanced at the opened folder in the inspector's hands.

He eventually nodded.

"Do you recognise this person?" asked Kaiden.

Brandon studied a post-mortem photograph of Yuen, along with a crimson-coloured post-It note that was stuck to his forehead, concealing the bullet hole in his skull.

Brandon flinched as he replayed the scene in his head. He pressed his eyes shut as the sound of Yuen's voice returned from the grave.

"I am Yuen. This is Franco."

He fast-forwarded through the scene, flicking to the frame where the gun went bang, Yuen's artwork suddenly painted with a starburst of brain matter.

"I watched him shoot Yuen like he was nothing," said Brandon in a daze. "He pointed the gun at his head and pulled the trigger."

"Who, Brandon? Who was the trigger man?"

"A big man with thinning hair, wearing a fur coat."

Kaiden rifled through Chow's folder in search of a different photo when the description matched.

"Is this the man you saw pull the trigger?"

Brandon assessed a black-and-white surveillance photo of Johnathan Zhang exiting his motorcade-like Cadillac at Stanley Bay, Dozer and Mr. Kile in tow.

"Who is he?" asked Brandon.

Kaiden stared at him wordlessly, hesitating, yet eager to share all in an attempt to get his man.

He stared at himself in the one-way glass and signalled to Chow, running his fingers across his throat.

He waited until the tiny camera light in the corner of the interrogation room went out, then thanked Chow with a wink.

"Big man in the picture is Johnathan Zhang," said Kaiden. "Was a People's Liberation Army former explosives expert. Little low-key nowadays, but utilises his old military contacts to conduct shady deals in smuggling, human trafficking, and illegal arms."

Brandon pointed to Dozer and Mr. Kile. "What about those two?"

"Zhang's muscle. Tall slender one with the albino skin is Mr. Kile, Zhang's lieutenant. Arrest record shows he's quite fond of throwing knives. He's got a sheet as long as my arm."

"And the wee man?"

"Goes by the nickname, Dozer. Former disciple of some Shaolin Monastery in Mainland China, brutally trained since he was a toddler in the fighting principles of Shaolin Kung Fu: iron body, iron palm. Don't let his minute frame fool you. What he lacks in size, he makes up for in power."

Brandon gulped at the photo; eyes transfixed in horror. "That's them."

"Who?" asked Kaiden. "Which one?"

"All of them. They were all there at Yuen's store, along with that pair of psychotic twins. You might remember barbequing one of them on the promenade."

"Mia and Kelly Kwon," said Kaiden. He stared at the one-way interrogation room glass, nodding at an invisible Chow on the other side, satisfied it wasn't all in his head. Kaiden finally had his man.

"Brandon, would you be willing to testify with everything you saw? The shooting and so forth?"

Brandon looked at Kaiden to cut him off.

"What's my mother's condition?"

Brandon held his breath when he found sorrow in the inspector's eyes.

He hesitantly flipped the lid of Chow's folder, extracted the medical report, and started to read.

"Your mother suffered a broken femur, dislocation of the hip, torn ligaments in her neck and back, but that isn't the main issue."

"What do you mean?"

Brandon's heart began to race, fearing the worst.

"Brandon, your mother is in a coma, due to a severe bleed on the brain . . ."

Kaiden trailed off when Brandon raced his face into his hands.

"How long she could remain unconscious is anyone's guess. Nothing can be done until the swelling comes down. The Department of Health is going to fly her to a specialised coma facility in Shenzhen City. It's only an hour away by plane, just over the border."

Brandon brought himself upright and wiped away the tears from his cheeks. "When do we go?"

Kaiden glanced at the floor, treading carefully with his response.

"Brandon, your mother has been granted special permission by the health minister to be flown to Shenzhen City. It might only be a short distance away, but it's Mainland China, not Hong Kong. I'm afraid you're going have to sit tight here with us for now."

Brandon glanced down at the folder in Kaiden's hands, studying a crime scene photograph from Yuen's store. He took it from the folder and looked at the gutted safe in the floor.

Brandon sharpened his eyes at Kaiden and held up the photo.

"Get me on that plane to Shenzhen City inspector and I'll tell you what was in that safe. Or kiss your testimony goodbye."

CHAPTER 19

"Hello, handsome."

Johnathan Zhang was salivating on the inside over the etched face of Benjamin Franklin. He took his time to study the flawless craftmanship of the counterfeiting plate, tenderly acquainting his fingertips with the plate's detailed lines and contours, caressing them like the hourglass curves of a woman.

"Outstanding," he said over the consistent roar of the Fleetwood.

Dozer drifted forward from the back seat and peered over his boss's shoulder.

"It's a work of art."

Zhang smiled in admiration, then reached around to pat Dozer on the back of his bald, melon-shaped head. "Dozer, my little friend. After we put this beauty into production, we will own this fucking city. It's time to take the power back."

Mr. Kile smiled as he steered the Fleetwood toward an enormous, oblong-shaped sign that read: "*Zhang Industries.*"

He pressed a red button on the dashboard and made the sign split in half, revealing the opening of two gigantic warehouse doors.

"Shit," said Dozer as the Fleetwood rolled inside. He rushed his teeny hand inside his jacket and palmed the tan-coloured grip of his .38 stub nose.

"No, Dozer," shouted Zhang, trapping Dozer's hand inside his coat. "There's too many."

Zhang stared in fascinated horror as a handful of uniformed infantry soldiers strategically stormed the Fleetwood, surrounding it on all sides, shouting crazily to the sporadic clicking of their AK-47 assault rifles.

"Show me your hands," roared their team leader. He hammered the bonnet of the Fleetwood with his fist, then regripped the shaft of his rifle.

Zhang discreetly stashed the counterfeit plate inside his cigar box, then offered the view of his open hands in the windshield.

"Okay, take it easy," said Zhang. He calmly pushed opened the passenger door of the Fleetwood with his foot and stepped out.

As the team leader approached, Zhang ran his eyes over the red and blue army patches on his shoulder, paying particular attention to the positioning of a red-and-white star.

North Korean Special Forces, he thought.

"Let's make it a little more dramatic, shall we?"

The voice arrived in echo, bouncing off the warehouse walls.

One of the soldiers reacted immediately to the words, slinging his AK-47 over his shoulder as he broke away from the pack.

He arrived at the warehouse entrance and rattled the dangling chains at the doors.

"I hope you have good news for me, Mr. Zhang," the voice snickered. "I don't enjoy these pointless endeavours to Hong Kong."

The gigantic doors closed with a *bang*, instantly cloaking the warehouse in darkness.

Zhang tracked the outline of the mystery man as he floated forward in the shadows, stopping a few feet short of the Fleetwood.

The team leader reached inside the driver's side window and flicked on the headlights, illuminating the highly decorated General Kim Myong-Su in uniform.

"I have news, General," said Zhang, his voice rising an octave. "Good news."

General Myong-Su glided around the grill of the Fleetwood and met Zhang head-on.

"It had better be."

The general nodded at his team leader, ordering his troops to haul Zhang's muscle from the Fleetwood, then directed Zhang with his hand.

"Walk with me."

Zhang offered Dozer and Mr. Kile a parting glance, while the troops did as instructed, viciously hauling Mr. Kile and Dozer from the Fleetwood. The soldiers pinned them against the car doors and stripped them of their weapons.

"May I lift a cigar from my coat?" asked Zhang as he arrived by the general's side.

"You may."

The general followed suit as the pair walked, hauling a slim-line cigarette case from his emerald-coloured jacket.

"Rumour has it that you and your associates ran into a little trouble earlier today, in some cosy tourist shithole just outside the city?"

Zhang offered General Myong-Su a strange look as he palmed his lighter.

"Oh, that was nothing, General. A minor inconvenience."

"Really? One that required you to put a bullet in another man's skull?"

Zhang paused as he lit his cigar, thrown by the intimate detail the general put up.

"General, I can assure yo—"

Myong-Su grabbed hold of Zhang's lighter hand, the sudden move forcing Zhang's words to die on his tongue.

The general slowly drifted forward and put his cigarette to the flame, staring fixedly at Zhang as he puffed his cigarette to life.

"Hong Kong Police say a young Australian man by the name of Brandon Willis was witness to the shooting. A witness that is still alive and breathing. You can see the drawback, I think?"

Zhang cleared his throat and discreetly wiped the sweat from his forehead. "Yes, General, I see."

General Myong-Su blew out a cloud of smoke and glanced at the burning cherry of his cigarette.

"Until the threat has been eliminated, our business is on hold. I can't have some murder investigation jeopardising our transaction. Do I make myself clear?"

"As a bell, sir. I'll see to it immediately."

"Splendid." The general flashed Zhang a dazzling smile and held out his hand for him to shake.

Zhang studied the scheming twinkle in the general's eyes, then glanced back at the Fleetwood in search of Dozer and Mr. Kile, wishing they were by his side.

"We understand one another, yes?" urged the general.

Zhang looked down at the general's hand, listening as every muscle in his body screamed for him to flee.

He shook the hand, then felt a sharp pain shoot through in his wrist.

General Myong-Su turned toward Zhang and performed a hand-shake wrist throw, laying him out cold on the warehouse floor with a thud.

Dozer and Mr. Kile rushed forward in protest, but the soldiers countered, ushering them back with the barrels of their AK-47s in their faces.

General Myong-Su smiled cruelly at Zhang, then brought down his army-issued boot like a guillotine, squashing the larynx of Johnathan Zhang.

"Listen very closely, you fat Cantonese pig. There an inspector attached to this case, goes by the name of Kaiden Chan. You remember Kaiden Chan, don't you, Mr. Zhang?"

"Kaiden Chan?"

Zhang gripped the general's boot with both hands, his eyes bulging from the pressure under his skin.

"He's a bum, General, an over-the-hill burn-out that belongs in a museum, not on the force. He's no threat."

Zhang gagged as the general drove his boot in harder.

"I'll decide who is and is not a threat, fat man."

He took a drag on his cigarette and positioned the burning cherry beside one of Zhang's wide eyes, ensuring that he was all ears.

"I don't want to see Kaiden Chan making a case out of you or any of those circus freaks you refer to as a crew. Do I make myself clear?"

The general pulled down on the skin under Zhang's eye to expose more of the eyeball.

"Yes, sir," Zhang said in suffocated whisper. "Yes!"

"See to it that Inspector Chan suffers the same fate as that of his father. Eliminate him, along with the boy and his mother. She is comatose and on life support, so all you have to do is flick a switch. Do you think you can manage that? Or do I have to draw it in crayon, like usual?"

"No, General. We will accommodate."

General Myong-Su stepped off of Zhang's pancaked throat and tossed his spent cigarette on the ground.

"You have five days to prepare the funds for our transaction. If you fail to meet my deadline, you and your goons will be found floating face down in Victoria Harbour. Do I make myself clear?"

Zhang rolled over onto his side, coughing in fits. "As a bell, General."

General Myong-Su straightened the knot of his tan-coloured tie and tipped his peaked hat.

"Good day to you, Zhang."

The general departed with a grin, screaming at his troops. "Doors!"

The soldier stationed by the door rattled the chains, parting the giant warehouse doors, filling the spacious floor with sunlight as General Myong-Su marched toward the entrance, arms proudly swinging by his sides.

The remaining soldiers unpressed the muzzles of their AK-

47s from Dozer and Mr. Kile's cheeks, leaving behind tiny, circular indentations in their skin.

The infantry unit broke away as one, headed for a stream of army-green Hummers that skidded to a halt before the warehouse doors. The North Korean unit climbed inside, slammed closed their doors, and left to the sound of screeching tyres.

"Mr. Kile," said Zhang as Dozer hauled him to his feet. "Liaise with your police contact, and do it quickly. If I know Kaiden, the boy and his mother won't be far from his side. They die tonight. All of them."

Mr. Kile viciously drew one of his throwing knives as a blood-red Ducati roared through the warehouse doors and squealed to a stop, lowering it again only once he'd seen the familiar face of Mia Kwon.

CHAPTER 20

B randon's positive ID of Zhang by way of photograph was
good enough for Kaiden, and if he wanted Zhang to spend
the rest of his days behind bars, he was going to have to meet
Brandon halfway.

He reacted quickly, bursting through the door of the interrogation room and ushering Brandon toward an unmarked police
sedan that was idling outside the precinct.

"Get in," said Kaiden as he scanned the street, prepared to
shoot anything that moved.

He got behind the wheel, stabbed the gas, and left.

Twenty minutes later, Kaiden and Brandon found themselves
probing their way through the early evening light, speeding west
along the Tsing Ma Bridge, headed for the outskirts of Hong
Kong and its International Airport.

"Kaiden, are you out of your mind?" screamed Chow on the
other end of the line.

"If the superintendent finds out that—"

Kaiden cut Chow off in Cantonese, eager to shield the
conversation from Brandon's ears.

"I'm not gonna give one of Zhang's thugs an opportunity to
pop up and put a bullet in this kid. He's too important."

"Then keep him here at the precinct where it's safe! We've
practically got cops coming out our ears in this building."

Brandon broke down the conversation in his head, battling to
translate, his Cantonese a little rusty. He frowned at a gathering
of storm clouds in the distance and pictured Zhang staring back
at him. The mob boss drew his Tacargi pistol in slow motion,
aligned his face with the gun sights, and made the gun go boom.

"Kaiden, you can't just take this kid to another country. He's a material witness in a goddamn murder case! This time, you've gone too far."

"Shenzhen City is only an hour away. It's practically just down the road."

"Down the road? Listen to yourself, Kaiden! Have you been drinking again?"

Kaiden chuckled in reply. "No, not since this morning!"

The inspector weaved through a stream of cars at high speed, then worked the wipers as rain lashed the highway.

"Look, Chow, the coma facility in Shenzhen City might just be the safest place for this kid right now, for him and his mother both. But all that aside, it's just the right thing to do."

Chow didn't respond. He couldn't. He didn't want to admit it, but he knew Kaiden was right. The further he got Brandon Willis and his mother away from the streets of Hong Kong, the safer they would be.

"You still there, partner?" asked Kaiden.

"Yeah, yeah. I'm still here. I'll have to inform the entire department, so watch your six. What am I meant to tell the superintendent?"

Kaiden smirked at the road, then replied in English. "You're smart inspector. Improvise."

Brandon anxiously gnawed at his nails as the exit sign for Hong Kong International arrived in his eyes. "How much longer?" he asked.

Kaiden observed his strung-out state, then guided the undercover vehicle onto the descending exit ramp. "Ten more minutes," he said softly "Just a few more minutes. Hang tight."

Kaiden swapped hands on the steering wheel and pulled his phone from his pocket when it started to jingle again.

"That was quick," said Chan, knowing who it was.

He looked at the screen and read the caller ID: "*Superintendent Yeung.*"

He smirked at the name as it ran from left to right on the

screen, opened the phone, and snapped it shut again, terminating the call as the unmarked sedan pulled up at a security gate.

"Inspector Chan," announced Kaiden.

He rummaged inside his trench coat and offered his badge to an oncoming airport marshal who greeted them with a friendly smile. "Good evening."

He flicked the water from his hands, then collected Kaiden's badge and Police Id through the window.

He waved his flashlight in Kaiden's face, then directed the light towards his credentials.

The faces matched.

"How may I be of assistance, Inspector Chan?"

"You can direct us toward Medical Air Services. We have a plane to catch."

"We?" he asked.

The marshal shone the halo of light through the bullets of rain and found Brandon in the passenger seat.

"And who is this good-looking young man?"

"Ahhhh, my new partner," joked Kaiden. "They keep getting younger every day."

"They most certainly do," the marshal laughed, then proceeded to shout directions over the bombardment of airport traffic.

"Head straight for about two miles and veer left when you find a series of small aircraft with blue-and-red pin-striped paint, medical symbols plastered on all their rudders. You can't miss 'em."

The marshal flicked off his flashlight and rehomed it inside his poncho.

"There is only one flight left tonight, headed for Shenzhen City. Leaves in around thirty minutes. Better hurry."

"Okay," replied Kaiden. He took his badge and Police Id from the marshal as a panel of iron bars rolled past the front of the sedan.

"Rough skies tonight, Inspector. I wish you and your offsider a safe trip."

The marshal waved the sedan onward through the rolling gate, then followed the tail lights with assessing eyes.

As the security gate drew to a close, the warm and accommodating marshal intentionally wiped the staged smile from his face.

He hauled a radio from his poncho and mashed the button.

"Mr. Kile, your guests have arrived!"

CHAPTER 21

K aiden shielded Brandon from the bulleting rain with his trench coat.

Side by side, they scampered up the narrow aircraft staircase and boarded the emergency room with wings.

Kaiden consulted with the medical crew in the galley on arrival. He flashed his badge and Police ID, then broke the news that they had just acquired two additional passengers for their flight to Shenzhen City, a demand that wouldn't be up for negotiation.

Brandon broke away from the pack mid-announcement, his eyes wandering when the sounds of a beeping heart monitor and hissing ventilator seeped into his ears.

He found a tiny hospital on the other side of the galley curtains, the aircraft cabin loaded with stretchers, defibrillators, and beeping screens that were monitoring their one and only patient's vital signs: Lena Willis.

For Brandon, it was like undesirable déjà vu. Again, he relived the horror of when he'd arrived at his father's bedside, watching his chest float up and down in time to the hiss of his ventilator, a gathering of tubes feeding neatly into his throat.

"Don't worry," assured a sweet-sounding voice from behind. Brandon turned to find a Medical Services flight officer and read her name badge: Anna Lee.

She offered him a warm smile, then reached across to peck at a glowing screen positioned next to Lena.

"What's that?" asked Brandon.

"This is a transport ventilator. It will assist your mother to breathe while she rests, and will fill her body with oxygen during the flight."

"Can I touch her?" asked Brandon as he reached for his mother's hand.

"Sure. You can talk to her, too. It might feel a little silly, but she can hear every word. You should let her know you're here."

Brandon leaned over the stretcher and gently drifted toward Lena's bandaged face.

"Mum," he softly whispered. "I'm here. Can you hear me?"

He stroked her cheek with his hand and stared at the concealment of her eyes.

"Don't worry, Mum. I'm in your corner."

Brandon lifted his watery eyes and found Kaiden's reflection in the oval-shaped passenger window. He was looking down at Lena with Chow's folder tucked under his arm.

"She looks calm, Brandon."

"Your job's done, Inspector," Brandon said suddenly. "I think someone else needs you now."

Brandon followed Kaiden's reflection as he turned away from the stretcher and took a seat with Chow's file, flipping the lid open to revisit what he suspected was the crime scene data from Yuen's store at Stanley Bay.

Brandon readjusted his eyes in the oval Perspex to flinch at the night sky. He frowned deeply when a storm cloud dispensed a ferocious crack of lightning, sending it crawling across the jungle backdrop of Lamma Island.

He reached over Lena and positioned his fingertips on the window shutter, preparing to haul it to a close, when a soundless flash of lightning illuminated a party of three scooting under the belly of the plane.

Brandon shifted his steady gaze to a gap in the galley curtains, where Anna Lee arrived, the sudden movement strange to his eyes, as if she had been delivered by way of force, ushered unwillingly into position.

He whistled at Inspector Chan and pointed toward the tail end of the aircraft cabin.

Kaiden robbed his eyes from Chow's folder and observed the fearful gaze in Brandon's. He turned in his seat, frowning over his shoulder to find a slice of Anna Lee's face oddly positioned in the gap of the curtains, as if her body had been bolted to the aircraft floor.

"Wait here," whispered Kaiden as he quietly rose to his feet. He cautiously made his way down the cabin aisle, contemplating what danger might be lurking on the other side.

The inspector stopped a few feet short of the curtain, now close enough to study a single tear that was cascading through the concaves of Anna Lee's cheek.

Brandon moulded himself into a human shield, inaudibly positioning himself in front of Lena when Kaiden's hand drifted inside his trench coat, probing for the falcon grip of his Glock.

The aircraft reeked of ambush.

CHAPTER 22

B randon gasped as the vengeful screams of Mia Kwon filled the aircraft cabin.

She savagely tossed Anna Lee aside and drove a push kick through the curtains, hammering Kaiden in the chest, her tremendous power sending him cartwheeling over one of the passenger seats.

The phony airport marshal followed. He drew a pistol from his poncho and rushed Brandon with it.

"Sit," he said, reversing Brandon back into his seat.

Brandon watched helplessly, a gun pressed against his head, while Zhang's posse stormed the aircraft cabin like a pack of wild dogs.

The inspector staggered to his feet and clumsily made a play for his Glock, slipping his hand inside his trench coat.

Dozer countered, thundering a hammerfist into Kaiden's gun hand, the force making him scream in pain.

Mia Kwon attacked from the other side. She propped herself up on an armrest and delivered a stabbing side kick to the meat of Kaiden's head, the blow returning the inspector to the cabin floor.

"On your feet, Mr. Policeman," screamed Mr. Kile. He snatched a bundle of Kaiden's black-and-white hair and viciously hauled him to his feet.

Mia and Dozer took turns, trading blow for blow, thundering combinations into Kaiden's face and midsection as if they were striving to obliterate the guts of a heavy bag.

Punch after punch, kick after kick, each strike found their devastating mark, their shots pulverising Kaiden with freakish power and accuracy.

Brandon found himself out of breath as the brutal attack unfolded. He began negotiations with himself: knock the gun away from the phony airport marshal's hand to turn the tide? Or remain by Lena's side, stay the course, and hold position as her human shield?

He looked at the craziness in the marshal's wide eyes and knew that if he intervened, the man would put two in his mother's head, ensuring she'd sleep forever.

Crack. Kaiden grimaced as one of Mia Kwon's bone-shattering kicks collided with his ribcage.

Brandon redirected his eyes toward the relentless dismantling of Kaiden Chan and found Dozer smiling in commentary.

He welcomed the sound of broken bones and thundered another fist point-blank into the inspector's face.

Mr. Kile repositioned his grip and threw a semi-conscious Kaiden into the aircraft cabin, the collision simultaneously ejecting a congregation of oxygen masks and tubes from the overhead compartments.

The vicious onslaught continued.

Dozer snatched an oxygen tube midair and looped it around Kaiden's throat, criss-crossing the ends behind his head.

"Your insides are gonna be nothing but fucking mush," screamed Mia Kwon as she delivered more punishment, driving a series stabbing side kicks into Kaiden's midsection, her eyes wild with murderous intent.

"Bring him here," ordered Mr. Kile.

He unbuttoned his black dinner jacket and showcased the family of holstered throwing knives around his waist. He hauled aside his curtain of hair and made preparations to end Kaiden's life.

Mia and Dozer ushered the inspector into position. Taking an arm each, they hauled him across the cabin like a prisoner of war about to face a firing squad.

Brandon's stomach contracted into a tight ball when Mr. Kile placed two fingers on one of his blades and plucked the handle from his belt.

He peered into the pistol mouth beside his eye and discovered the attention of the phony marshal had conveniently wandered off.

For the second time today, Brandon had found an opening—only this time, he wasn't going to repeat the same mistake twice.

He slapped the gun away with his hand, clenched the marshal's poncho, and threw a devastating right hand into his jaw, the shot sending him to ground, knocking him out cold and forcing the gun from his hands.

The bold move awakened something inside Kaiden Chan, the unexpected punch prying his mind away from the saddening thought that he was about to meet his maker.

He pinched the oxygen tube from around his neck, jumped off the ground, and drove the soles of his shoes into Mia Kwon's face.

He let out a war cry as he reached behind his back, grabbing onto the only part of Dozer that was yet on the tender side: his pecker. Dozer's eyes bulged as the inspector aggressively gripped his package in his hand and twisted, the vicious contortion of testicles forcing a high-pitched squeal from the iron hamster.

Kaiden spun out of the clench and took the opportunity to return the favour, repeatedly mailing closed fists into his unprotected face. "Eat that, ya fucking circus midget!" he screamed.

Brandon rushed Mr. Kile as he put one of his shiny friends to work. He cocked his arm behind his head and sent one of his blades slicing through the air.

"Kaiden, look out!" Brandon screamed.

Kaiden reacted to the warning and turned, running his arm across his chest.

He screamed as the knife went in, the steel blade neatly driving itself between the bones of his forearm and coming out the other side.

Brandon delivered a dynamic kick combination that started at Mr. Kile's foundation and wrapped with a wheel kick to the face, sending the knife-wielding Mr. Kile to the cabin floor.

"Brandon, my gun," said Kaiden as his hand wandered inside his trench coat. "Help me!"

Brandon caught the inspector in midair as his legs gave out beneath him, clutching at his torso from behind. Together, they brought out Kaiden's pistol, working as one, hands overlapping on the charcoal falcon grip, Kaiden's finger on the trigger, Brandon's trembling hand guiding the sites.

"Come on!" screamed Mia Kwon as the distant sound of wailing airport sirens filled the aircraft cabin, prompting an immediate retreat. "Move!"

She pulled Mr. Kile to his feet and towed him through the galley curtains, his vengeful eyes locked on Brandon while he wiped a string of blood from his mouth.

Dozer quickly trailed, shuffling like an eighty-year-old man riddled with arthritis after the vicious contortion of his package.

Heaving in breath, Brandon and Kaiden lowered the gun, satisfied the brutal ordeal had come to an end until two of Mr. Kile's throwing knives ripped through the galley curtains and into the marshal's chest.

CHAPTER 23

Kaiden Chan looked like a packet of bloodied meat.

"You look like stir-fried shit, Kaiden," said Brandon as he watched the inspector wriggle on the bench seat of the moving ambulance.

"Do it now," ordered Kaiden, referring to the highly polished blade lodged in his forearm.

Anna Lee turned, cautioning the inspector against such an act.

"We have to wait until we get to a hospital. I can't work like this while we're mobile."

The ambulance driver gently applied the brakes and twerked the rear-view mirror.

"Get cosy people. Next three blocks are jammed."

"There, you see?" said Kaiden. "We've stopped. Now get on with it"

Anna Lee observed the discomfort in his eyes and let out a sigh.

"Bite down on this," she said, handing him a white ambulance blanket. "It'll help."

He rushed it in his mouth, biting down as instructed.

"Ready?" she asked, as the ambulance idled at a set of lights. Anna Lee gently palmed the handle of the blade, curling her rubber-gloved fingertips around Mr. Kile's steel.

"Ready as I'll ever be," Kaiden growled around the towel. "Do it already."

He grabbed at his forearm and prepared to mask the pain.

"I'm gonna to count to three," she whispered.

Brandon squeezed Lena's hand in the stretcher and held his breath.

"One . . ."

"ARGH!" Kaiden screamed as Anna Lee reefed Mr. Kile's blade from his forearm, extracting it before there was a *two*.

Brandon rushed his eyes away, bowing toward Lena when he found Kaiden's blood painted on both sides of the knife.

They had left the tarmac of Hong Kong International in their wake, their so-called ride to Shenzhen City now a murder scene likely crawling with cops and airport police, not that they had stuck around to find out.

Within seconds of the phony airport marshal's demise, they had high-tailed it out of there, piling into a nearby ambulance with the aircraft's skeleton crew, just in case Zhang's band of killers decided to return for round two.

"You're going to need some stiches there," said Anna Lee. She dabbed at the letterbox slit in Kaiden's arm, her hands still a little shaky from the worst pre-flight checklist in the history of aviation.

"I'll stitch you up as soon as we get to the safe house."

Brandon stared at Kaiden as the ambulance got some green.

"Safe house?" he protested. "What do you mean, safe house?"

"It's a secure location," answered Kaiden. "Somewhere we can guarantee your safety."

"I know what it means, moron, but you can forget it. I've seen more than enough movies to know that safe houses are anything but safe, especially if it's anything like that 9-11 re-enactment of a hijacked aircraft you just put us on."

Kaiden's eyes wandered off in thought as he started to piece it all together.

"How did they know we'd be at the airport?" he asked himself.

Kaiden found it odd that Brandon had thought of it sooner, then realised it must have had something to do with the bombardment of elbows and knees he took to the head while inside the aircraft cabin. Zhang must have had someone on the inside, a rat in the force, someone who was playing both sides.

"Kaiden!" Brandon interrupted over a beeping horn as he caught the inspector studying the ambulance floor for answers.

If Kaiden wanted to keep Brandon and Lena alive, he would have turn his back on the force and everyone in it. Men and women he had trusted with his life.

Anna Lee pinned a square, snow-white gauze over Kaiden's forearm while he fished for his phone, diving into a bloodied trench coat pocket.

He started punching numbers, then raised the phone to his ear.

"Yeah, Kenneth, guess who?" Kaiden abruptly shouted down the reply on the other end of the line and barked instructions.

"Prepare the presidential suite. I'll be there in an hour, checking in a party of five with no questions asked."

He snapped his phone shut and shouted at the ambulance driver in Cantonese.

"Take us to Whompoa Garden in Kowloon. I'll direct you from there."

CHAPTER 24

"Go in the back way," said Kaiden. "I don't want anyone to see us pulling up at the front."

The driver nodded, then made the tail lights of the ambulance wink.

"What the hell is this place?" asked Brandon when a mammoth wall of glass arrived in his eyes.

He studied the reflection of city lights in its glass panels and turned to Kaiden for answers.

"It's called the Harbour Grand Hotel. Welcome to Whompoa Garden."

"A hotel? This is your bright idea?"

Kaiden didn't reply, instead opting to retrieve a much-needed Chesterfield from his trench coat.

He pulled a bent, snow-white cigarette from his pocket and stuck it in his mouth.

The ambulance arrived undetected, rolling quietly into the belly of the Harbour Grand Hotel, its loading bay a discreet entry point for deliveries, honoured guests, celebrities, royalty, and apparently, critically ill comatose patients.

Kaiden opened the double rear doors of the ambulance, then directed its two-strong skeleton crew. "That way," pointed Kaiden. He paused mid-instruction when it occurred to him that the skeleton crew needed a third, so he gave them one.

"Brandon! Help the crew with whatever they need. We'll use the freight service elevators to get to the seventy-fifth."

Brandon shook nervously as Anna Lee began prepping Lena to disembark the ambulance.

"Brandon, say hi to Ethan," she said.

Ethan sent a nod Brandon's way as he climbed through the seats and arrived in the back.

"Brandon, you're going to ensure Lena has enough oxygen while we're in transit to the room, okay?"

Brandon sheepishly nodded in reply. He unglued his eyes from Lena and watched Anna Lee work the screen of the transport ventilator.

Ethan and Anna Lee conversed in Cantonese, rapidly collaborating on how best to move Lena while they fiddled with the ventilator and packed first-aid kits, stripping the ambulance cabinets bare of supplies.

Brandon gulped when the ventilator died, its LED lights blinking once before shutdown, as if they were drifting off to sleep.

The skeleton crew gently extracted the cluster of tubes from Lena's throat, forcing a subtle hiss from her gaping mouth.

"Here, Brandon," said Ethan.

He placed a manual ventilator over Lena's face, positioned his shaky hands on the pump and locked eyes with him.

"Once we arrive upstairs, we'll reconnect her back to the transport ventilator, but until then, you will be her air, okay?"

Brandon pushed down the lump in his throat. "I don't . . . I don't know if I can do this."

"It's okay. I'm going to guide you. There's nothing to it."

"Like this?" Brandon asked while he squeezed the pump in his hands.

"Yes, very good, but not too fast. Keep it rhythmical. Slow and steady."

"Slow and steady," he repeated. "Okay, got it."

"Man's alive," cheered a voice at the rear of the ambulance.

Brandon lifted his wide eyes from the ventilator and found a short man hauling Kaiden Chan into his arms. "Good to see ya, pal," he said.

In between the hissing pumps of the ventilator, Brandon

decided Kenneth to be legit. He scanned the golden-edged name tag that was pinned to his ivory-coloured hotel jacket, then looked at the security ID that was attached to his hip.

"Jesus Christ, what the hell happened to you?" asked Kenneth. He nudged the inspector away, pressing him with his hands to study the combination of bruising and dried blood caked to his face.

"Road rage," Kaiden joked. He lit his bent Chesterfield and blew smoke away from his face.

"I'm sorry for coming here like this, Kenneth, but there was nowhere else to turn."

Kenneth reacted to the dragon hiss of the ventilator and curiously turned his eyes toward the belly of the ambulance. He followed Brandon's hands as they pumped oxygen into the comatose patient on the stretcher.

Kenneth studied the weary eyes of the skeleton crew, eyes that looked defeated, battered, and war-torn.

"Whatever you need, my friend." He returned to Kaiden and squeezed his shoulder with his hand. "Whatever you need."

The seventy-fifth floor of the Harbour Grand was a quiet one, a trickle of spacious and luxurious rooms that ate up the entire floor. Rooms set aside for royalty, celebrities, and rich banking tycoons who had come to do business in Asia's world city.

Brandon's eyebrows went up as the double doors to room 7543 opened.

He felt like he was in an episode of MTV's *Cribs*, taken in by the twinkling chandeliers that dangled from the ceilings and the mammoth, oblong-shaped window that showcased Victoria Harbour and the distant city lights of Hong Kong.

"One, two, three," Anna Lee and Ethan said in sync as they lifted Lena from the stretcher and placed her in a gargantuan bed that could accommodate an NBA centre.

They fired up the transport ventilator and gently fed the tubes into the opening of Lena's mouth.

"Okay, Brandon, step back," Ethan said.

Brandon took away the pump ventilator and collapsed in a chair, sighing with relief when the transport ventilator lights winked at him, the machine once again working to fill Lena's lungs with air.

Relieved beyond words, Brandon rested his forehead on Lena's hand and whispered, "It's over."

Kaiden exited the bathroom with a damp face-washer in hand and took to a framed mirror made of gold. He began chipping away at the dried and crusted blood stuck to his face, pausing when Kenneth arrived, whispering words at him in the glass. "So, now what?"

Kaiden eyed Lena in the mirror, then looked at Kenneth.

"Can she rest here for around seventy-two hours? It's too risky to move her again."

"Of course. Of course," assured Kenneth. "I'm the manager of the hotel. I can do whatever I want."

"I'm sorry I can't tell you more, but you're better off not knowing," Kaiden said. He dropped the blood-stained washcloth in the trash and ran his fingers through his hair. He pulled his Glock from his trench coat and checked the magazine, failing to recall if he had spent any rounds on the flight that never left.

"I need to get back on the streets and find Johnathan Zhang before he finds us."

"The boy and his mother will be safe here," advised Kenneth as his hotel radio squawked on his hip.

Kaiden rehomed his pistol and sighed at Brandon in the mirror. He was stuck to his mother like glue, squeezing her hand and caressing her bandaged forehead.

Kaiden crossed the room to sit across from Brandon, listening to him whisper in Lena's ear, ensuring her that everything was going to be all right.

"Brandon," Kaiden hesitantly whispered, "we need to leave."

Brandon lifted his eyes from Lena and frowned.

"What do you mean, leave? I'm not going anywhere."

"Brandon, I can't protect you here, not like this. I need to be back on the streets, where I can see them coming."

"No. No way. Forget it." Brandon shot out of his seat and began circling the hotel room, a storm brewing inside his head. "She needs me here. I'm not going anywhere."

"Have you forgotten about Johnathan Zhang?" asked Kaiden. He left his seat and went after Brandon.

"I don't give a fuck about Johnathan Zhang."

Kaiden rushed into Brandon's path and clamped onto his shoulders.

"Right now, Zhang and his goons are tearing this city apart, leaving no stone unturned until they put a bullet in your skull. You saw him kill a man—the only person that has ever seen Zhang pull the trigger. Do you think he's gonna let that slide?"

Brandon broke away from the clench and pushed the inspector away.

"If Hong Kong Police can't protect us, then I'll find someone who can."

He plucked the hotel telephone from its cradle and started to dial.

"Brandon, what are you doing?"

"Calling the Australian embassy."

"Like hell you are." Kaiden marched toward the wall and ripped the phone line form its socket.

Brandon lowered the receiver from his ear and drilled the inspector with his eyes. "Plug it back in."

Saying nothing, Kaiden stood his ground.

"Fine, I'll plug it back in myself," said Brandon as he drove his shoulder into Kaiden's chest and went for the phone line on the floor.

Kaiden took hold of Brandon's wrist and pushed back against the youngster's driving force.

Consumed by his rage, Brandon dropped the receiver and threw a right hand toward the inspector's face.

Kaiden blocked the punch, locked his arm behind his back, and pinned him face fist against the wall.

"Brandon," Kaiden said forcefully, loud enough to cut through Brandon's snarling cries, working tirelessly to contain his explosive strength. "Not like this, Brandon. Not like this."

"I hate you," said Brandon, seething with anger. "I fucking hate you!"

Kaiden took in a breath and released his grip when Brandon broke down in a barrage of tears.

"Then hate me," he said with a sigh. "But we gotta start someplace."

Kaiden turned Brandon over on the wall and placed his hands on his shoulders.

"Look at me,"

Brandon lifted his tear-soaked eyes and looked at Kaiden.

"The further you are away from Lena, the safer she is. Remember, it's you they want."

Brandon glanced at Lena and considered Kaiden's plea. He didn't want to admit it, but the inspector was right. If leaving the Harbour Grand Hotel would ensure Lena's safety, he'd go willingly.

He wiped the tears from his eyes, took a deep breath, and then nodded.

"Okay. All right, then," said Kaiden, dropping his hands from Brandon's shoulders.

He headed across the suite and huddled with Kenneth and the skeleton crew, dishing out instructions.

"Okay, phones—let's have 'em." Anna Lee and Ethan glanced at one another in confusion, then redelivered their eyes to Kaiden.

"Come on, come on. Phones, now," Kaiden continued. He

snapped his fingers in the air, tipped the room's complimentary fruit out onto the floor and sat the glass bowl on a table.

"Phones, now!" he repeated. "Quickly."

Kaiden took the phones one by one from the ambulance officers, placed them in the bowl, and pulled a bottle of water from the minibar.

The skeleton crew turned to one another and watched in horror as Kaiden twisted the bottle cap and flooded the bowl, turning their glowing cell phone screens into useless chunks of plastic.

"Kenneth—nobody in, nobody out, except you. Keep your radio and phone handy at all times. I'll call every few hours to check in."

He pulled his backup pistol from his ankle holster and approached Ethan.

"You know how to fire a gun?"

"I guess," Ethan replied with a shrug.

"I'll ask again," said Kaiden, unhappy with the response. "Do you know how to fire a gun? Yes or no? Answer quickly!"

"Uh, it's been a while, but yes, I do, Inspector."

Satisfied, Kaiden slapped the handle of his .38 in his hand.

"Here. Safety is on. It's not a movie, so don't walk around with the gun stuffed in your pants. I don't want a call from Kenneth telling me you've blasted your dick off. Never look in a direction the gun isn't pointed, shoot anything you see move."

"What if it's both of you?"

"You won't see us coming."

Anna Lee moved in with her emergency kit and went for Kaiden's arm. He blocked her hand.

"The window for stitches has now been and gone. Concentrate on Lena," he said.

"At least let me re-bandage."

Kaiden winced silently as Anna Lee wrapped his arm. He

looked at Brandon and witnessed his goodbyes, contemplating if he was doing the right thing, tearing away a teenager from a mother who had sustained life-threatening injuries, especially when she was in desperate need of specialised care, not a lavish hotel suite.

"Mum, can you hear me?" Brandon whispered. "I've gotta leave for a little while, but I'll be back. That's a promise." He towed the silk sheet up under her chin and kissed her on the cheek.

"It's time, Brandon," said Kaiden as he rolled down the sleeve of his trench coat.

Brandon hesitantly rose from his chair and looked at the inspector. "Where are we going?"

Kaiden considered his reply. He smirked at Brandon to lighten the mood.

"Back in time."

CHAPTER 25

Dozer, Mia, and Mr. Kile returned to the Zhang Industries warehouse empty-handed, their daring assault on the hospital with wings nothing short of a king-sized failure.

They trickled into Zhang's office, one by one, tails tucked neatly between their legs and prepared him for bad news. The botched job was not well received.

"God*damn* it," roared Zhang as he viciously upturned his office desk in a fit of rage, sending stacks of papers and telephones flying across the room.

Mr. Kile calmly reached in, grabbing at Zhang's shoulder in an attempt to curb his anger when Zhang responded with a move of his own.

Seething with anger, Zhang plucked one of Mr. Kile's blades from his knife belt without invitation. He trapped Mr. Kile's offending hand against the wall and stabbed it with the blade, pinning him to the wall.

Mia rushed to Mr. Kile's aid, only to feel the back of Zhang's hand across her cheek, the force sending her tumbling backward and flying over his tossed office desk.

Dozer cautiously stood back, gulping at the gut-wrenching screams pouring out of Mr. Kile.

"You are fucking with my timetable here, Mr. Kile." Zhang cupped his hand over Mr. Kile's mouth to mute his agony. "I stand to inherit the largest shipment of arms this country has ever known, and *no one* is gonna stop me from collecting it, do you understand me?"

"Mr. Zhang, I think—"

Zhang drew another knife from Mr. Kile's belt and pointed the blade at Dozer's head.

"Shut your hole, Dozer, or the next one goes in your eye."

Having seen the crazed look in Zhang's eyes before, Dozer took a backwards step.

"I cannot stand stupidity." Zhang left Mr. Kile to clutch at the knife in his hand and parked himself in front of a window. He sharpened his eyes at the round, silver moon hovering over the South China Sea.

"You had one fucking job." He pulled a handkerchief from his trouser pocket and dabbed at Mr. Kile's blood on his hand. "Find and kill a seventeen-year-old boy. And instead of that, you let some over-the-hill, obsolete relic of a police inspector get the drop on you all."

Zhang pocketed his handkerchief, drew his Heckler and Koch pistol, and then faced his war machines.

"I think it's safe to say you've all just qualified for positions on my shit list."

One by one, they took their turn, eyeing the pistol by Zhang's side as he tapped the barrel against his leg. "What does our newfound friend at Hong Kong Police have to say?"

Mr. Kile struggled through his reply. "Kaiden has gone off the trail. It appears they've ventured underground, somewhere he can keep the boy and his mother hidden. Not even Kaiden's fellow officers have been able to trace them since the airport."

Zhang's lips curled with disgust. He scratched his forehead with the barrel of the Heckler, then ran a hand through his thinning hair.

"If Kaiden has gone underground, Mr. Kile, it's because he smelled a rat. He knows there's a dirty cop in the ranks."

Zhang plucked a cigar from his jacket pocket, sat on the edge of his upturned desk, and stuck it in his mouth. Dozer arrived without request, lighter in hand.

Zhang took his time, puffing his stogie to life when an old photograph resting in the scattered papers on his office floor arrived in his eyes.

Zhang went to ground and collected the oxidized black-and-white still, smirking at the three people in the picture: a young boy, a father, and an elderly man. Zhang nodded in realisation and tucked it inside his trouser pocket.

He lifted his head and monitored the pleading eyes of Mr. Kile through a stream of cigar smoke.

"Okay," he said suddenly, as if awakened from a deep sleep. "We have a witness running wild in the city, one that can lock me up for the next thirty years and throw away the key, and we have no idea where he is. I don't know about you dim-witted fools, but I'd say that increases my problem exponentially."

He sucked in a puff of his cigar, his mind swirling with options.

"Dozer."

"Yes, Mr. Zhang."

"Scoop that phone off the floor and send message to the hangar: fuel the Blackbird immediately."

Zhang stuffed the Heckler back inside his coat and approached Mr. Kile, staring deep into his frightened eyes.

"Let's see if we can find someone to wipe this egg off Mr. Kile's face, shall we?"

Dozer did as instructed. He took to the floor and began pecking away at the phone, placing the receiver to his ear.

Mr. Kile sucked in a breath and drove his teeth together as Zhang tore out the knife, sending his whimpering lieutenant to the ground, cradling his butchered hand along the way.

Zhang followed, crouching next to the injured man. He positioned the bloodied tip of the blade next to Mr. Kile's wide eye.

"Fail me again, Mr. Kile, and I'll drive one of these blades you love so much straight through the meat of your heart."

Mr. Kile nodded fretfully as Mia hauled him to his feet.

"Start the Fleetwood," announced Zhang as he headed for the door, leaving a trail of cigar smoke in his wake.

Dozer reacted quickly. He slammed the phone into its cradle

and used Zhang's upturned table as a springboard. He sailed through the air, draping Zhang's fur coat over his shoulders while in transit.

"Where do we go, Mr. Zhang?" asked Dozer as he trailed his master out the door.

"The Northern Islands of Japan. It's time to resurrect an old friend."

Sujin Yamamoto remained as still as humanly possible, seeking reprieve from the bulleting winds in a snow-covered tree well, the tattered remains of his clothes the only thing keeping him from turning into a human ice cube.

Sujin squinted through the haze of racing snow, repeatedly asking himself the same question over and over again: *Am I in the right place?*

Sujin couldn't be sure.

He scanned the area as best he could, blinking excessively at the crystalised sleet that arrived in his eyes like shards of glass, trying to recognise anything familiar.

He bowed his head momentarily, excusing his face from the onslaught of weather when the howling winds whisked away a patch of powdered snow.

Even in the dark of night, the sight was unmistakable to Sujin's eyes: a weathered patch of cracked and dilapidated tarmac that belonged to an abandoned runway.

Sujin smiled behind his rag-covered face when he found it. He crawled out of the tree well and started scouring the patch with his bare hands, wiping away the snow to confirm his discovery.

He had been ordered to brave the blizzard all by his lonesome, even if it killed him.

He did this willingly, knowing all too well that the person who gave such an order would go un-challenged. Sujin knew better.

The elderly Japanese caretaker pulled a woven basket from his shoulder, then started hauling out bunches of cylinder-shaped logs that had been bathed in kerosene.

He took his time, carefully positioning the cut timber in groups on top of the snow-covered tarmac, strategically stacking and constructing tiny pyramid-shaped objects that would become beacons: landing lights for a plane.

One by one, Sujin ignited the pyramids, then stood back to observe his minute creations come to life, the structures pluming blackened toxins and whirling flames into the frozen air.

Who in their right mind would want to attempt to land a plane amongst this madness? thought Sujin. *It will be nothing short of a miracle if the jet doesn't slam into the runway and burst into a ball of flames, its pilot and passengers screaming in terror until their last breath.*

Sujin squinted at the blackened sky when it began to rumble. He scanned left, then right, then left again, his eyes on high alert, anticipating an aircraft to emerge from the darkness.

The sound of the Blackbird's waning engines arrived in Sujin's ears, just before its amber marker lights emerged from the blizzard, winking on the wing tips of the aircraft.

Satisfied that his landing lights had done their job, Sujin took shelter in his Kubota: the miniature, all-terrain vehicle that had bought him to this discontinued runway.

He peered through the Kubota's square-shaped windshield and made the wipers work overtime, whacking snow from the glass as the Blackbird aquatinted itself with the tarmac and snow.

A miracle, indeed, he thought.

Moments later, Sujin found Johnathan Zhang trudging through the snow, headed for the Kubota, towing his fur coat closed in transit, flinching at the bombardment of ice and snow.

"Jesus Christ," shouted Zhang as he dropped uninvited into the Kubota, his fat frame shaking snow from the roof. He raced the door closed behind him and shut out the storm.

He observed the robe-covered head behind the wheel and assessed a familiar set of eyes that were staring back at him.

"How have you been, Sujin?"

Sujin didn't reply. He twisted the ignition key and the Kubota rumbled to life, his eyes still narrowed slits painted on Zhang.

"Great to see your social skills are still in order, my old friend," smiled Zhang.

He drove a fresh cigar in his mouth, winked at Sujin, and pressed the Kubota's cigarette lighter.

"Take me to see the man."

CHAPTER 27

In a bid to steer clear of the city streets, Kaiden Chan commandeered a harbour vessel—a ferry, to be exact. He slipped inside the bridge of the ferry and flashed his badge, forcing the uniformed captain to leave his passengers stranded at the terminal. The inspector demanded total radio silence.

Brandon frowned at the mammoth skyscraper as it started to shrink, the ferry carrying him further and further away from Lena and the lavish Harbour Grand Hotel.

He set his eyes on the seventy-fifth floor, studying the extravagant, chandelier lights of the presidential suite when they suddenly went dark, extinguished by Ethan and Anna Lee for some much-needed shut-eye.

"Don't worry," assured Kaiden as he arrived by Brandon's side. "They'll sleep in shifts. Lena will be watched the entire time."

Brandon watched Kaiden as he scanned Victoria Harbour, searching for any abnormal vessel movements, suspecting that he knew all too well that Zhang had eyes and ears all over the city.

"Those people looked really pissed," said Brandon when the protesting faces of the ferry passengers returned to visit him. "Or maybe you just tend to bring that out in people?"

"They'll get over it." Kaiden tossed his spent Chesterfield overboard and coughed out the remainder of its smoke from his charred lungs.

Brandon leaned on the rail at the back of the ferry and looked down. "What the hell?" he yelled, as the trailing seawater at the back of the ferry started to flicker with shades of highlighter green.

The surrounding skyscrapers erupted to life, pouring out orchestral music into the harbour like he was at a music festival.

"Symphony of Lights," said Kaiden. "Each night, the harbour showcases the spectacle for locals and Hong Kong tourists. Do you like it?"

Brandon smiled at the pulsating decorative lights and stabbing laser beams that shot into the bleak harbour sky. "I've never seen anything like it."

Kaiden discreetly smiled at Brandon, pleased by the ecstatic gleam in his eyes.

"I gotta be honest," Brandon yelled over a display of pyrotechnic fireworks. "When you said 'go back in time,' pictures of a DeLorean came to me."

Kaiden looked at him stupidly.

"DeLorean?" he asked.

"Yeah, DeLorean. You know, scientist with crazy white hair, teenage sidekick?"

Kaiden shook his head and made a face. "Doesn't ring a bell."

"Really?" Brandon laughed out loud "That film is older than I am. It's one of Mum's favourite movies."

Somewhere in between the wave of sweeping lasers and criss-crossing searchlights, Brandon's joyful smile faded from his face. "I wish she could see this."

Brandon turned away from the lights and returned to the rear of the ferry. He leaned on the railing and stared into the churning seawater below, hit by a sudden wave of guilt for even having raised an eyebrow at the strobe lights and wondrous symphony in the sky.

There, he fantasised about revisiting his old friend, the one who could welcome him with open arms and take away the pain. He imagined how good it would feel to lock a toilet door at Trinity, shielded by a box of melamine walls in a party for one, the incomprehensible wave of warmth just moments away.

He bunched his eyes together, took a deep breath, then exhaled, fighting to destroy the chemical romance in his mind.

"You ever have that sinking feeling you're all alone?"

Kaiden chuckled to himself and looked up at the lights. "I invented it. It's mine."

"We were meant to be starting our new lives tomorrow—a new school, a new job—and now she's stuck inside a motel, the last place she needs to be right now."

Brandon gripped the railing tightly as his bottom lip started to tremble. "I keep seeing her lying in that bed with the tubes stuck in her throat, and I, uh . . . I can't help her."

Kaiden reached out his hand and squeezed Brandon's shoulder.

"She'll be okay, Brandon. That's a promise."

Brandon wiped away a tear from the side of his face and shrugged off Kaiden's hand.

"How 'bout you quit playing fucking counsellor and we skip to the part where you get these guys?"

Kaiden nodded. "Tell you what, a deals a deal. What was locked inside the safe at Yuen's store?"

Brandon turned back to the rear of the ferry and stared deeper into a trail of mixing seawater, his mind going back in time to revisit the horror of Yuen's store. It played inside his mind as if he were fast-forwarding through scenes in a movie.

"It was a plate," Brandon whispered, reciting the words of Johnathan Zhang.

"Benny took a great deal of money to arrange the creation of a specialised plate."

"A plate? What kind of plate?" Kaiden waited during the intermittent pause, then waved his hand in front of Brandon's stargazed eyes.

He broke away from the youngster, eyes wandering around the ferry deck, piecing his words together.

He pulled out a Chesterfield, lit it, took a drag of his cigarette, and let the smoke ooze out. "Yuen Lau was an engraver," he said out loud. "An artist."

He rubbed a hand down his face and tore the cancer stick from his lips.

"Brandon, was it a counterfeiting plate?" he asked, eyes beaming.

Brandon eventually looked over his shoulder and nodded.

"One minute," interrupted the captain suddenly.

Kaiden leaned over the railing and found the ferry captain pointing out the window, stabbing his finger toward Hong Kong Island.

Brandon arrived at Kaiden's side and looked out at the glittering lights of Hong Kong Island.

"Are you gonna tell me where we're going, Inspector?"

Kaiden found a look of renewed confidence in Brandon's eyes.

"You look like you might be warming to the idea of trusting me a little."

"Not really, but we're joined at the hip now, and I'm willing to do whatever is needed to get my mother out of that hotel room."

For a cinematographer, it would have been a wet dream.

The pair stood side by side at the rear of the ferry, facing the breathtaking remainder of the sweeping lasers as the Symphony of Lights prepared to wrap.

"Don't go thinking this makes us pals or anything," Brandon said, taking it upon himself to have the final word.

"Perish the thought," Kaiden replied with a smirk, flicking the spent cigarette into the sea.

"Good, because I still want to punch you in the face a little bit."

CHAPTER 28

Deep within the valley walls of backcountry Hokkaido, Sujin's Kubota was about to arrive somewhere off the beaten path, a location that had been a place of secrecy for hundreds of years, a place now lost somewhere deep in the sands of time.

Kinjo Temple was purposefully hidden from the eyes of the outside world, strategically positioned in the distant mountains of Hokkaido, camouflaged by cruel winters of ice and snow.

"Shibisaki will see you now," said Sujin as he abruptly squashed the Kubota's brake with his foot.

Zhang shot forward in his seat and rushed his hands to the dashboard, the sudden movement preventing his fat body from bursting through the square-shaped windshield of the Kubota.

"Thanks for the ride," said Zhang. He sharpened his eyes at Sujin, plucked his cigar from his mouth, and kicked opened the Kubota door with a scoff.

"Where's the temple?" he shouted over the howling winds.

Zhang hauled himself from the Kubota and shielded his eyes as the hellish, ice-cold wind nipped at his face.

Sujin stabbed the gas pedal with his foot and abruptly departed, the take-off force plucking the handle from Zhang's hand and automatically closing the passenger-side door as he skidded off into the night.

"Fucking tip rat," he scowled under his breath.

Zhang towed his coat closed and trudged through the snow, breathing out clouds of frozen air, screwing up his face at the weather, pleading for it reveal the whereabouts of Kinjo Temple.

"My god," he said suddenly when the temple remains arrived in his eyes, the sight stopping him dead in his tracks.

Zhang studied the bedraggled timber relic, balking at the raging winds that were threatening the temple's existence. He ran his eyes over an ambush of frozen plant life that was wrestling the warped exterior and took a moment to reflect, flicking through the stored images inside his mind, using them to revisit the face of the temple in its prime.

He closed his eyes and found the temple graced under skies of blue and white, with lush, native fauna that lined the hand-crafted river stone staircases, springtime offering the unmistakable scent of cherry blossoms, their pale pink petals scattered throughout the temple grounds.

Now, the temple is undoubtedly an abandoned house of horrors, thought Zhang. A dark and twisted hideout that would have suited the bones of Bruce Wayne's alter ego.

Zhang cautiously made his way up the crumbling staircase, battling the merciless winds, weaving between a fast-flowing line of snow-covered rats, his shoes disappearing between them one by one in the snow.

"Goddamn vile rodents." Zhang trapped one with his boot, snapping its back with a squeal, mashing its tiny bones and cartilage with a skin-crawling popping sound.

He anxiously pinned back the strings of hair on his head at the entrance, though he didn't need to. There was no one here to impress—at least by physical appearance.

No, Zhang did it because he was buying time, prolonging the eventual moment where he'd have to venture inside. Listening to the wooing winds inside the temple sounded like listening to gangs of ghosts. Zhang reached for the torn cloth curtain that was flapping at the entrance.

"Arrrgh," he screamed suddenly as a minute school of vesper bats shot through the curtain in rapid succession, screeching and squawking like tiny vampires fleeing the bowels of hell.

Zhang dropped to his knees, his arms raised overhead, shielding his face as the winged rodents took to the sky, wildly disappearing one by one into the blizzard's haze, looping and spiralling out of control until they were consumed by snow and darkness.

Rising, Zhang arrived through the curtain and scanned the remains of Kinjo Temple, disgusted by the stink of decay, as if mounds of animal carcasses were decomposing in one big heap.

He weaved through clumps of destroyed furniture, using the chaotic congregation of flickering crimson candlelight to avoid the endless mounds of rat feces beneath his feet.

"That repulsive aftershave is nearly as vile as your Cantonese skin," a voice whispered in the dark.

Zhang squinted at the shadows, using the flickering candlelight to pinpoint the voice that boomed off the temple walls in echo.

"I keep getting it for Chinese New Year," joked Zhang.

He approached a Kagizuru, the temple's traditional Japanese fireplace that was loaded with snow-covered logs.

"Would a fire kill ya?" Zhang flipped up the collar of his coat and tightly crossed his arms.

He stepped back suddenly when the fireplace erupted to life, the snow-covered logs igniting, melting away the layers of snow.

"Well, it's good to see your skills haven't waned after all this time at least."

Zhang eagerly leaned toward the fire and rushed his hands to the flames.

"Thought I asked you and your Cantonese parasites to forget I ever existed."

"Yeah, well, things have changed," said Zhang. "I have a situation in Hong Kong, a . . . delicate matter that requires someone with your skill set."

"Not interested."

"Yeah, well, I knew you were gonna say that, so how 'bout I make it worth your while?"

Zhang lifted his eyes from the Kagizuru just in time to catch a glimpse of the whispering man who went by the name, Shibisaki. He was moving behind the crumbling rows of temple pillars, drifting silently, as if he was on a tiny platform of wheels, the candlelight dimming just for him.

"Are you going to emerge from the shadows, or are you going to keep lurking back there like some kind of jackal stalking me in the dark?"

Zhang wiped the sweat from his forehead when there was no reply.

"We both know you have nothing of interest that can entice me. I have no use for Cantonese currency."

"It isn't money I've come to offer you. Here me out."

The drifting shadows came to a halt, and Shibisaki spoke. "Go on, then. Lure me with your wares."

Zhang returned to the fire and a devilish smile arrived upon his lips.

He put his cigar in his mouth and cautiously leaned toward the flames, puffing his stogie until it came to life.

"Two days ago, a young tourist boy inconveniently caught my trigger finger in action. I set my dogs of war on him, but they turned a clean sweep into a total cluster fuck, and now, he has slipped into the hands of the Hong Kong Police."

"And why on earth would that interest me?"

Zhang offered Shibisaki a soundless reply. He hauled the photograph from his pocket with a smile and placed it face down on a busted table.

Shibisaki's grubby hand emerged from the shadows, the visible parts of his skin covered in grime and filth. He flipped the photograph with his chipped fingernails, then held it in his hand.

Zhang puffed on his cigar with great satisfaction when he saw the image brew a storm inside Shibisaki, his hand progressively trembling with rage as he studied the oxidized black-and-white still, gawking at the three figures in the photo.

"It's all very simple," said Zhang. "Hong Kong Police have

taken this boy underground. I need you to track him down and close the book on him. I get to abandon the idea of spending the next thirty years in prison, and you, my old friend, get to settle a score you've always dreamed of."

Zhang studied the ferocity in Shibisaki's butchered face as he emerged into the flickering candlelight, revealing a ghostly white, redundant eye that was mad with hate.

"I'll wait outside." Zhang tossed his spent cigar into the flames and left the temple. "You have twenty minutes to gather your things."

Shibisaki hauled the photograph back into the shadows for safekeeping.

CHAPTER 29

Shibisaki rested in the tray of the Kubota, rocking from side to side while Zhang and Sujin tackled the mountain terrain up front.

The people in the photo had awoken something dark inside him, had made his blackened heart thump so hard it was about to burst through his chest.

He gazed up into the undercarriages of pine trees as they whipped by, thinking how badly he wanted to kill things. He reacquainted his grubby fingertips with the hideous scarring on the right side of his face and held his breath, revisiting the past, memories that were etched into his mind forever.

To a stranger, the horrendous marks and unsightly eye could have been from the mauling of a dog, a vicious attack that had been left to self-heal without the care of a physician, care that could have delicately stitched and realigned the facial tissues, making Shibisaki appear more human and less like someone who had endured the teeth of Hannibal Lecter and lived.

He tore a strip of cloth from his tattered robes and folded it over the lower half of his face, creating a fukumen: a temporary mask that would conceal his butchered skin from the bitter cold.

He tied the knot behind his head and dipped his hands into the pre-packed arsenal by his side, his fingers lovingly seeking each familiar item in turn.

First, an escrima. Shibisaki gripped the hardwood, cylinder-shaped fighting stick and thought about the vast number of skulls he had opened with it, the bones it had shattered, the men, women, and children he had crippled with it, memories that comforted him.

He returned the escrima to its former home, sliding it inside the sleeve of his tattered robes, perfectly aligned with his forearm. The sound of a primer pin clicked as it locked the escrima in place.

Next, the kusarigama sickle. Shibisaki felt the cold metal chain in his hand and smiled. The terrified screams of his victims returned to visit him, unchallenging prey who had fallen under the slash of the sickle. He pictured hundreds in movie montage, falling one by one after the weighted chain swung in large circles over their head, entangling its prey and reeling them in to take them apart with the curved blade that looked like the scythe of a grim reaper.

And last, his beloved ninjato. Shibisaki tenderly whispered to the sword in Japanese. He clenched the handle, removed it from its sheath, then thrusted the blade at the sky.

He stared at the square cross guard and ran his amber eye down along the length of the blade, the steel devastatingly sharp as ever.

"One minute," shouted Zhang through a tiny window of the Kubota.

Shibisaki sheathed his sword and rolled over onto his knee to find the Kubota hitting the abandoned runway, heading for Zhang's Blackbird that was still parked in the snow, surrounded by Sujin's burning beacons of light.

Shibisaki bumped forearms with Sujin, and then he was gone, the Japanese caretaker skidding back off into the night, headed for Kinjo Temple, where he would await the return of his master in secret.

"Fire the engines," yelled Zhang as he signalled the pilot through the cockpit windshield. "I want Planet Hoth to be a distant memory inside of five minutes."

Zhang stuffed his hands in his coat and waited for the staircase to grow from the belly of the plane. Shibisaki clutched at his sword when Mia, Dozer, and Mr. Kile rushed out past Zhang to get to the tarmac. One by one by one, they headed for Shibisaki, encircling him, analysing with scrutiny, despising the very sight of him.

On any normal day, the three-piece detested the presence of any outsider, but especially ones who were now in Zhang's employ to finish a job they couldn't.

"So, this is the man you've brought in to mask our incompetence?" asked Mr. Kile as he glared at Shibisaki's white eye.

Zhang yelled as he took to the staircase. "Mr. Kile, get on the fucking plane."

Mia moved toward Shibisaki and scoffed as his rotten-temple odour stung her nostrils. "This man smells like trash."

Dozer studied the square cross guard of the sword by Shibisaki's side and analysed the tattered remains of his ninja-yoroi, an outfit worn by ninja.

"Stay back," warned Dozer as Mr. Kile got in Shibisaki's face, close enough to find his own reflection inside his whitened eye.

"Nobody joins Zhang Industries without my signature, Mr. Zhang," he shouted over the howling wind. "Do you mind if we try before we buy?"

Shibisaki felt a sudden urge to unsheathe his ninjato and separate Mr. Kile's head from his body.

He tilted his head to the side and placed his working eye on Zhang, seeking approval to engage in a little bout of warfare on the snow-filled runway.

Zhang stared back at Shibisaki and retuned the slightest of nods.

"Make it quick."

Dozer spotted the tip of Shibisaki's kusarigama sickle tucked inside his ninja-yoroi and moaned out loud. "I don't think this is a good idea."

"Shut up, Dozer." Mia Kwon swore in Cantonese, eagerly on board with dismantling the time-worn apparition standing in front of them.

Mr. Kile moved to within an inch of Shibisaki's face. "How 'bout it, trash man? Wanna dance a little?"

On the surface, Shibisaki appeared calm and steady, his eyes expressionless, unintimidated by the taunts of Mr. Kile. Down below, however, was a different story. Down below, Shibisaki was cunningly busy, making preparations to introduce his separator.

With the slightest of movements, he used his thumb to push up on the square cross guard of his sword, exposing the blade to the frosted mountain air of Hokkaido.

CHAPTER 30

S hibisaki felt the swift, striking movements of Mr. Kile.

He retreated quickly, his feet sliding backward in the snow, unfazed and untested by the deadly combinations that were coming for his head, combinations that would have made an ordinary man crumble.

Hook, hook, jab, overhand right—Shibisaki made Mr. Kile miss with ease, shifting from side to side, sword still sheathed in hand.

Mr. Kile took a knee when the sound of tiny feet crunching in the snow fell in his ears.

Shibisaki took position, fixing himself in a defensive stance as Dozer used Mr. Kile's back as a springboard to launch himself through the air.

Shibisaki watched as the five-foot-nothing ball of Cantonese muscle came for him, screaming wildly over the roaring winds, his tiny concrete fist curled into a ball to deliver a hammer punch.

Shibisaki calmly waited, acting as if he had all the time in the world, filling Dozer with hope that his punch was about to land with devastating effect.

Click.

Shibisaki twerked his wrist and his escrima stick arrived suddenly in his hand.

He raised the hardwood club in the frozen air and swung it at Dozer.

Crack.

The strike forced Dozer to spiral into a backflip, like he had been coat-hangered by a tree branch in midair, the blow forcing an explosion of blood from his mouth as he landed in the snow.

Shibisaki lowered his club and turned toward the window-shattering screams of Mia Kwon.

She drove her signature push kick through the haze of snow and Shibisaki countered.

He watched Mia's face shift from rage to despair as the soles of their feet collided like an explosion, the force of Shibisaki's kick lifting her off the ground and sending her flying through the air, her arms and legs flapping wildly in the wind before crash-landing in the field of snow.

Dozer returned, screaming wildly, fists clenched, probing through the snow like a miniature torpedo.

Shibisaki pulled his kusarigama sickle and swung the weighted chain in circles overhead.

Dozer grunted when the chain found a home around his neck, seizing him like a head of cattle.

Shibisaki tugged on the chain and tossed the iron hamster in a Judo-style throw, plucking him from the snow-covered tarmac and hurling him through the air.

"Incoming," yelled Zhang. He shielded his head with his forearm as Dozer collided with the body of the aircraft, leaving behind a perfect indentation of his minute frame in a panel of the plane.

Shibisaki turned quickly as a slicing sound met his ears. He unsheathed his ninjato and attacked the air, deflecting a series of Mr. Kile's blades in rapid succession, sending them ricocheting off into the blizzard.

Cringing, Mr. Kile offered up his hands in surrender.

"Bravo," laughed Zhang. He peeled his gloves from his hands to clap in admiration. "Now, lick those wounds, and get on the fucking plane."

Shibisaki offered Dozer and company a parting glance as he made way for the Blackbird.

The fight was over before it began. Shibisaki couldn't be touched.

CHAPTER 31

K aiden led Brandon through the honeycomb alleyways of
Hong Kong Island, drifting from shadow to shadow,
using what remained of the night to sneak through the city
streets undetected.

Kaiden knew by now that Hong Kong Island would be
crawling with police, fellow officers he considered friends,
marching as one, eager to seize the rogue inspector along with
his witness.

He thought about Zhang's gang of thugs, pictured them out in
force, moving undetected amongst the uniformed officers of
Hong Kong, unaware that the mob boss was actually travelling
through the skies overhead, returning from his visit to the frozen
ground in Northern Japan.

"This is it," said Kaiden. "White Crane Wing Chun."

He palmed Brandon's chest to stop him from entering a
shower of orange streetlight.

Brandon found an oblong-shaped sign filled with Cantonese
characters across the road. He studied a circular drawing of a
defending crane doing battle with an attacking snake and
frowned.

Something about it was familiar, as if he was experiencing
déjà vu.

"How are you so sure we'll be safe here?"

He watched Kaiden stare at the sign. "I haven't stepped inside
those walls for almost eight years. Trust me, nobody will be
looking for us here. I'm not welcome, and the whole city
knows it."

"Can't say I'm surprised. I've only known you for five
minutes, and I hate you already."

He turned to Kaiden and raised his eyebrows. "No offense."

"None taken," said the inspector. He shook his head and lost a large chunk of his cool.

He studied a towering wall of bamboo scaffolding that was positioned next door to White Crane Wing Chun. "We'll wait until there's a break in traffic, then we're gonna climb that neighbouring bamboo structure and drop down into the school. You're not scared of heights, are you?"

Brandon ran his eyes up the towering structure and gulped when it disappeared into the night sky.

"Who, me?" said Brandon with a wild note of hysteria. "No sweat, but what's wrong with the front door?"

Kaiden smiled at the fear in Brandon's eyes.

"It's too risky to allow anyone to see us enter the school from the street. Zhang has eyes and ears everywhere."

He scanned the passing cars and patiently waited for an opening. "Okay, let's go."

"I'll race you to the top, old man," joked Brandon as they took to the bamboo structure.

He scooped in two lungful's of air when he found Kaiden racing up the rows of bamboo like a long-tailed macaque. The inspector hooked his legs over a bar of bamboo, hung upside down, and playfully pounded his chest like an ape. He regretted it immediately, clutching at his sternum where Mia Kwon had kicked him.

"No fair! You need to be drug-tested by an official," cried Brandon.

He frowned at Kaiden clutching at his chest. "What's wrong?"

Kaiden winced in agony, then unhooked his legs to pull himself upright. "My chest is still killing me from when that bitch kicked me."

"Oh, it hurts?"

"Yeah."

"Hurts bad?"

"Yeah."

"Good."

Brandon felt a little woozy when he arrived at the top. He looked down and followed a stream of vehicles that were now the size of remote-controlled cars.

"Okay," said Kaiden. "Now, all we gotta do is jump down into the school and we're home free."

Brandon peered over the edge. "How far is it? Wait, I'll rephrase: where is it?"

"Geez, I don't know. Can't be more than thirty feet"

"Oh, really? Okay, that's fine. Yeah, it's just thirty feet. That's not too far." He grabbed a fistful of Kaiden's trench coat and glared at him. "Are you out of your mind?"

"Brandon, calm down. It's roughly thirty feet to the ground inside the school's quadrangle, but it's only around fifteen to the roof."

"Yeah, the roof we can barely see."

"Look, I'll go first, and you can follow me down, okay?"

"Yeah, okay. No problem. I can do this." Unsure, Brandon sucked in a deep breath and watched Kaiden move into position.

"Okay, here we go." Kaiden let go of the bamboo structure and dropped feet first toward the school.

Brandon let his ears be his eyes as the flaps of Kaiden's trench coat seeped into the shadows.

A crash of roof tiles followed, then silence, then a loud slapping sound when Kaiden's shoes found the terracotta tiles inside the quadrangle.

"Army roll when you hit the roof," Kaiden whispered. "Then land feet first in the quadrangle. It's okay. Pretty soft landing."

Brandon moved into position. "I swear to god, Kaiden, if I break my neck . . ." he said to himself.

He rested his forehead on a bar of bamboo and closed his eyes, working overtime to calm his racing breath.

"On three," Kaiden whispered form the shadows below. "Ready?"

Brandon shook his head as Kaiden kick-started the count, hating every second in the lead up to the eventual moment where he'd find himself letting go.

Brandon felt his stomach tie itself into a knot somewhere between two and three as he lifted his hands from the bamboo and fell toward the school.

"Fuck you, Kaiden," Brandon said out loud as he plummeted toward the earth.

He freaked when he felt his body travel through the roof of White Crane Wing Chun at an alarming rate, failing to army roll off and land inside the quadrangle as Kaiden had instructed. Instead, he shot through the ceiling, bounced off a cabinet, and crashed through a wooden table, smashing it to smithereens.

"Brandon, are you okay?" panicked Kaiden as he shifted through the rubble, waving away clouds of plaster from his face. "I said roll off the roof, not smash through it like a crash-test dummy."

"Holy shit," said Brandon as he coughed out clouds of plaster. He wiped the dust from his eyes and found a barrelling silhouette charging at Kaiden, its fists raised, raging toward him with murderous intent.

"Kaiden, move!"

Kaiden Chan didn't know what hit him, the force deadly, fast, and accurate.

Brandon got to his feet and went into battle with the moving shadow as Kaiden abruptly left the scene, sent to collide face-first into a brick wall.

Brandon made a fighting stance, attempting to bob and weave around the shuffling fists that were headed for his head at an alarming rate.

He grimaced as the flurry of fists hit their mark, knocking the wind out of his chest, conditioned knuckles slapping into his face with a brutal style that frightened him.

He'd never seen or felt punches like these before. The strikes were fast, deadly, and freakishly accurate.

He screamed when the attack finished with a stabbing kick to the chest, one that sent him exploding through a wall of decorative lattice like a rag doll.

"Elizabeth," a voice rasped in the dark.

Brandon shielded his eyes as the school's florescent lights flickered awake.

He sat up, clutching at his ribcage, looking at a frail Cantonese man at the end of the hall. He leaned into his timber cane and slid his hand from the light switch on the wall.

Brandon looked at the skilled attacker and wrestled with his ego when he found a young woman who may have been all of twenty-one years of age. She was dressed in a scarlet robe with laced frog button fasteners.

"Elizabeth, help them up. I think there are two of them," said the old man.

Brandon watched the old man press against the walls with the palms of his hands, as if he was searching for a light switch in the dark. He studied the foggy grey surfacing of his eyes and found no pupils.

"What are you looking at?" snarled Elizabeth, spotting Brandon's intrusive stare. "Haven't you ever seen a blind man before?"

Elizabeth formed a blockade in front of the elderly man and took a breath, her fists still tightly clenched.

"Stand back, Sifu," she said. "Let the police take care of them."

There was something else that irked Brandon about his attacker. He experienced another strange sensation of déjà vu and couldn't help shake the feeling that he knew the girl who had just kicked his arse.

It was her name. *Elizabeth*, he thought.

"Wait," said Brandon as he struggled his feet. "We can explain."

"You can explain it to the police when they get here," she said.

"There's no need. We have a real-life cop here. Look."

A cough came from underneath the rubble, followed by a groan as Kaiden almost revisited consciousness.

Elizabeth pointed her finger at Brandon. "Don't move. You stay right there."

She started to clear the timber from the struggling man's back, attempting to roll him over to make sense of his slurred speech.

Elizabeth froze when she saw the man's face, her eyes burgeoning with tears.

"Dad?" she whispered in confusion.

Elizabeth growled as she grabbed two fistfuls of trench coat, hauling the semi-concussed inspector to his feet.

There, she glared at him in disbelief, clenching her teeth, torn between hugging the man who had given her life and rearranging his face for a second time.

"Wait, hold up," said Brandon. "This crazy guy is your father?"

She turned to Brandon and glared at him. "I don't have a father."

With little regard for his welfare, Elizabeth let go of Kaiden, dropping him like a piece of trash, sending him back to the pile of rubble beneath his feet. The inspector didn't feel a thing.

Suddenly, it dawned on Brandon why she seemed so familiar and he gawked at her as Elizabeth charged away, using her satin robe sleeve to rub the water from her eyes.

He returned to the scene on the plane, where Lena had handed him a book: *The Six Forms of Wing Chun*.

He whispered her name as she charged down the hall, swearing loudly in Cantonese.

"Elizabeth Chan."

CHAPTER 32

The aroma of rum and wine filled the air inside Yuen's store.
It all unfolded in slow-motion. Johnathan Zhang strolled through a haze of cigar smoke, his cold, dead eyes painted on his target. He hauled his silver-plated pistol from his fur coat, cocked the hammer, and winked at the sights. Brandon shook nervously in anticipation when the barrel arrived an inch from his forehead—

The sound of a car exhaust went *bang!*

Brandon woke to the thunderous boom, the sound of a back-firing taxi spooking a flock of pigeons from the rooftops of White Crane Wing Chun.

He wiped the sweat from his forehead and opened his eyes, his facial expression still stretched into a mask of terror.

He sat up in bed and listened to the drowning hum of Hong Kong Island, its streets now filled with beeping car horns, pining trams, and hissing tourist buses.

He spotted the White Crane quadrangle through an arched window, the beautiful setting towing him toward the window on auto-pilot, like he was still in a dream.

He scanned the majestic layout of White Crane Wing Chun, marvelling at the stone-carved dragons fixed in fighting positions, the rich flower arrangements set in Chinese decorative pots, row upon row of hand-painted scrolls, and crowds of cherry-red lanterns that hung from the eaves of the school.

A rapid knocking sound derailed Brandon's dreamlike state. He quickly switched windows and moved to the neighbouring framework, folding his arms on the window sill.

He found Elizabeth Chan inside the quadrangle, moving swiftly, spouting screams that sounded like war cries. She tossed her deadly fists into a combination dummy: a fake person hand-carved from timber, designed specifically for the art of Wing Chun.

Brandon cringed, riddled with discomfort when he felt the shockwaves from Elizabeth's raw power.

She circled around the wooden dummy, fighting voice raging while she viciously bombarded the padding of the dummy, her fists and feet blurring before Brandon's eyes.

Elizabeth braked suddenly, appearing fixed in thought. She placed her hands on her hips and steadied her heaving breath. Brandon gulped when Elizabeth turned toward the arched window, sending a venomous glare filled with hatred through her beautiful brown eyes, eyes that intended to deliver a very clear message: *"Get out."*

The cold and uninviting stare made Brandon feel like some kind of foreign disease.

She smashed the combo dummy a final time and stormed off, departing the quadrangle in long, angry strides.

"Argh!" An unexpected cry came from a room behind Brandon.

He slid open the paper-windowed door and found the old man from last night dabbing at the knife slit in Kaiden's forearm. He was dipping a folded cloth into a concoction of water-soaked herbs, then returning it to the wound where Mr. Kile's knife had been.

"Smell's interesting," said Brandon as he ran his own forearm across his nose.

The old man lifted his face from Kaiden's arm and offered a warm, inviting smile in the direction he believed Brandon to be standing, showcasing the foggy grey surface of his blinded eyes.

"This is one of Sifu's signature remedies," grumbled Kaiden. "He believes healing comes from nature, not from a physician."

"Sifu?" Brandon asked.

"Yeah, you know, like a sensei. It means 'father.'"

Brandon scanned a row of framed pictures overhead,

portraits that were painted in black-and-white by an unnamed artist. "Who are all these guys?"

Kaiden followed Brandon's inquisitive eyes to the paintings.

"They're the heart and soul of White Crane Wing Chun," he said. "Generations of masters. Men who handed down their knowledge, from father to son, teacher to student." Kaiden looked at Sifu and smiled. "You'll have to make room on that wall for Elizabeth."

Sifu smiled at Kaiden and finished the fresh wrap on his arm.

Brandon watched as Kaiden carefully guided Sifu to his feet.

"His English is a little rusty, Brandon, but here goes. Brandon Willis, meet Grandmaster Wong. You can call him Sifu."

"I've heard many great things about you," said Sifu in a flattering tone. He took his time to search for the right words. "Kaiden has spoken very highly of your martial art. I believe you saved his life?"

Kaiden laughed awkwardly. He stumbled around the remark, eager to derail the conversation.

"Forgive me," said Sifu with a warm smile. "I have to see about cancelling classes until further notice."

"Here, let me help you." Kaiden went for Sifu's frail arm.

"It's okay. I know my way. Give Brandon tour of school. He may find many things of great interest. Nice to have met you, Brandon."

"Yeah, likewise."

Brandon watched Sifu trudge through the door, aided by his hand-carved timber cane.

"Is he your . . . ?"

"Father?" asked Kaiden as he hauled a Chesterfield from his soft pack. "No. But he might as well be."

They made their way through the meditation chamber and headed for a small side balcony.

"My mother left shortly after I was born, and then, when my father died, Sifu raised me here."

Brandon recalled Elizabeth's venomous glare in the quadrangle.

"So, when you said you weren't welcome here anymore, you meant by Elizabeth, right?"

Kaiden blew out a cloud of smoke and regretfully nodded.

"So, now what?" asked Brandon.

"I'll return one of the hundred and thirteen missed phone calls I received from Chow yesterday and get to work. See if we can find out where the leak came from on the inside. It wasn't by chance that Zhang and his goons stormed that Medical Services flight at Hong Kong International."

Brandon studied Hong Kong Harbour through a window and found the lavish Harbour Grand Hotel in the distance, a sight that was within reach, but still felt worlds away.

"I'll get an update on your mother," said Kaiden, when he found the anxious stare in Brandon's eyes.

"But for now, Brandon, just sit tight. I know it sounds easier said than done, but be patient. Work with me, and this will all be over as soon as possible."

Kaiden flicked his smoke over the railing and headed for his trench coat. He pulled out his Glock, inspected the loaded clip, and rammed it home.

"Stay out of sight, keep away from the windows, and above all else, under no circumstances leave this school. If anyone comes around, Sifu will know what to do. I've filled him in on everything."

Kaiden took to a set of stairs suddenly, driving his arms into the trench coat.

"And stay away from Elizabeth" he shouted as he disappeared out of sight.

Brandon arrived at the railing. "She's not my type."

"I meant for your own personal safety."

CHAPTER 33

L indsey Chow looked like he hadn't slept in a month, having pulled a double at the precinct, his phone locked on speed dial, desperately trying to reach Kaiden, begging for him to pick up.

Frustrated, he tugged at the choking Windsor knot around his neck and kicked open the doors to his apartment building in West Kowloon.

He froze as he took to the stairs, suddenly remembering what was waiting for him three floors overhead. He frowned deeply into the empty staircase, then returned to a chair in the foyer, slipping off a pair of sunglasses to reveal reddened eyes.

He jerked his wallet from his jacket pocket and flipped it open.

A momentary look of discomfort arrived in the inspector's eyes when he found the face of a familiar-looking business card sliced in half by the pouch.

He slid it out, revealing its bone-shaded face and raised lettering, then ran his eyes over the company title in its entirety: *"Zhang Industries."*

The card's best days had been and gone, filled now with creases and ripped edges, as if the card had been repeatedly brought out and shoved back inside over a duration of time.

He flipped the card over and found a "Mr. K" scribbled in black pen, a cell phone number written beneath.

He squeezed his eyes shut and scrunched up the card in his hand, his fist trembling like he wanted to turn the spent card into confetti.

He dropped the expired cardstock on the floor and returned to the wallet.

He smiled lovingly as he turned it sideways, staring at a photo of his then four-year-old son: Lei. Happy and healthy. Smiling wide for the camera in one of his playschool photos.

The inspector caressed the photo with his thumb and sighed, questioning if there even was a God.

"Kaiden," he said out loud as his phone rang. He pulled it from his pocket and recognised the incoming number.

"Where the hell are you?"

"I can't tell you that, Chow. Besides, you're better off not knowing."

"What do you mean?"

"They knew, Chow. They knew. About the Medical Services flight to Shenzhen, they knew the plane, where to find it, what time it left, everything. Zhang has got someone on the inside. There's a rat in our division. I'm sure of it."

Chow nodded regretfully, then sighed. "Yeah, I kinda got that feeling also when you disappeared so suddenly. That phony airport marshal, the one at Hong Kong International? Two years ago, he was arrested for drug trafficking, spent just six hours in lockup, and then he was out. Guess who posted his bail in full?"

"Johnathan Zhang?" asked Kaiden.

"Correct."

"Son of a bitch. I knew it! Any luck tracing that explosive from the safe?"

"Yeah, report came in. It's not good. The explosive used on Yuen's safe was a standardised charge, one that's used on hundreds of demolition sites every day. You can buy it anywhere with as little as a driver's licence or passport, in both Hong Kong and Mainland China. Too common to trace the sale."

"Oh, that's wonderful."

"Where's the boy and his mother?"

"I've stashed them somewhere safe, for now."

"Come on, Kaiden. You're not even gonna tell me?"

"I wouldn't tell the Dalai Lama."

Chow shook his head in disapproval, then took to the stairs, fishing for his apartment keys.

"Any luck locating Zhang?" Kaiden asked.

"Nothing. It's like you both suddenly disappeared off the face of the earth last night. Only thing we know for sure is his private jet returned from a sudden trip to Japan this morning. Airport police seized it moments after its arrival, found one of those spent cigar butts on board that you're so fond of, but no Zhang. It was empty, much like your apartment!"

"My apartment?"

"The superintendent had a squad of uniformed officers turn it upside down last night. I think it's safe to say our beloved leader thinks you're involved with some unsavoury characters. It must have something to do with your sudden Houdini act at the airport. You know, the one where you stole an ambulance, its crew—two of which are still missing—their patient, and her son who just happens to be a witness in a murder case." Chow ran out of breath and took another. "No biggie."

"Chow, listen. Zhang and his goons were at Yuen's store for a plate, a specialised counterfeiting plate that Yuen Lau must have made for Benny. I think Benny took the front money from Zhang and tried to jump the border. When Zhang found out, he took away the use of his legs."

"Steal, and you'll be disfigured," said Chow, reciting Kaiden's words at the murder scene on the fishing trawler.

"That's right," replied Kaiden.

"Are you sure about this plate? There's no evidence in that shop to suggest one had been created. They could have stolen anything from that safe."

"We have a material witness in a murder case that says different. We find that plate, we find Zhang. What's the matter with you, Chow? Are you with me on this, or not?"

"Okay, okay. Don't go getting unhinged, Inspector. Tell me what you need?"

Chow hauled his tiny notepad from a pocket and pressed it against the wall, penning Kaiden's instructions, trying to keep up with his racing voice.

"Start digging! See if there have been any newly approved leases, ones that have been obtained in the past twenty-four hours. Look for warehousing, storage facilities, anywhere large enough to handle the production of a counterfeit operation, then check—"

"Yeah, yeah, got it, partner. That's it. I've gotta sleep first. It's because of you I've had none."

"We'll sleep next month. We have—"

"*I* have to spend some time with my son," Chow replied, his voice roaring in echo, bouncing off the concrete walls inside the apartment stairwell.

The power in his voice was met by a wall of silence on the other end of the line.

Chow turned away from his apartment door and palmed away the bloodshot tears in the corners of his eyes.

"The doctors told Lynn to take Lei home, to keep him comfortable and get our affairs in order."

"I'm sorry, Lindsey."

Chow cleared his throat and wiped his nose. "If his AB-Positive blood type wasn't so incredibly rare, there would be a glimmer of hope, but the chances of finding a donor are probably worse than the odds of winning the Lotto."

Kaiden exhaled on the other end of the line.

"Chow, listen. Go inside, hug your wife and kid, and get some rest. I'll call you later, see how you're all doing."

Chow pushed away from the railing and returned to his door, apartment key in hand.

"You better stay in the shadows, Kaiden. If Zhang or the superintendent catch up with you, they'll fit you for a toe tag."

"Yeah, way ahead of ya."

"Where will I reach you?"

"Don't! I'll reach you."

Chow heard Kaiden perform his customary clapping of the phone in his hand before the line went dead. He slid his key in the door and jerked the lock, his mouth breaking wide apart in yawn.

"Hello, I'm home," Chow whispered softly.

He pulled off his gun and badge, resting them on the kitchen counter beside his keys, just as he did every day after arriving home from work.

The bedroom door opened with a creak before Chow stuck his head inside.

He scanned the ill-lit room and found his wife, Lynn Chow, resting in a recliner chair, fast asleep, a blanket towed up around her neck, holding on to the frail and tiny hand of their six-year-old son, Lei.

Chow smiled lovingly as he eyed the congregation of miniature Iron Man images plastered all over Lei's pyjamas, shooting across the sky in his red jet suit.

He pulled the covers over Lei's scrawny frame and placed a kiss on the top of his hairless head.

"I love you, son," he whispered.

Click.

Chow froze at the unexpected sound.

Knowing what it was, he thought about rewriting the entering of his home, drafting a script where he opted to keep the loaded pistol attached to his hip instead.

He turned to find the threatening silhouette of a man standing in the doorway.

The man quietly raised his silver-plated Heckler and Koch pistol and placed Chow in its sights.

CHAPTER 34

B randon paced the empty quadrangle of White Crane Wing
Chun, anxiously gnawing at his nails, contemplating Lena's
condition in the presidential suite at the Harbour Grand Hotel.

He arrived at the school's now heavily barricaded gates and
peeked through a keyhole.

He found a wave of identical red-and-white taxis choking the
laneways, their drivers angrily stabbing at their car horns,
shaking closed fists and hurling abuse in Cantonese.

A group of small children suddenly whisked by, neatly
dressed in school uniforms, humming joyfully to drown out the
barrage of beeping horns and shouting voices.

He turned his back on the gates, groaning in complaint when
he couldn't shake the feeling he'd been incarcerated, forced to be
an inmate rather than a visitor or student of White Crane Wing
Chun.

Brandon spotted Elizabeth's wooden dummy in the middle of
the quadrangle and contemplated striking it as a way to vent his
frustration.

He approached it, curious, scanning the still quiet quadrangle
to ensure it was free from spying eyes, eyes who could pan or
mock his punches if they didn't land correctly.

Brandon awkwardly positioned his feet and placed his hands
in front of his body.

He delivered a sporadic shuffling of fists, trying to mimic the
chain-punching style of Wing Chun, attempting to impersonate
Elizabeth's raw power and lightning speed. He failed miserably.

The past twenty-four hours had taken its toll, the stress and
trauma showing in the visible signs of wear and tear in Brandon's
weakened punches.

He threw a careless straight right hand into the padding of the dummy, sending it rocking back and forth inside its foundations, as though it had been shaken by an earth tremor.

"That's not the way to do it," a voice snickered suddenly.

Brandon turned and found Elizabeth Chan's threatening eyes charging toward him.

"You've gotten rid of all my students, so now, I will teach you."

For many, Elizabeth's words may have sounded like an invitation, but they weren't. Far from it.

To Brandon, it was nothing more than a spiteful remark, one that filled him with intimidation.

Elizabeth spoke over him, shutting down his half-hearted reply like a drill instructor.

She began lecturing, circling him on the spot like a shark, her eyes locked to his as she spouted the proper technique.

"The Wing Chun punch is very different from other types of punches. It's vertical, and uses one precise point to punch with."

Elizabeth opted to circle back in the opposite direction, her eyes still bolted to his, fierce and focused.

"Our punches pierce, instead of being thrown, like a sharp knife penetrating flesh. They come from our centre, from our heart, from our soul."

She stopped in front of Brandon and stared him down. "Put up your hands."

Brandon hesitated. He swallowed the dryness in his mouth and cautiously raised his closed fists.

"Like this?"

Elizabeth nodded. "Now, hit me."

Brandon pushed an easy-going straight right hand Elizabeth's way, pretending to hit her.

"I said, hit me," she shouted. Elizabeth aggressively slapped away Brandon's forearm and glared at him. "I'm not made of silk."

Brandon frowned when he caught Elizabeth positioning her

feet. She raised a closed guard to her face and sharpened her eyes. "Hit me. Stop hesitating, and do it."

Her aggressive tone sparked something in Brandon. Suddenly, he felt threatened, like he was back within the walls of Trinity College, preparing to defend himself against the cowardly taunts of Mr. Johnson.

Brandon closed his fist and threw a powerful right hand towards Elizabeth's head.

Brandon's eyes took on a haunted look when Elizabeth's shuffling knuckles drove the wind from his lungs before his punch had travelled even half the required distance to take off her head.

Before Brandon knew what had happened, he found himself skidding across the quadrangle on his back, wildly clutching at his chest like he'd been tagged by the blast of a shotgun.

"Elizabeth," Sifu yelled in protest when he heard the commotion.

Brandon rolled over in agony, struggling to race air back into his lungs.

He found a blurry Sifu limping toward him, the butt of his timber cane stabbing into the pavement of the White Crane quadrangle. "Elizabeth, you know better."

Letting his ears be his eyes, Sifu crouched down beside Brandon. He hauled him upright and brought his arms up over his head in a bid to open his lungs.

"It's okay, Brandon. Just breathe, slow and steady."

Sifu looked skyward when the soles of Elizabeth's shoes scraped the paved surface of the quadrangle. He frowned in her direction as she departed, saddened by her vulgar display of power.

"I'm sorry, Brandon. For Elizabeth, this is out of character."

"What's her deal?" He watched Elizabeth storm out, once again departing in long, angry strides. "That's twice she's kicked my arse."

"There is real pain inside," said Sifu. "Memories from the past.

The return of her father has stirred many emotions, emotions she is unsure how to express."

Brandon didn't have to weigh up Sifu's words. He felt them.

His eyes wandered through the network of pavers in the quadrangle, his mind ticking as the physical trauma she'd bestowed upon him dissipated. Suddenly, he became over-whelmed by a deep sense of anguish and loss, raw, painful emotions he knew like the back of his hand. In many ways, they were alike.

CHAPTER 35

S hibisaki cruised the warehouse catwalk overhead, lurking in the shadows, monitoring Zhang's pop-up operation from above in secret.

Kaiden had read Johnathan Zhang like a book, spot on about his requirement to secure a space large enough to kick-start his counterfeit operation. Somewhere far off the beaten path, a warehouse non-affiliated with Zhang Industries, one that had most likely been obtained by a phony name: a Cantonese Jane or John Doe, perhaps.

To Shibisaki's one working eye, Zhang stuck out like a sore thumb, with his rounded frame and balding head cruising from aisle to aisle, puffing on a cigar while he barked orders at his crew.

"I want this operation run air-tight, Mr. Kile. Make it like a cocaine plant."

Zhang pointed from worker to worker. "Strip them down to their underwear, Dozer. Toss all the clothes in the incinerator when you're done. I don't want these commoners growing ideas about leaving this warehouse with wads of cash once Benjamin Franklin arrives in the flesh."

Zhang stopped suddenly, peering over an artist's shoulder who was placing the finishing touches on Yuen's counterfeit plate by way of a microscope. "Any discrepancies?" he asked.

"It's the finest work I've ever seen, Mr. Zhang."

"Excellent. I want the test press underway within two hours, no exceptions."

The artist pulled away from the microscope lens, closed his eyes, and nodded.

Zhang scanned the rows of computer techs who were calibrating and refining the money's imagery on their screens, critiquing the digital files, adjusting process data, aligning Benjamin Franklin's face with the margins, eliminating possible defects that could be detected by the human eye.

Zhang smiled proudly and imagined endless rows of Carbine MP4s, AK-47s, and M13 assault rifles, tightly bunched and cradled in storage crates, resting next to a lifetime's supply of ammunition.

He blew out a cloud of smoke toward the warehouse rafters and found the outline of Shibisaki positioned overhead, staring back at him, concealed by the shadows.

"After a rich man gets rich, his next ambition is to get richer," Shibisaki whispered as he heard the heels of Zhang's shoes clapping on the catwalk behind him.

"This isn't about greed or money, my old friend. It's about power and taking it back."

Shibisaki considered the quote and held his position, offering Zhang nothing but a view of his back.

"So, it is with the people where your loyalty lies. I mistook you for a warmonger. How noble."

"None of which is your concern right now, might I add." Zhang ran his fingers through his hair in frustration. "Shouldn't you be out in the city by now, kicking in doors, tearing homes and buildings apart brick by brick, getting me what I need instead of picking apart my operation like a meaningless film critic?"

Shibisaki turned to Zhang and lightly tapped his temple, the one next to his milk-white eye.

"Everything I need is right here."

Zhang cringed when he found the reflection of his balding head in Shibisaki's spent eye.

He pushed down the lump in his throat and made a face.

"Just get me what I need. I don't care if half the city is in flames by nightfall. Just make sure Brandon Willis burns along with it."

Zhang stubbed out his cigar on the railing, then squashed it under his shoe.

"After that, you are free to rewrite the past."

CHAPTER 36

Kenneth monitored the movements of the Hong Kong Police from the presidential suite while they scurried around on the ground like a pack of angry ants. He stood on the window ledge, pressing the side of his face against the glass window, and smiled when his phone rang.

"Kaiden," he answered without checking the caller ID.

"Kenneth. How is she?"

"No change in condition?" he asked out loud, turning toward Anna Lee and Ethan to confirm.

Ethan nodded in reply with a thumbs-up.

Kenneth returned the phone to his ear and looked back outside.

"She's doing well, a fighter."

"Good."

"I'm just busy spying on your friends from afar."

"Huh, what do you mean?"

"Hong Kong Police received an anonymous tip. Some squealing member of the public said they saw the tail end of an ambulance roll inside the guts of the Harbor Grand Hotel yesterday evening, roughly an hour after your trouble at Hong Kong International."

"Shit," swore Kaiden.

"Don't worry. We have it covered. Their search of the underground carpark came up empty. We rehomed the ambulance and chucked it inside a locked garage downstairs, then sealed the seventy-fifth floor for unscheduled maintenance that's never gonna happen, just in case the boys in blue get creative and decide to do a thorough search of the hotel floors."

"Phew, good work."

"Hang on a second." Kenneth turned up the TV with the remote when a large sign for Zhang Industries flashed across the screen.

"What is it?" Kaiden asked.

Kenneth waited for the reporter to wrap his lines before replying.

"Nothing much. Seems your friends raided a Zhang Industries warehouse way out on Lantau Island. Didn't find anything, it seems."

"Then that might be a good place for me to start."

"How so?"

"Maybe they've overlooked something. At least I can be assured they've been and gone. I'm practically flying blind at the moment."

"Urgh," said Kenneth suddenly.

"Now what?"

"They just showed a picture of you on the TV."

"How do I look?"

"Like shit." Kenneth laughed into the mouthpiece.

"They've had you and your newfound friend plastered all over the tube for the last three hours. Fresh report every thirty minutes or so."

Anna Lee arrived by Kenneth's side and tapped him on the shoulder.

He turned to her and held his hand over the mouthpiece while she spoke.

"Can you please ask the inspector how his arm is?"

Kenneth nodded and returned the phone to his ear.

"How's the arm getting on?"

"It stings like a fucking son of a bitch."

Kenneth's mouth hung open in reply. He stared blankly at Anne Lee, stumped as to how best to translate. Finally, he leaned toward her ear and whispered, "He said it still stings a little."

Kenneth cleared his throat and returned to the glass window to look outside.

"Looks like your friends have given up on the Harbour Grand. They're piling back into their vehicles as we speak. Perhaps they've decided the sighting was bogus. I don't know where you've stashed the Willis kid, but you better make damn sure the police don't think to look there—or Zhang, for that matter."

"Don't worry. He's safe. They'd need a crystal ball or a friggin' psychic to find where I've stashed him."

CHAPTER 37

Shibisaki hoisted himself up into the warehouse rafters. Stretching from beam to beam, he moved deeper into shadows, eager to detach himself from Zhang's obedient sheep on the factory floor.

He took position on a platform of planks, crossed his legs, and closed his cunning eyes.

Shibisaki wanted a world, a world he'd be able to see unobstructed through his mind's eye, a world that stretched far beyond the limits of mortal minds.

Slipping into a dreamscape, Shibisaki crossed over, wandering through valleys of endless paths inside his mind, open spaces of matter filled by strangeness and mystery.

It was here he waited, in search of someone who could unconsciously offer an open invitation, a foreign pathway, someone who could keep Shibisaki from having to kick down every door in the city, or tear foundations apart brick by brick as Zhang had described.

Thirty-two miles to the east, resting deep in the heart of Hong Kong Island, he found that person, someone consciously unaware that they were destined to commune with an outside force, unaware that they were about to go mind-to-mind with a ghost.

Sifu was peacefully practicing mindfulness, resting in a lotus pose, breathing deeply inside his meditation chamber, contemplating Elizabeth's outburst towards Brandon, longing for solutions he might never find, when something dark and mysterious distorted his thoughts.

He placed his frail hand on his heart and took in a deep breath, attempting to calm his mind, to discard the unexplained arrival of his rapid heart palpitations.

Sifu opened his eyes suddenly, desperate to end the session, when he discovered he couldn't move. It was as if he'd been bolted to the floor.

An unknown force arrived, sending shockwaves through his body, hitting him like the blast wave from an explosion.

He started to scan his meditation chamber with his ears, his face laden, stricken with fear as the environment started to shift around him.

His ears picked up the sound of sliding furniture, skimming across the meditation chamber floor as if they were being pushed by an invisible force.

Ceramic pots fell on their sides, spewing clumps of blackened soil and tree roots out onto the ground.

Framed pictures slid from their walls and exploded on impact, showering the floor with shards of glass, as if Hong Kong was enduring an earthquake.

He experienced a cold he had never felt before, brutal and unforgiving.

A cruel frost started to eat at his skin, forming blisters on his body like he had been subjected to severe frost bite. He opened his mouth, breathed out a cloud of frozen air, then vanished from the meditation chamber of White Crane Wing Chun, fading into the atmosphere like a ghost.

Sifu found himself on an ice-covered floor, his vision blurred and warped, the atmosphere twisted and bent out of shape. He lifted his head and found himself face to face with the beady eyes of a rat.

The rat tilted its minute head, tinkered with its whiskers from side to side, and then scurried away.

In the midst of the chaos, Sifu found time to smile to himself.

He propped himself up onto his knees and opened his hands. He smiled as he ran his eyes over the network of lines in his skin, wondered by them, his sight somehow restored.

"So, powerful Kung Fu man, we meet again," Shibisaki's voice arrived in whisper.

Sifu scanned the shadows, his cold eyes narrowed to slits when Shibisaki revealed himself in the limited light.

He studied the wretched man from head to toe, inspecting the lower half of his face that was concealed by a fukumen, the strips of cloth dangling from his ninja-yoroi, his tattered tabi boots plastered in dried rat feces.

"You can't place me, can you?" He studied the confusion in Sifu's eyes.

"Cast your eyes, Grandmaster. You will know."

Sifu scanned the floor for answers, every muscle and bone shaking as he found a rusted ninjato sword resting in the corner of the room, sprinkled by a dusting of snow.

Next to sword, he found a faded and rotted timber sign with Japanese text carved into the planks. He whispered the text out loud in Japanese: "Kinjo Temple."

"That's it," said Shibisaki. He spotted the dreadful realisation in Sifu's eyes and smiled.

"Now, look at me!"

Shibisaki rolled toward Sifu as if he were on a platform of wheels. He lowered the fukumen from his face and revealed his network of scars.

"Give me the boy, and I promise I'll kill you quick. Refuse, and I'll burn every martial arts school in Hong Kong until I find the right one."

Sifu studied the scattered remains of Kinjo Temple. "Like you did here?" he said. "Killing me or Brandon Willis won't mend the shame you have woven into your dark heart."

Shibisaki viciously drew his ninjato from behind his back as a warning.

"Do not challenge me. If I kill you here, it's for real, old man. Now give me the boy."

Sifu shook his head in reply, cringing against the cold. He

squeezed his eyes closed, desperate to break free of the invisible chains that had him anchored to Shibisaki's mind.

"It's cold, isn't it?" asked Shibisaki as Sifu clutched at his chest, jetting clouds of white mist from his mouth in rapid succession.

"Tell me where the boy is now, and I'll send you back, provide you with warmth, allow you to die comfortably in your bed many days from now."

"Never." Sifu knew Shibisaki's words were a lie.

"Sifu . . . ?" A young voice echoed suddenly within the walls of Kinjo Temple.

Shibisaki arrived by Sifu's side, eyes wandering, his ears investigating the echo.

He softly placed his hand on Sifu's head and closed his eyes, eager to seep deeper inside his mind.

"No," Sifu screamed. "No, Brandon, get out!"

Shibisaki used the pathways in Sifu's mind to travel to White Crane Wing Chun. He found himself wandering Sifu's meditation chamber with his mind's eye, utilising his powers of invisibility, listening for voices, trying to identify anything that would give away the location.

Shibisaki studied Brandon as he arrived, calling out for Sifu, standing up the overturned furniture and inspecting the bed of broken glass.

Shibisaki examined a circular emblem stitched to the cuff of a Kung Fu robe that was lying on the floor: the circular symbol of a defending crane doing battle with an attacking snake.

The symbol of White Crane Wing Chun.

Shibisaki smiled and opened his eyes, as if awakening from a pleasant dream.

Sifu reappeared suddenly with a scream, returning to the meditation chamber of White Crane as if he had been teleported by force.

"Sifu!" yelled Brandon. "What's wrong?" He placed his hands

on Sifu's shaking body in an attempt to calm him. "Holy shit, you're freezing. Elizabeth, get in here!"

Brandon pulled the Kung Fu robe from the floor and draped it over Sifu's trembling body.

He held the old man's face in his hands and watched the greying mist seep back into his eyes, returning his peepers to darkness.

CHAPTER 38

K aiden quietly weaved through the tall grass of Lantau Island, darting from hiding place to hiding place, Glock pressed firmly in hand as night consumed everything in sight.

Kaiden found his target resting quietly beyond a sea of swaying reeds.

He took a knee, patiently using his time to study the Zhang Industries warehouse from a distance.

To the inspector's eyes, the warehouse looked like a trap: dark, motionless, and abnormally quiet.

He tweaked the bandage on his forearm, then revisited the ambushed Medical Service's flight behind his eyes.

Kaiden didn't want history to repeat itself. This time, he'd be ready, fiercely alert, willing to reveal his licence to kill.

He switched off his phone and cautiously started to move in, unified by the dark.

He criss-crossed his forearms before entering the gaping warehouse doors, positioning the muzzle of his Glock side by side with a minute torch, ensuring his bullets would travel anywhere the light went.

The halo of light picked up gutted filing cabinets, tossed and busted furniture, and smashed computer screens scattered across beds of broken glass.

To a stranger's eyes, it looked as if the Zhang Industries warehouse had been ransacked, burglarised, or ravaged by some rogue gang of youths who had nothing better to do.

As Kenneth had mentioned on the phone, Hong Kong Police had done their thing, had been and gone, their search for Johnathan Zhang unsuccessful and now, most likely on to the next possible location.

He started sifting through the rubble, picking through scattered paperwork, flipping open manila folders with his shoes, searching for anything that could connect the dots and provide a link between the counterfeiting plate and Zhang's whereabouts.

He found a piece of paper, torn from a notepad, almost chewed to pieces from the ransacking.

He put the torch on it and whispered the text: "Jasper's Dream, February Fifth."

A code of some sort? he thought. Perhaps the name of a parade, a racehorse, a whore house?

Nevertheless, it was something. Clues at this point were almost non-existent.

With little thought, he folded the piece of paper and stuffed it in his pocket.

Click.

Kaiden froze, his search interrupted when a gun behind him made a snapping sound.

"Bang, ya dead," laughed a familiar voice in the dark. "It's okay, Kaiden. Look, no bullets." The man presented his empty gun to a strip of moonlight, then floated forward to reveal his face.

"You gotta be kidding me." Kaiden heaved in breath as he leaned over a table, relieved beyond words when he found Inspector Chow's smiling face grinning in the moonlight.

"Well, that was embarrassing," Chow laughed. He drove the loaded clip back into his gun, yanked the barrel, and stuffed it in his holster.

He joined the party, hauling out his own minute flashlight, assisting in examining the warehouse floor.

"How did you know I'd be here?" asked Kaiden.

"Come on, Kaiden. I know you better than you know yourself."

Kaiden nodded in agreement, then rehomed his Glock while

Chow prattled on, both of them now scouring the glass-filled floor in sync.

"When you refused to tell me where you were, I tried the next best thing—tracing Zhang's final movements before he fell off the radar. I knew we'd eventually cross paths somewhere. I must have waited at Yuen's store for a couple of hours before deciding to move on. You know, the forensics team still haven't cleaned his brains off the wall inside his market stall yet?"

Kaiden found Chow's laugh just as unsettling as the gruesome remark. Suddenly, he couldn't shake the feeling that something felt out of place.

Kaiden shone his torch on Chow, lighting him up as though he was on a stage.

He felt a chill down his spine when Chow turned his head, staring fixedly into the light, his eyes cunning and laced with anger. It was a look he'd expect to find on Johnathan Zhang, not his partner.

"You ever see blood in the moonlight, Kaiden? It appears quite black."

Kaiden found himself intensely monitoring Chow, his thoughts starting to race.

He considered why Chow had decided to venture out here alone, oddly separating himself from the pack, especially when he had a dying son at home.

"Any luck with the warehouse's storage facilities?" asked Kaiden, acting as if everything was as it should be.

"Oh man, look at this." Chow tore his eyes away from the light.

"Glenfarclas." Chow collected the head of a broken bottle from the ground and lit up the label with his torch.

"Zhang is gonna be pissed. You know, this is a sixty-year-old bottle of scotch. Must be worth thousands."

"Never heard of it." Kaiden's fingertips began to crawl across his midsection, headed for the handle of his gun while Chow studied the glass in his hands.

"Ah, sorry Kaiden, where were we? Uh, warehouses? I thought we might skip that and go straight to the part where you tell me where Brandon Willis is."

Chow drew his gun suddenly. He dropped the bottle head and pointed his pistol toward Kaiden's face.

"I'm sorry, Kaiden. I thought I had it in me to wound you on arrival as you came scooting through those warehouse doors. Turned out, I was wrong. I even robbed the clip from my gun to keep myself from accidently shooting you for real. But as of right now, I realise my options are fading fast."

Kaiden's hands slowly rose toward his head.

"Any luck with leads on locating that rat in our division, Inspector Chow?"

Chow analysed the disappointment in Kaiden's eyes and laughed half-heartedly.

"What the hell happened?" asked Kaiden.

Chow rubbed the barrel of his gun on his forehead, then began rambling like a madman.

"Hmm, okay, well, let's start with the life-sucking whore known as leukemia. You ever see cancer gnawing away at the bones of a six-year-old child?"

Kaiden didn't respond. He studied the intense agony in his friend's eyes and chose to hear him out.

"They don't die quietly. Oh no. The effects of chemo are far from quiet: round-the-clock vomiting, anaemia, hair loss, ulcers of the mouth, the tongue, the throat, veins so black they look like they've been lined with motor oil! It's no day at the beach, let me fucking tell ya!"

Kaiden fearlessly drifted towards Chow's gun. "Chow, listen. It's not too late. We can talk—"

Chow silenced Kaiden with the barrel of his gun, stabbing it into his chest.

"I'll only ask this one time, Kaiden. Where is the Willis boy? And by god, it had better be the truth. No games. I need him if my son is going to survive!"

"Survive?" Kaiden asked. He scanned the desperation in Chow's eyes and raised his hands again.

"Without a bone marrow transplant, Lei will die. Zhang has agreed to provide us with a donor, someone who matches Lei's rare blood type. I keep the force off his back, allow him to complete his deal, help bring in the Willis boy, and Lei gets the donor."

Kaiden protested. "You really think a crook like Zhang is going to save your son once he gets what he wants?" Chow flinched and looked away, his eyes beginning to wander in thought.

"Chow! Use your head! Zhang probably manipulated data in the registry to create a donor. Think about it: he offers a desperate inspector hope, one who'd do anything to save his dying son, and he gets what he wants without lifting a finger. He's using you like a chess piece, positioning you to get what he wants, and once you have served your purpose, he will kill you, your wife, and your dying son."

Chow's mind started to tick, realising in a fleeting moment that Zhang had swindled him.

Suddenly, he felt worthless and ashamed, the last shred of exhausted hope he'd been clinging to torn apart before his eyes.

"I can't trust him . . ."

Kaiden shook his head empathetically and slowly raised a hand toward the barrel of Chow's gun.

"Give me the gun, Chow. You don't want to do this. You're a good man, a father, a husband. You're not a killer."

Kaiden followed the rows of tears running down Chow's cheeks, confident he had abandoned his murderous rage and was now lost in feelings of remorse.

"There's so much pain here. Too much pain. I won't watch my son suffer anymore. I can't."

Chow suddenly took a step back from Kaiden, knocking his hand from the gun and placing the barrel next to his own temple.

"Please, Chow, give me the gun,"

"No. I am in hell, Kaiden. *Hell.*" Chow pressed the muzzle of his pistol against the wall of his brain, like he was attempting to drive it inside.

"Please don't do this, Chow."

Chow pulled away the gun from his head suddenly, unable to pull the trigger.

He held it out with both hands and took aim at Kaiden.

"You'll help me. You can help me. Tell me where he is!"

"I can't do that," yelled Kaiden.

"I'm going to count to three. Please, I can't watch my son die. Tell me where to find Willis."

"Chow, please."

Chow roared over Kaiden. "Do it now, or I *will* kill you. Understand? Look into my eyes, Kaiden. Draw your piece, or I'll orphan the only daughter you pretend you don't give a shit about. The daughter you turned your back on!"

Kaiden watched Chow's lips move as he started the count, pleading through a stream of tears, his trembling voice a childish whisper.

On the count of three, Kaiden drew his Glock, aimed it at Chow's heart, and pulled the trigger.

CHAPTER 39

The unmistakable greed in Zhang's wide eyes was a sight to see.

He eagerly paced the catwalk above his adopted warehouse floor, chain-smoking cigar after cigar, monitoring his funny-money operation from above, one that was now coasting through production.

The custom-built hydraulic press invented by Zhang Industries travelled up and down, stamping proprietary paper stock into Yuen's custom-engraved counterfeit plate, creating thousands of high-grade Federal Reserve notes that came complete with security ribbons and textured ink.

Mr. Kile arrived behind Zhang and placed a hundred-dollar bill under his snout for inspection.

"Hi, Benjamin," said Zhang. He ran his eyes over the lines in Mr. Franklin's face, smiling proudly as he silently mouthed the detailed text from the Declaration of Independence emblazoned on the bill.

As the hours drifted by, Zhang continued to watch his operation unfold like a Rocky montage: guillotine paper cutters sliced and diced the proprietary paper into individual notes, while hired hands shuffled bills, banding wads of cash into sums of thousands and packing them neatly into rows of enormous, plastic-clipped cases.

At the end of the warehouse floor, more workers pitched in, forming a human chain, coordinated in endless lines of delivery-men, working to place the concealed cases into vans and slamming closed their doors.

As the final van door closed, Dozer found himself swearing at the warehouse PA system, wildly shaking his fat little fists at the control panel in tantrum, infuriated by its inability to function.

Mr. Kile smiled when he found Dozer erratically flicking a host of switches, his tiny feet dangling off the ground like a child in a high chair.

He made a miniature fist, sharpened his eyes, and tossed it into the face of the control panel, rattling it to the core with a monstrous *boom*.

Zhang turned away suddenly and cupped his ears as the PA suddenly squealed to life with a high-pitched scream. He jerked his ear canals with his index fingers and found Dozer looking back at him, smiling awkwardly, his tiny thumb pointed toward the warehouse ceiling, signalling to Zhang that he was now on the air.

Zhang swiped the microphone and faced his workers, who were still in their underwear. He smiled proudly when he found them prepared to hang on every word, neatly aligned in rows like an infantry battalion.

"First, there was a dream. Now, there is reality." He was quiet for a clock's worth of seconds, his voice booming off the warehouse walls. "In days gone by, Zhang Industries was an organisation without a home, cast aside by corrupt government officials. Tomorrow, we will reshape them as ours."

The warehouse workers stabbed closed fists in the air and chanted to Zhang's words.

"History is written by victors, conquerors, the strong, the determined. It is our turn to write our own pages of history, and you will all bear witness to the revolution."

Zhang stabbed both fists in the air, and the crowd erupted as one, roaring wildly in approval.

Zhang watched Shibisaki descend from the shadows, lowering himself from the warehouse rafters to land on the catwalk.

"Well?" asked Zhang as Shibisaki arrived.

"I know how to find them."

Zhang snapped his fingers in the air to summon Dozer, Mia, and Mr. Kile.

Together, they huddled as one while Zhang dished out the plays like a coach to his quarterback.

"Dozer, Mia, Mr. Kile: take the Fleetwood and go with Shibisaki. Obey him. Do whatever he asks. And above all, get this job done."

CHAPTER 40

E lizabeth wiped down the deep lines in Sifu's face with a cloth, then glanced at Brandon with imploring eyes.

"What the hell happened?"

"I dunno." His breath left him without speech for a handful of seconds.

"I came into the meditation chamber when I heard the sound of broken glass, and he just appeared out of nowhere. He was lying on his side, like he is now, shaking, frozen to the bone."

One of her brows slanted with scepticism, and she studied the frown on Sifu's forehead. She caressed the left side of his face, trying to soothe the elderly grandmaster, urging him to drift off to sleep.

"His colour is returning," she said. "Let him rest here."

Brandon felt her affection for Sifu, the tender gaze in her eyes revealing a side of her he hadn't yet seen.

"You really care about him, don't you?"

She neatly folded the cloth in her hands and stared at the ground. "He's all I have left."

She looked at Sifu and frowned deeply.

"When my mother died, Sifu took care of me. He trained me, raised me as his own."

Brandon nodded. He took a moment to consider the inspector's role in the family's checkered past, wondering where Kaiden sat in the family tree. "And Kaiden?"

The very mention of Kaiden Chan filled Elizabeth's eyes with disdain. The snarling eyes Brandon had been introduced to were back.

Annoyed, she rose to her feet and turned away, staring

intensely at her wooden combo dummy in the middle of the White Crane quadrangle.

"Just because someone shares the same blood doesn't make you family. Blood makes people related. Loyalty makes people family."

"Sounds a little cold-hearted," said Brandon.

"I don't expect a Westerner to understand. Besides, unless you've lost a parent, you wouldn't know what I'm talking about."

"You're wrong," he said, answering almost immediately. Brandon gulped and summoned the courage to share his pain, realising now that Elizabeth and he wore matching scars. "My father, he—"

Before Brandon could finish, a flock of wedge-tailed pigeons exploded from the roof of White Crane. They flapped their wings in a cacophony of sound, bolting into the Hong Kong evening sky as if they'd been startled by an unknown presence.

Brandon and Elizabeth both turned wide, startled eyes to the ceiling, wondering what on earth had spooked the pigeons, fearful the White Crane was now secretly under attack.

They jumped away from one other as a body arrived between them, falling upside down through the newly created hole in the roof from Brandon's botched arrival.

They each made a fighting stance, preparing to defend themselves, but instead found a man trapped inside his own trench coat, wriggling around on the tiled floor, rambling like a crazed mental patient.

"Nice entrance, Inspector," said Brandon as he lowered his closed fists from his face.

He grabbed onto Kaiden's arms and attempted to haul him upright.

"Get your hands off me."

He slapped away Brandon's hands and spat a mouthful of blood on the ground.

"I don't need your goddamn help."

Brandon and Elizabeth eyed one another, analysing the slurred speech of Kaiden Chan.

"Run out of booze where you were, did they?" asked Elizabeth as Kaiden crawled to his feet, swaying back and forth on the spot like he'd just recovered from a vicious knockdown.

"Correctomundo," he said.

He wiped a blood trail from his chin and plucked a half-finished bottle of Jack Daniels from his trench coat pocket.

"Can I buy either of you two losers a drink?" Kaiden screwed off the bottle cap and swigged.

Elizabeth shook her head. "So, you came all the way back to White Crane to show us you're still a drunk? Congratulations. I already knew that."

Kaiden tripped towards his daughter, stabbing at his chest with his finger, angered by the remark.

"I'm not a drunk. This is nothing. I'm just merry." He held out his arms and turned in a wide circle, like he was boasting on a stage. "I'm not as think as you drunk I am."

Appalled, Elizabeth analysed his droopy, drunken face. She closed her fist and picked out a spot to mark up if and when the time came.

"Hey," Kaiden pointed suddenly over Elizabeth's shoulder. "Who's your silly-looking friend?"

Kaiden brushed past Elizabeth and stumbled out into the quadrangle, his drunken eyes aimed at her Wing Chun dummy.

"What's your name, buddy?"

He gripped onto the forks of the wooden dummy to keep himself from going to ground and cunningly whispered in the dummy's imaginary ear.

"You haven't got a spare Chesterfield, have ya?"

He set his bottle of booze on the ground and went to work, as if performing a bust on the city streets of Hong Kong.

"Come on, Mister. Don't you hold out on me. Come on now, empty those pockets!"

Brandon and Elizabeth frowned at one another, eyes oddly racing back and forth as Kaiden searched the dummy, patting down the trunk, feeling for its hips and pockets that weren't there.

"Kaiden Chan, you're demented," Brandon whispered, loud enough for Elizabeth to hear.

"No. He's just a worthless alcoholic."

"Come on. Take a free shot." Kaiden bumped his head on one of the timber forks. He stood back and slapped at both sides of his face in anger, then shouted at the dummy. "You think I'm afraid of you? Huh?" Agitated by what he believed to be an imposing threat, Kaiden drew his Glock and fired a shot at the dummy, shaving a thin piece of timber from the side of its trunk.

"You're a terrible example for our people," screamed Elizabeth as she lowered her hands away from her ears. "A humiliation and a disgrace."

Kaiden gazed around awkwardly, pretending to be dumb-founded by the remark.

"Are you talking to me?"

He holstered his pistol and stumbled toward Elizabeth, placing both fists in front of his bloodshot eyes.

"Come on, then," he laughed. "Teach me a lesson. Rattle me once."

He slapped both sides of his face to antagonise.

"Come on. It'll be like old times. I'll go easy on ya."

Elizabeth shook her head in disgust, struggling to keep a lid on her rage.

"I don't fight drunks."

She glared at Kaiden for a moment, then departed in long, angry strides, arms folded, swearing under breath when Kaiden spat loudly, the sound stopping her dead in her tracks.

She glanced over her shoulder and found Kaiden's blood-filled saliva rolling down the trunk of her combo dummy.

"Okay, wait a minute," said Brandon, morphing into a human blockade between the pair.

"Stand aside, Brandon." Elizabeth held Kaiden in her sights.

Brandon felt his legs shoot out from underneath him, Kaiden performing the same leg sweep that took him to ground on the promenade in Stanley Bay.

"Step aside, round-eye." Kaiden lifted his intoxicated gaze and found a rampaging Elizabeth.

She drove a one-inch punch into her father's midsection, the freakish force lifting him off his feet and sending him skidding across the quadrangle on his back.

Coughing and sputtering, Kaiden spat blood from his mouth and raced air back into his lungs.

He smiled at his daughter and got back on the horse.

"I was waiting for that," said Kaiden as he floated into position, making a fighting stance. "Now, let's see how much you've really learned."

Brandon watched from the ground as the freakish skills of Wing Chun erupted within the belly of White Crane, father and daughter going head-to-head in the quadrangle, hurling an endless barrage of chain punches at one another, neither able to seize the advantage before Sifu arrived out of nowhere, armed with a long wooden dragon pole.

He went to work, effortlessly hooking their legs from underneath them, sweeping and tossing them across the quadrangle one by one like someone who could see what they were doing.

"Stop this," yelled Sifu. He threw the dragon pole to ground and growled with furious anger. "We are family!"

Elizabeth scrambled to her feet to scream in protest.

"Just because we're related doesn't mean we're family. All that changed the day he left us."

"Aw, boo-fucking-hoo." Kaiden pulled a handful of change from his trench coat pocket and threw it on the ground. "Here, I'll even chip in a few bucks. Go call someone who cares."

Seething, and willing to finish the job, Elizabeth went for Kaiden, but found herself entangled in a Sifu's arms.

"You've never been around when anyone needed you!" she screamed.

Kaiden shook his head, his shoulders drooping with shame.

"Jesus Christ, Elizabeth. I had to leave after the funeral. Can't you understand that?"

"We all wanted to leave. But you know what? *We* stayed. We aren't cowards, unlike you."

Tears leaked into the corners the inspector's eyes as he returned to his feet, but when he finally responded, he was screaming. "I was afraid, all right? You wanna hear me say it? You wanna break me down? There it is! I was afraid, and I'm sorry. I'm sorry, Elizabeth. I was too afraid of failure."

Elizabeth found herself wanting to accept the half-hearted apology, desperate to mend the brokenness inside her heart. They stared at one another for what seemed like the longest moment in time, the truth finally out in the open.

"The pain in my heart was just too great," Kaiden said, softer now. The anger that held him up deflating. "I'm sorry, but I couldn't help you."

"I didn't need help. I just needed you. We should have been afraid together."

Kaiden lost his balance and fell on his backside. He unscrewed the lid off his bottle of booze and swigged.

Elizabeth shrugged out of Sifu's grasp and walked forward, toward her father.

"Instead of sticking together, you turned your back on us to become a fucking drunk, spending night after night wallowing alone in self-pity."

Elizabeth grimaced as Kaiden hitched a hiccup and drooled onto his shirt.

"That's it, Sifu," she said, disgusted by what she saw. "I'm done.

I don't need him. I don't need White Crane. I'm fucking out of here. Fuck him."

Sifu gave chase as Elizabeth departed, desperately calling out for her to return.

Kaiden Chan responded by doing what he knew best: he wiped his tears, drew a fresh Chesterfield from his soft pack, and stuck it in his mouth.

He crashed out on his back in the quadrangle of White Crane and lit his smoke, blowing rings at the moon until sleep came for him.

Brandon sighed at the closing of the inspector's eyes, looking around at the empty quadrangle.

He scooped up the handful of Kaiden's coins and stuffed them in his pocket.

"Goodbye, Inspector." Turning, Brandon made his way toward the White Crane barricade.

CHAPTER 41

Brandon had grown tired of his incarceration-like existence at White Crane Wing Chun, the cunning leg sweep by its warden the final straw. No more.

He found himself back on the streets of Hong Kong Island, working from memory, reusing the mental map of honeycombed alleyways that Kaiden had given him, a map that would lead him back to the ferry dock and eventually, to Lena's bedside at the Harbour Grand Hotel.

Brandon smiled as the ferry gate came to a close in the corner of his eye, proud that he had done it alone, confident that he had been sly enough to move throughout the city streets and to board the ferry undetected.

He took a deep breath when the top floor of the Harbour Grand Hotel arrived in his eyes.

He thought about Lena, sleeping in fits, her breathing hitching from the transport ventilator he hoped was still going strong, pumping oxygen into his mother's lungs.

"Next stop: Whompoa Garden," squawked the tiny maritime speaker behind him.

Brandon followed the ferry passengers as they moved to their feet, collecting their belongings of briefcases, backpacks, and shopping bags as they ushered tightly together at the door like cattle.

He decided to blend in, taking a position in the middle of the pack, head bowed, shoulders up around his ears, eager to remain undetected from the searching eyes of Hong Kong Police, or worse yet, Zhang and his dogs.

In the carpark, Brandon slowly broke away from the pack and started jogging, glancing over his shoulder every couple of strides as he made his way toward the Harbour Grand Hotel, leaving the ferry terminal and its CCTV cameras in his wake.

Brandon studied the entrance to the hotel through the eyes of a cop, casing the layout, scanning its entry and exit points, watching guest after guest arrive and depart in limos, Audis, and lavish sports cars.

Gaining entry to the Harbour Grand Hotel would be easy. However, gaining entry undetected, evading its surveillance equipment, and finding a way to the top floor where Lena was, was a totally different ball game.

He considered imitating a rich, snobby hotel guest, causing a scene where he'd march up to front desk to complain about the service, demanding to speak with the manager—i.e. Kenneth—but it was too risky.

What if Hong Kong Police were now searching the hotels? What if Zhang and his crew were in the area? What if someone recognised him and reported it? The stunt would inadvertently put Lena at risk.

Brandon's eyes suddenly landed on a Harbour Grand employee: a doorman who was walking quickly, peeling off a pair of snow-white gloves and hauling a packet of cigarettes from his custom-made, tuxedo-like jacket.

Brandon floated toward the edge of a box hedge, using its thick, lush foliage to secretly monitor the man. He paced past a cigarette smoking sign and disappeared into a walkway.

The trail of the doorman's cigarette smoke was easy to follow—rancid, chemical, and poisonous.

Brandon stuck himself to the wall like glue. Skimming along the smoothed marble surface, he crept in the corridor of shadows to avoid detection.

He peeked around the corner and found the doorman flattened against the wall, one hand in his pockets, the other guiding the cancer stick toward his mouth as he puffed out clouds of smog.

Brandon summed up the size of the doorman and quickly envisioned himself in the jacket. He looked at the ground, deciding where best to position his feet as the doorman puffed away, unaware that spying eyes were on him.

Brandon attacked suddenly, using the roof of his shoe to deliver a controlled roundhouse to the face.

Brandon cringed after the kick hit its mark, bouncing the back of the man's head off the marbled wall behind him and knocking him out cold.

He moved in, feeling for the man's pulse, listening for the booming heart inside his chest.

"Sorry about that, buddy." He smirked as he started to undress the man.

"Thank you for not smoking," he whispered.

Brandon fixed the cuffs of his tuxedo-like jacket as he headed toward the hotel entrance, hoping to blend in as he had on the ferry and move to the floor of the presidential suite undetected.

He entered the lobby, opened the door for a hotel guest, and then moved inside, viewing the spiralled marble staircase that intertwined between dozens of twinkling chandeliers overhead.

He examined the lobby around him, hunting for the elevators, when he heard a pinging sound over his shoulder.

He turned to find the two-strong ambulance crew, Ethan and Anna Lee, inside the elevator.

Brandon parked himself behind a fern in the lobby and held his breath when he observed the sorrowful look in their eyes.

Brandon tried to stop his bottom lip from trembling as the ambulance crew guided Lena's bed out of the elevator, her motionless body concealed head-to-toe by a white sheet.

Brandon started to step backwards in disbelief, then turned his back on the saddened skeleton crew.

He bolted out of the Harbour Grand Hotel, scared out of his mind, crying as he ran.

When his grief took his legs out from under him, Brandon

collapsed on the boardwalk in a dishevelled heap, afraid he was about to go insane from the gut-wrenching sobs that tore through his chest.

He sharpened his tear-filled eyes at Victoria Harbour and tracked the ferry boats, watching them as they bobbed up and down in the ocean's chop.

He took a deep breath and reached for boundary railing, clutching it tightly with his hands, envisioning the throat of Johnathan Zhang as he screamed at the sky.

CHAPTER 42

The following morning, Kaiden's mouth reminded him of a rainless desert.

He parted his shrivelled lips and sat upright, cringing at the pounding, beer-induced hammer inside his head.

"Argh," he said suddenly, referring to the random squirt of pigeon shit that arrived on his shoulder.

He nodded at the mayonnaise-coloured poo and spoke to himself. "Guess I deserved that."

He dabbed at the patch of dried blood where his head had collided with the pavement of the quadrangle, then vaguely recalled passing out, lit Chesterfield in hand as an amalgamation of beer, mild concussion, and fatigue stole the night from his eyes.

He struggled his way to his feet and examined the handle of his Glock by his hip.

More memories returned from the night—including the worst one yet.

Kaiden squeezed his eyes shut as a snapshot of Chow arrived in slow-moving black-and-white against his mind's eye, that dreadful moment when Kaiden's bullet had departed his gun barrel in a burst of fire and travelled across the warehouse to enter Chow's chest, spouting an explosion of red-blackened blood.

Chow's words echoed inside his head:

"I keep the force off his back, allow him to complete his deal."

"Deal," said Kaiden as he opened his eyes. "What deal?"

He remembered the piece of paper from Zhang's pockets and fished it out of his pants.

"Jasper's Dream, February fifth," he said as he unfolded the paper, thoughts of last night running through his mind. "The name of a parade, a racehorse, a whore? A street name? A ship?"

He stopped pacing the quadrangle and looked toward the sky, rubbing at his neck when he found Sifu sitting quietly on one of the many balconies of White Crane, his face positioned toward the humming drone of the city, feeding a flock of pigeons by his feet.

Kaiden searched for his Chesterfields and lit one as he walked upstairs, arriving on the balcony. He stood silently in the doorway, put the note back in his pocket, and looked toward the city with Sifu, Chesterfield smoke oozing from his nostrils.

"They say it is meant to be good luck." Sifu smiled at the city, knowing what the pigeons had done.

Kaiden wiped the poo from his shoulder with a nearby towel and smiled.

He joined Sifu on the bench seat and tapped the ash of his cigarette into an empty bottle.

"When you were a boy, I used to sit out here," Sifu whispered. "While you slept. I would feed the pigeons, waiting for you to wake while your father practiced in the quadrangle."

Kaiden smirked at the memory and watched Sifu's pigeons peck at the feed.

"I have early memories of us watching him train," said Kaiden. "Watching his power, his skill—that deadly right hand of his." Kaiden paused for a moment, and his shoulders fell toward the ground. "Before the accident took him from us."

Sifu started to breathe heavily. He bowed his head and dropped the paper bag of pigeon feed from his frail hand. The pigeons took to the sky, as if they'd been spooked by Kaiden's words.

Kaiden looked at him, studying his sudden unsettled state.

"Sifu, what's wrong?"

He lifted his head and pointed his eyes up to the sky.

"Forty-four years is a long time to hold on to a secret, a lie that has eaten a part of my soul very slowly over time."

"What the hell are you talking about?"

Sifu turned his flat grey eyes to Kaiden and frowned.

"Your father didn't die in a car accident like I told you, Kaiden . . . he was murdered."

I f it were a cinematic flashback, Sifu would have prattled off a narration as Hong Kong arrived to us in reels of black-and-white, a caption in the year of 1977 signalling the shift.

A continuous shot would have floated through the skies of Kowloon, in search of an apartment while he spoke, his voiceover setting the scene for what would soon transpire.

"Many years ago, when your father was an inspector, he got too close to Johnathan Zhang and his many Cantonese business partners. They put a contract out on him, employed the services of a Japanese assassin from the Kinjo Temple in Japan: a cruel and unforgiving abomination of a man.

"Legend has it there would be nothing but concrete jungle . . . and then a ghost . . . and you would be dead.

"In the northern tip of Japan, he was ninja, an ordinary man known as Shibisaki, but in the underworld of Hong Kong, he was quietly known as the Ghost Ninja of Hong Kong Island . . .

Kaiden's six-year-old eye peered through a gap in the doorway, heart pounding as he watched his father, Yoson Chan, hanging on for dear life, blood streaming from his nose, one hand clasping at the forearm of the Ghost Ninja, the other desperately searching for the police-issued revolver on his hip.

The sword tip of the ninjato was near, edging closer and closer to his father's heart when a younger version of Sifu arrived, barrelling through the apartment door, stouter, stronger, in his prime, his eyesight alive and well.

Sifu took to Shibisaki, viciously kicking and striking with both his hands and feet, knocking the ninjato from his grasp, yet unable to land a single blow, the ninja too fast, too quick, too strong, and too skilled for the moves of White Crane Wing Chun.

Kaiden followed Yoson as he rolled off the table. He drew the revolver from his hip and took aim, the pistol barrel wandering, waiting for Sifu to move, waiting for a shot.

"Duck, Sifu! Move!" pleaded Yoson as he cocked the revolver's hammer.

Kaiden brought his hands to his ears as a streak of fire departed the muzzle of Yoson's firearm, discharging a single round toward the tussling duo.

Kaiden gulped as Shibisaki winced in agony, clutching at his shoulder as the bullet exited his back and exploded through a glass-screen balcony door, raining shards of blood-stained glass onto the ground.

Shibisaki desperately countered, tossing a ball-shaped bomb into Sifu's face, where it exploded on impact, showering a blinding, crimson-coloured powder in his eyes.

Sifu screamed. He ran his trembling hands toward his burning eyes as Shibisaki delivered a heel kick to his chin, the strike rendering him unconscious, freeing him of pain and rag-dolling him to the floor.

Kaiden peered through the crimson, powdery haze to find Yoson cursing wildly at the jammed wheel of his revolver.

Shibisaki took advantage of the gun's jam. He hauled a star-shaped shuriken from inside his robe and took aim at Yoson.

Before Kaiden knew what had happened, he had left the doorway, his heart and eyes set on the ninjato that was resting within the low-lying crimson haze by Shibisaki's feet.

Kaiden arrived in an army roll, scooping the ninjato from the floor and delivering the Japanese steel to Shibisaki's face, striking him with his own sword, the body of the blade obliterating his right cheek and piercing the eye.

"Move Kaiden," pleaded Yoson as he tossed his revolver and leapt over the table, kicking Shibisaki in the chest. The kick drove the Ghost

Ninja through the obliterated glass door, flipping him over the railing and into black-and-white city lights below.

Kaiden felt the cold wind rush his face as he stepped out onto the balcony, hand in hand with Yoson.

Together, they clasped onto the railing and peered over the edge, hoping to find the masked assassin some thirty stories below, sprawled out on the road, dead.

Instead, they found the bustling traffic of Hong Kong Island, unobstructed by a falling body that should've been there, bringing traffic to a halt . . .

The Ghost Ninja was gone.

Kaiden felt the tension in his father's hand slip away suddenly.

He looked up to find Shibisaki's shuriken lodged in Yoson's hip, a trail of blood cascading down his leg towards his knee.

"Father," Kaiden screamed as the poison-tipped shuriken went to work, coursing its way through the inspector's veins as he slid toward the balcony floor, his face now white as snow.

Present-day Kaiden was indeed listening to Sifu's tale, trying to swallow it all in one big gulp as long-repressed images surfaced, supporting Sifu's claim.

"After the death of your father, I only allowed you to remember what you needed to, so your mind would not be clouded with pain."

Kaiden frowned at the floor.

"It used to come to me in my dreams: a room full of strangers shouting voiceless words, heads filled with dark, empty spaces where faces should have been . . ."

The cigarette fell away from Kaiden's hands. "Somehow, I think I've always known."

"Over time, I made you believe it was all a dream, through intense White Crane meditation and delicate manipulation of the mind. I only let you remember what you needed to know, so the memory couldn't haunt you and I could keep you from racing off to seek revenge. Yoson would have wanted it this way, would have begged me to make it this way. But now, the Ghost Ninja has returned from the frozen ground of Japan. He has returned to regain his honour and to rewrite the past."

Kaiden growled inwardly, his mind skipping into high gear.

"Eventually, Shibisaki will find White Crane," said Sifu. "He mustn't find you here. You, or Brandon."

Kaiden rushed to his feet and tossed his spent Chesterfield over the balcony.

"I'll get Brandon, and we'll move to another location."

Sifu rose from the bench seat and followed Kaiden inside.

"I'm afraid that time has already been and gone, my friend."

Kaiden stared at Sifu, shaking his head in question.

"Brandon left sometime during the night."

Kaiden studied the floor for answers. He drew his phone from his pocket, arming it to make a call.

"I think I know where to find him."

CHAPTER 44

B randon spent the night alone, paralysed by his grief, staring out into the sea until the morning sun met with his face.

He hung his head, staring blankly into oblivion, exhausted from zero sleep and countless hours spent crying.

He rubbed at his forearm, gripping it tightly, wishing he was back at his dreaded Trinity, a place where he would still have his mother, and a warm friend who could provide a comforting wave of numb.

"Brandon," Kaiden whispered softly from behind.

Brandon looked into the corner of his eye and found Kaiden kneeling at the railing, clapping closed his phone, the sea breeze flapping at the tails of his trench coat.

He stared at the torn state of the gutted youngster, watching him rock back and forth in a seated position. Kaiden stared at the ocean with Brandon, thinking about Kenneth's words, the news of Lena's passing the hardest of truths.

"If you would have just let me stay in the room with her, I wouldn't have been rotting away at that Wing Chun school while she was dying."

Kaiden frowned, thinking how Elizabeth would have felt the same degree of hopelessness when her mother passed.

Kaiden crossed his legs and sat with Brandon.

"You know, when Elizabeth's mother died, I didn't want to know nothing from no one, not even from my own daughter. I was filled with so much hate and rage that I was terrified I'd kill someone with my bare hands if I was rubbed the wrong way. I let the anger, the fear, the hate, consume every part of me. I let it swirl so bad inside that it robbed me of every good memory I ever had of her."

Kaiden held out his hand and placed it on Brandon's shoulder. "Do you understand what I'm trying to say?"

Brandon pressed his eyes shut and nodded, working hard to subdue his rage.

"If you give into your anger, if you focus solely on revenge, it will swallow you whole. You'll rob yourself of all the good memories held deep inside."

Kaiden scanned the harbour, monitoring the boats, Zhang and the Hong Kong Police on his mind.

He stood and held out his hand.

"Come on. It's not safe here."

Brandon took Kaiden's hand and made it to his feet.

"Now what? Where are we going?"

"Back to White Crane. We have to get Sifu, find Elizabeth, and get out of the city. Things have changed."

CHAPTER 45

F or the first time in a long time, Sifu had White Crane all to himself.

He should have been resting inside his meditation chamber, enjoying the peace and quiet, but instead, he found himself shuffling back and forth across the quadrangle, using memory to guide his straw broom across the leafy tiles, thinking about Elizabeth, wondering where she'd stormed off to, and more importantly, when she'd be back.

It was only a matter of time, thought Sifu. *Only a matter of time until Shibisaki finds the school, until he traces the origin of the White Crane Wing Chun emblem he spotted on the jacket sleeve during his commune.*

Sifu froze mid-sweep when he felt the atmosphere shift all around him.

The sound of scattered leaves racing across the quadrangle arrived in his ears, as if they had been directed by a force, shown what to do, and how to do it.

He stood still as a statue in the middle of the quadrangle, letting his ears wander, the broomstick clutched tightly in his hands, feeling threatened by a dark presence that felt moulded to the very walls of White Crane.

"Hello again, old man," hissed a voice in the swirling wind.

Without warning, Sifu felt the handle of the straw broom roll from his fingertips, the curved stick knocking into the quadrangle pavement by his feet as he interpreted the sadistic hiss that was delivered in Japanese.

Sifu quickly tuned his ears, desperately trying to pinpoint the voice when Dozer, Mia, and Mr. Kile showered him with laughter, playing the role of chuckling schoolyard bullies: cowardly cornering their prey to ensure they couldn't fight back.

"We'd like a Kung Fu lesson," mocked Mia Kwon as she placed a stick of gum in her mouth.

"Can you teach us how to defend against an incoming attack?" asked Dozer.

Mr. Kile charged at Sifu and stabbed him in the chest with a palm strike, the brutal force sending him crashing into the pavement on his back.

Dozer smiled at the fall, then proceeded to mock Sifu's milk-white eyes.

"I bet you didn't see that one coming."

The cowards laughed as one, hovering over Sifu, kicking him repeatedly in the ribs as he tried to return to his feet.

"You have to watch out for those strong typhoon winds, old man. They'll blow you right of your feet," laughed Mr. Kile as he placed the sole of his shoe on Sifu's hand, crushing it into the pavement.

Shibisaki remained in the shadows, arms folded while Zhang's wolves had their fun, listening to Sifu wheeze in agony as Mr. Kile worked to pancake his hand.

He hauled a pamphlet from his robes and read the cover: "White Crane Wing Chun."

Below the name of the school was the school's address, along with their trademark emblem: a circular symbol housing a defending crane doing battle with an attacking snake. Shibisaki tore the pamphlet in half with a grunt and tossed it on the ground.

"Enough," he bellowed into the quadrangle. "Bring him to me."

Mr. Kile and Mia swooped in and took a hold of Sifu. Taking an arm each, they presented the grandmaster to Shibisaki on his knees.

Shibisaki came from the shadows, drifting out from under the eaves of the White Crane, studying the harrowed look on Sifu's face, considering how best to mutilate him.

He found the straw broom on the ground and kicked it up into his hand.

"For centuries, Shaolin monks have worked tirelessly to condition themselves."

Shibisaki snapped the broom handle across his knee and handed it to Dozer.

"The body, the arms, the legs, the head, and the hands."

Dozer slapped the shortened broomstick in his tiny mitt, like a child-sized policeman wielding a club.

"Shall we test your conditioning, *Sifu?*"

Shibisaki nodded at Mr. Kile, directing him to hold out Sifu's knuckles for inspection.

Sifu worked to slow his breath as Mr. Kile placed his frail hand out for Dozer.

Crack. Sifu yelped as Dozer brought the stick down, shattering the knuckles in his hand with a sickening blow.

"There are a total of fifty-four bones in the human hand, Sifu. Do not make me ask you fifty-four times. Where are Brandon Willis and Kaiden Chan?"

"Never heard of them," cried Sifu. He spat into the quadrangle pavement.

Dozer smiled at his agony, excited by the lie. He turned to Shibisaki, waiting for his blessing.

Shibisaki replied with a nod, granting his permission.

Crack.

Sifu screamed again, louder this time, the pain magnified as Dozer landed the second blow, shattering his other knuckles.

"He'll never use chopsticks again," laughed Mia Kwon as a speckle of Sifu's blood landed below her eye.

Dozer smiled again, wider this time, amused by Sifu's pain.

He wilfully cocked the broken broom handle behind his head and prepared for round three.

Shibisaki took a knee, positioning himself in front of Sifu, lifting his chin to direct Sifu's foggy eyes toward him.

"Where are they, old man?"

Sifu aimed his face at the sky, savouring the warm sunlight on his skin, imagining the cloudless sky that hovered overhead, using the pleasant imagery inside his mind to derail the pain.

"It can all stop now," said Shibisaki with a ghoulish smile. "Just cry out the words, cry out their location, and it can all be over."

Sifu returned his face toward Shibisaki. He twerked his lips before he spat into the ninja's milk-white eye.

"I'll never betray my family," he said in Japanese. "Never."

Shibisaki calmly wiped the spit from his eye and faced Elizabeth's Wing Chun dummy in the middle of the quadrangle.

"Rack him," he roared.

Mr. Kile and Mia dragged Sifu to the wooden dummy, his head slumped, the tips of his shoes skimming along the pavement, blood dripping from his hands.

The trio flattened Sifu into position, strapping his torso to the trunk of the wooden dummy, stretching out his arms and binding his wrists to the wooden forks as though he was about to be crucified.

Dozer scrambled to the peak of the dummy, like a small child exploring a tree, using the forks as branches to reach the summit. He pinned Sifu's head against the trunk of the dummy, then secured it to the timber.

Sifu felt Mia, Dozer, and Mr. Kile part like the sea, making way for Shibisaki as he moved in, handing off his sheathed ninjato to the trio, his cruel, unforgiving eyes set on Sifu.

Sifu smiled as he took a moment to reflect. He tilted his face toward that cloudless sky, savouring the warmth on his face, longing to see it in the flesh one final time before death was handed down.

CHAPTER 46

Brandon rushed his eyes to Kaiden when a harrowing scream came from within the walls of White Crane. They reacted quickly, breaking their gaze, throwing themselves at the scaffold of bamboo, mountaineering toward the sky to bypass the barricaded school entrance.

Brandon stopped halfway up the structure, turning away from the wall of bamboo, trying to pinpoint the screams.

He gulped when he found Elizabeth screaming for help, cradling a battered Sifu in her arms.

"Sifu," screamed Kaiden as he took his turn, glancing over his shoulder to eye the horror unfolding in the quadrangle.

Brandon quickly followed Kaiden, bombing into White Crane from the bamboo structure, arriving in army roll, scrambling to their feet and racing across the pavement.

"I just got back and found him like this," cried Elizabeth.

Brandon arrived out of breath, watching Elizabeth caress the side of Sifu's trembling face.

"I found him like this," she repeated. "He's not good."

Brandon scanned the quadrangle for answers, expecting Zhang and company to emerge when the wooden combo dummy caught his eye.

He moved toward it, studying a map of red and blackened blood caked to its trunk.

It was if a person had been tied to the dummy, then lashed one hundred and fifty times, bound by the leather straps that were still anchored to the timber, looped at the ends where wrists had been.

As he moved around the timber, he saw something flicker in the wind—a piece of paper perhaps? A card of some sort?

It was an old photograph, its surface time-worn and oxidized, purposefully nailed to the bloody dummy by someone who'd wanted it found.

He plucked it from the timber as Kaiden's investigative fingertips wandered, attempting to lift Sifu's blood-soaked shirt to assess the damage.

Elizabeth ran a hand to her mouth and stepped back when Sifu's torn midsection arrived in her eyes.

Parts of the grandmaster's ribcage were exposed, protruding through skin, broken bones coated in blood, as if he'd been stuffed into a bag and beaten with metal pipes.

Sifu screamed as Kaiden made contact with the bloodied skin. "Don't touch it! It's too late."

"We've gotta get you to a hospital," said Kaiden as he hauled out his phone.

Sifu raised his bloodied hand in reply, trapping the phone inside Kaiden's grasp.

"It's not up for negotiation. There is something more important now."

"Sifu, who was it? Who did this?"

Sifu tried answering, but couldn't. He rolled to the side and coughed out lines of blood.

"Sifu," again Kaiden pleaded. "Who did this?"

Brandon moved in and gently placed the photo in Sifu's shaking hands.

The feel of the photo ignited something inside him. He lifted his head and aimed his foggy eyes at the picture, frowning at the photograph he couldn't see.

He purposefully brushed a fingertip along the jagged edges and smiled.

Kaiden noticed the smile and looked at the picture.

The inspector found a six-year-old version of himself standing next to his father, Sifu standing on the outer edges of the frame.

"The Ghost Ninja has returned," Sifu said.

Kaiden's eyes wandered, the name forcing him to remember the man who took his father's life.

He pictured the handle of the ninjato gripped tightly in his hands when he was six, scared out of his mind as he drove the blade into the assassin's face, obliterating his skin and eye.

Brandon whispered the name, pondering the spooky title, looking to Kaiden for answers while Sifu fought for every word that came from his mouth.

"He has separated himself from nature, branching out, defying the laws of mortality. Laws that would take the life of an ordinary man, parts of him that died a long time ago."

Kaiden gently pulled Sifu closer and held him tight.

"How do we defeat him? If he's not a man, how do we kill it?"

"There is only one way . . ."

Sifu set the photo on his chest and used his dwindling strength to search for Kaiden's hand.

He took the inspector's hand from his cheek and placed it on top of the photo.

Sifu reached out again, this time for Elizabeth's hand. He took it and sat it on top of Kaiden's.

"No one here is powerful enough to defeat him alone."

Sifu reached out a final time and took Brandon's hand. He reeled in the youngster's hand and placed it on top of Elizabeth's.

"Your only chance is to unite, together, as one. It's the only way."

The three of them looked at one another, eyeing their hands stacked on Sifu's sunken chest, considering his desperate plea, his dying wish.

Brandon thought about Lena as he watched the light fade behind Sifu's eyes, wondering if Anna Lee or Ethan had cradled her in their arms, caressing the side of her face as she drifted off to the other side.

Elizabeth wiped her tears from her checks and fought to

control the trembling state of her mouth. "Sifu," she said lovingly, caressing his face with her spare hand. "Don't go. Please."

The trio held their stacked hands on Sifu's chest, feeling his shallow breath move his broken lungs up and down until it stopped.

Brandon turned away and wiped his eyes.

He stared into a puddle of Sifu's blood, confused when the outline of man arrived in it. He slowly tilted his head and found a man housed in tattered robes, his face covered in a torn fukumen, the handle of a sheathed ninjato sword resting behind his shoulder looming against the skyline above.

"Kaiden," Brandon whispered. "The roof. Look."

Kaiden wiped the tears from his cheeks and followed Brandon's eyes. He stared at the roof, at what remained of the man he met forty-four years ago.

One by one, three random doors of White Crane Wing Chun opened, delivering Mia, Dozer, and Mr. Kile into the quadrangle, each on different sides, taking position as they eagerly waited for Shibisaki to give the order.

Kaiden drew his gun quietly and eyed the competition, wondering if he was still fast enough to get four shots off in time.

He considered the heavily barricaded gates behind him and knew it to be their only way out.

"Brandon, help Elizabeth to her feet."

"No, I'm not leaving Sifu," she cried, swatting away his hands when Brandon reached forward to comply.

"Elizabeth," Kaiden begged, "look at me."

She turned to him, glaring with renewed anger.

"He's dead. We can't help him. Now, come on."

Elizabeth kissed Sifu on his forehead and gently laid him to rest inside the quadrangle of White Crane.

Brandon guided Elizabeth to her feet.

"Both of you, get behind me," said Kaiden as he started to pace backward, the muzzle of his Glock shifting from target to target as they began arming themselves.

Dozer palmed his stub nose .38 and cocked the hammer, Mia Kwon drew her Walther PPK from her thigh, and Mr. Kile plucked a pair of throwing knives from his belt.

Shibisaki crept across the roof and twerked his wrist, bringing his escrima stick to his hand. He gripped it tightly, pondering whose skull to open first when a noise disturbed his thoughts.

Shibisaki froze and looked out into the city, staring at a barrage of Hong Kong Police that were weaving their way around the dawdling traffic, headed straight for White Crane Wing Chun.

He looked back at Kaiden and found him smiling at the sound, the barrel of his police-issued Glock still aimed at his head as he ushered Elizabeth and Brandon backward.

They soon found themselves at the barricaded gate of White Crane, their backs flattened against the mammoth timber doors.

"Elizabeth, help Brandon remove the barricade," said Kaiden, knowing they now had a get-out-of-jail-free card.

Elizabeth and Brandon took to the barricade and lifted it from the cradle.

Kaiden pressed both his palms onto the falcon grip of his Glock as the timber barricade hit the quadrangle pavement with a thud.

He thought about shooting him, the man who'd murdered his father, imagined how satisfying his death would be, but behind him was his daughter, a material witness he'd sworn to protect, and a corrupt police force. He didn't have time for revenge.

Shibisaki held out his hand and grunted, instructing his newly obtained trio of killers to holster their weapons and vanish.

Kaiden, Brandon, and Elizabeth used the opportunity to slip outside the doors of White Crane Wing Chun, closing them in their wake.

CHAPTER 47

T he taxi driver slammed on his brakes and offered a view of his open hands.

He cried out his driver-side window, pleading for his life when he found Kaiden Chan in the middle of the road, pacing toward his car, gun drawn and screaming demands.

"Get out of the taxi. Police business."

Brandon and Elizabeth put two and two together. They popped open the rear passenger doors and slid into the back seat, waiting on Kaiden to take hold of the reins.

"Hang on," yelled Kaiden as he dropped the column shift in the cab and made smoke pour from the wheels.

"Are they chasing us?" he asked as he sent the taxi into a drift, turning it sideways, the wheels screaming through an intersection, narrowly missing Hong Kong Island traffic.

"No," yelled Brandon. "No police, either." He clung tightly to one of headrests, struggling to see through the rear window of the taxi.

"Look again."

"I'm looking right now, and I'm telling ya, no one's chasing us. All I can see back there is a bunch of terrified people clutching at their steering wheels because you're driving this taxi like a *NASCAR*. Slow the *ef* down already!"

"Look," Elizabeth said suddenly. She pointed her finger at the rear windshield. "Up there."

Brandon followed her fingertip and found Shibisaki in pursuit, leaping from rooftop to rooftop like a superhero.

"My bad," advised Brandon, his eyes wide in disbelief. "That evil-looking homeless guy is hot on our tail."

Brandon rushed his eyes to Kaiden, pleading for answers

when he found his hand tweaking the driver-side mirror, desperate to get eyes on the masked assassin.

Shibisaki arrived inside the glass suddenly, growing larger in the vibrating rear-view, swinging from building to building, gliding through the air, using the chain of his kusarigama sickle to latch on to the surrounding infrastructure.

"Who is the hell is this guy?" asked Brandon "Some distant cousin of Peter Parker?"

"Who's Peter Parker?" asked Elizabeth as the taxi went round another sharp corner.

"Never mind! Kaiden, put your clog down! I've ran faster than this before."

Brandon turned his back on the speedo and redirected his eyes at Shibisaki, peering through the rear windshield of the taxi as the Ghost Ninja took to the rooftops of cars, navigating vehicle after vehicle, bouncing from car to car like he was on springs.

"He's gaining."

"I know."

"Kaiden, he's fucking gaining!"

"I heard you the first time."

Kaiden spotted a rare sight in the corner of his eye: an empty street in the heart of Hong Kong, a lunar eclipse the only thing capable of rivalling its rarity.

He stabbed at the brake pedal, turning the wheel at speed, tyres squelching furiously as the nose of the taxi entered the long, narrow straight.

Kaiden placed his eyes in the rear-view mirror and found Shibisaki tackling the corner his own way, kissing the face of a skyscraper at speed, banking himself on a wall of glass panels with his tabi boots, sprinting sideways as if he was moving on flat ground.

"Brandon, when I call ready, I want you to take the wheel."

"What?"

"Just be ready, and do as exactly as I say."

Brandon took a deep breath when Kaiden jerked the Glock from his hip and flicked the safety with his thumb. "Elizabeth," he shouted, "I'll need you to be Brandon's eyes."

Elizabeth nodded and quickly repositioned herself at the rear windshield.

"Hang on," yelled Kaiden as he yanked the hand brake and turned the wheel, sending the taxi into a one-eighty, then throwing it in reverse.

"Now, Brandon. Take the wheel."

Kaiden stabbed at the gas pedal, forcing smoke from its wheels, enabling the taxi to recommence its journey, barrelling down the empty street in reverse.

Brandon launched himself at the wheel, stealing possession from Kaiden's hands as he witnessed brilliant yellow flashes of fire exiting the muzzle of his Glock, spouting bullets at Shibisaki's sideways manoeuvre across the glass wall of the skyscraper, narrowly missing his head, shattering panes of glass until the gun went dry.

"Left," screamed Elizabeth as the rear end of the taxi started to drift toward the edge of the street, dangerously headed for a collision with a brick wall.

Brandon accommodated, shutting off his breath and running his eyes closed as he jerked the wheel, guiding the rear end of taxi back into the middle of the street before Kaiden rehomed his hands, retuning them to the steering wheel.

"Brandon, do you know how to reload a gun?" asked Kaiden as he aimed his eyes at the rear windshield, steering the taxi in reverse, pedal to the metal.

"Huh?" Brandon found the gun in his hands suddenly, smoke still oozing from the barrel.

"Do you know how to reload a gun?"

"Here," cried Elizabeth as she plucked the spent Glock from

Brandon's mitts and drew a fresh magazine from her father's trench coat.

Elizabeth took out the redundant clip and supplied a new one, yanking on the barrel and slapping the gun back into Kaiden's waiting hand.

"Hold on to something," screamed Elizabeth as she peered through the front windshield of the taxi and found the grill of Zhang's Fleetwood Cadillac headed straight for them.

Brandon stared at the sadistic smile of Mr. Kile in the driver's seat, hauling aside his Dracula-black curtain of hair beside Dozer's child-sized eyes hovering over the dashboard, licking his lips before impact.

The trio braced themselves as the fenders collided, Zhang's mammoth chrome grill obliterating the front end of the taxi.

They hung on tight as the much heavier Fleetwood provided a sudden boost, sling-shotting the taxi even faster in reverse, as if the tiny four-cylinder engine had just been injected with NOS.

Kaiden peered over his shoulder, his eyes sharpened, desperately trying to navigate the out-of-control taxi that felt like it had just been shot out of a cannon. "Hang on!"

"Gun," alerted Brandon as he ducked his head and covered his ears. Mia Kwon arrived through the sunroof of the Fleetwood, blowing a sensual kiss at the taxi before squinting at the gun sights of a Carbine MP4.

"Hello, cutie," she mouthed.

She wasted no time pulling the trigger, showering the iron skin of the taxi with bullets that made it sound like it was being bombarded with hail.

"Both of you, listen to me," yelled Kaiden. "Grab a hold of something—quickly!"

Kaiden placed the Glock on his lap and took his foot off the gas.

He turned the wheel suddenly, correcting the taxi, spinning it back the right way round with another one-eighty, offering Mia Kwon's bullets nothing but the rear end of the taxi.

Brandon took a peek through the rear-view mirror as it shattered and found the grill of the Fleetwood viciously gaining again, preparing for round two.

Mr. Kile gripped the steering wheel and ploughed into the rear of the taxi, the impact prying Kaiden's grip from the steering wheel, delivering another unwanted boost.

Kaiden lost control, the back end of the taxi smashed and sent swerving left and right, sliding out of control as if a drunk driver were behind the wheel.

Brandon shut his eyes and pressed his palms into the ceiling of taxi when the left tyre blew out.

The front end of the taxi dipped into the road, corkscrewing its body through the air before coming down on its roof with a tremendous *boom*, the remaining passenger windows exploding on impact.

Brandon reached for Elizabeth's hand when she screamed suddenly, stricken with fear as sparks spilled inside the taxi like they were grinding metal.

"Hang tight, Elizabeth. It'll be okay."

Mr. Kile returned for round three, smashing the grill of Zhang's Fleetwood into the taxi for the third and final time, arriving again with a thunderous *boom*, shunting the taxi upside down toward a new intersection, this one filled with lots and lots of people.

Brandon read the sign upside down: *"Central Station Hong Kong Island."* Pedestrians tore themselves apart at the seam, scurrying left and right, screaming as they found an upside-down taxi headed right for them.

"Hang on!" screamed Kaiden.

The trio screamed as one as they eyed the entrance to the train station, but welcomed it with open arms, relieved they'd soon be free from the clutches of Zhang's Fleetwood and Mia Kwon's endless spray of bullets.

The taxi entered the train terminal at frightening speed, descending on a concrete staircase, arriving upside down in the belly of Hong Kong's Mass Transit Railway.

CHAPTER 48

B randon wriggled his way out of the passenger window, shuffling across a bed of broken glass on his back, his ears ringing from the defining arrival of the taxi, as if a bomb had gone off in Central Station.

He struggled to his feet, only to fall sideways suddenly, crashing into the wall of the taxi, his legs still a little rubbery.

He peered through the stairwell and eyed the trail of destruction, flinching against the rows of obliterated fluorescent lights that hurled sparks at his face.

His breath hitched, starting to race as Shibisaki arrived in the distance, staring back at him from a distant rooftop. As Brandon watched, he reached out his arm, pointing into the belly of the train station.

One by one, Mia, Dozer, and Mr. Kile arrived in the stairwell, their eyes fixated on Brandon until a friend yanked him out of harm's way.

Brandon struggled to keep his eyes open as Kaiden placed him against the wall. He stared at the bloodied lines webbed across his face and followed Kaiden's lips as they mouthed voiceless words.

"Brandon. Brandon, can you move?"

"It's okay. I've got him," yelled Elizabeth as she swooped under Brandon's arm and guided him away from the wall, trying to kickstart his legs.

Brandon watched the passengers of Central Station flatten themselves against the walls, terrified by the sight of Kaiden's gun, cringing at the unsightly map of blood on his face, screaming as more sparks spouted from the busted fluorescent lights overhead and showered the floor.

Kaiden took point, gun in hand, dabbing at the blood in his eyes, waving the passengers away with his pistol.

"Brandon," Elizabeth shouted. "We have to move faster. Come on, Brandon. Move your legs."

Brandon opened his eyes at her voice, as if awakening from a dream.

He wriggled his finger inside his ear, working to end the distorted ringing sound.

He followed Kaiden and Elizabeth as they clambered over the ticket turnstiles and entered a new staircase, one that would take them further underground, deeper into the heart of the Hong Kong railway.

"Where are we going?" asked Brandon in a daze.

Kaiden glanced at him with a look of relief. "Glad to have you back."

He holstered his Glock and took Brandon's arm, guiding him down the stairs with Elizabeth.

"Come on. We're on the first train out of here."

As they reached the bottom of the stairs, Kaiden broke away and showed Brandon and Elizabeth the palm of his hand.

"Wait here."

Brandon watched Kaiden enter the deserted platform, scanning left and right with his gun, ready to shoot anything that moved.

"Elizabeth, take Brandon and wait by the doors."

Brandon studied a map of the MTR that was positioned overhead above the doors.

He scanned the train line and found the asterisk that said, "You are here - Central Station."

"It's the Tung Chung rail line," said Elizabeth, noticing Brandon's eyes at work. "It'll take us back to the mainland and toward the outskirts of Hong Kong."

Brandon kept his eyes on the line and arrived at the end to

find a tiny little picture of a gondola cable car, hovering way up in the sky under a sign that read: "*Ngong Ping 360.*"

"The train is coming," announced Elizabeth as the glass panels started to rattle in their frames.

Brandon turned to find Kaiden's eyes locked deep inside the stairwell, the barrel of his Glock pointed up into the opening. The inspector was studying the sounds of footsteps as they bounced off the walls in echo. Kaiden winked at his gun sight.

"Stay by the glass. Be ready to get on that train," he said.

He slid into position, sheltering his body around the corner, his stance sliced in half by the brickwork.

"Jesus Christ," Kaiden said suddenly. He lifted his finger from the trigger, legs almost giving way beneath him when he found a tiny Cantonese child arrive in his gun sights, clinging to a Baskin-Robbins' double chocolate-chipped ice cream.

Brandon rushed over to find the toddler standing inside the stairwell, chocolate topping dripping between his fingers in time with the aligned rows of tears.

Brandon's eyes grew wide as Mr. Kile appeared out of nowhere to scoop up the child and use him as a human shield. He unleashed one of his throwing blades with his free hand, sending it slicing through the air, hitting the barrel of Kaiden's gun, knocking it from his hand.

"Leave it!" yelled Brandon as Kaiden went for his gun.

"Come on! We can lose them in here."

Brandon grabbed a fistful of Kaiden's trench coat and towed him toward the pinging station doors.

They boarded the train as one, Elizabeth now on point, weaving her way through a stream of transit passengers, pacing from car to car, hopeful that Zhang's trio of killers had missed the train.

"Wait," demanded Kaiden.

He propped himself up on a seat and stared back into the crowd.

"Anything?" asked Brandon.

Kaiden held his tired eyes on passengers who were looking back at him, inspecting the map of bloodlines on his face.

"No," he said. "There's nothing. I think we're clear."

Brandon found relief in Kaiden's eyes as he blew out a breath, satisfied that Zhang's psychopaths weren't on board the train. Adrenaline fading, Brandon slumped into the seat across from Kaiden, dropping his head into his hands as exhaustion loomed.

"What? What is it?" Elizabeth asked suddenly.

Brandon glanced up, eyes darting back to Kaiden. Fear reignited when he saw the crazed look on the inspector's face. He frowned at the passengers as they started to separate in the middle of the train, as though being torn apart by an invisible battering ram.

He blinked when the carriage doors opened suddenly, as if an invisible person had made the sensors drive the doors apart.

"Look out," Kaiden yelled, surging to his feet.

Brandon shielded his head when a vicious-looking Dozer erupted from the crowd, bombarding him with his concrete fists.

Mr. Kile arrived shortly after and squared off with Kaiden, drawing two throwing blades from his knife belt, while Mia Kwon charged at Elizabeth, arriving last to pit her Tae Kwon Do kicks against the skills of White Crane Wing Chun.

B randon screamed with frustration as his left hook was trapped in midair, brilliantly caught by Dozer, who countered quickly, placing Brandon in a wristlock and throwing him across the carriage, legs cartwheeling overhead in an Aikido-style throw.

Brandon scrambled to his feet, trying to calm his rage as he squared off with Dozer.

He placed a defensive guard under his eyes, clenched his fists, and prepared to cave in the small man's head.

Brandon mailed a straight, righthand punch to Dozer's face, but he dipped his head just before the moment of impact, exposing his crown.

Whack.

Brandon screamed in pain, wildly shaking his hand. It felt like his knuckles had collided with a river rock.

"You like that, Brandon? Stings, doesn't it? Top of the head, hardest part of the body. It's like concrete."

Brandon felt his rage swell inside him when he found Dozer standing still as a statue, taunting him with his thinly cut eyes.

Brandon attacked again, stabbing a vicious side kick at Dozer's head, but the minute missile was too fast, too ready. He blocked Brandon's ankle with his wrist and slapped it, turning him away to expose his back.

Brandon screamed in agony as the punches landed, arcing his back as Dozer delivered a lightning-fast combination, hammering his iron-plated fists into Brandon's spine and kidneys like charging pistons, the force driving him across the carriage, sending him on a collision course with the passenger car's fire extinguisher hung against the wall.

Brandon shook off the pain and screwed up his face at the extinguisher, the thought of being schooled by an iron-plated hamster not what he had in mind.

He growled at the fire extinguisher, then unhooked it from the wall, turned around, and locked eyes with Dozer.

"I got a new game!" he yelled. "It's called Tag the Midget. Trust me, you're gonna love it."

Brandon put the extinguisher to work, swinging it wildly overhead like a crazed maniac.

Dozer strategically used the carriage to his advantage, calmly ducking and weaving between the pole grips, jumping off the seats and barrel-rolling across the floor of the aisle.

Brandon felt himself starting to tire, his lungs burning, ready to give in when he finally tagged Dozer.

Bull's-eye. Brandon let out a breath, relieved beyond words when he found Dozer stumbling backward, grabbing at his face after striking him in the head, the connection as loud as the beating of a gong.

Brandon observed the dent in the extinguisher and looked back at Dozer, wide-eyed in disbelief when he found him still standing, rocking back and forth on his heels, trying to shake off the blow.

Brandon aimed the extinguisher nozzle and worked the lever, showering Dozer's eyes in white foam, forcing screams out of him until he went to ground, crashing out flat on his back.

Brandon tossed the extinguisher and climbed on top of the diminutive man to deliver a barrage of closed fists to the face, brutally finishing the job Trinity-style until the small man lost consciousness.

CHAPTER 50
MIA KWON vs. ELIZABETH CHAN

Elizabeth Chan skilfully retreated, working to evade the powerhouse legs of Mia Kwon, surviving a brutal introduction to the kick work of Tae Kwon Do.

She used her size to her advantage, weaving backwards through the pole grips of the passenger car to create distance between herself and Mia Kwon.

Elizabeth dropped to the floor when she ran out of road, performing the splits on the spot to evade a powerful hook kick, the foot narrowly missing her head and slapping into the glass doors beside her, sending cracks running to the edges of its frame.

Elizabeth's eyes bulged with terror when she felt the hands of Mia Kwon grip tightly around her throat, the immense pressure sealing off the air to her lungs.

The much bigger Mia Kwon viciously hauled Elizabeth to her feet and stabbed a push kick into her chest, the brutal force driving Elizabeth through one of the pole grips of the passenger car, tearing it from its footings.

Elizabeth let out a *woof* sound when she collided with the wall.

She wiped away a trail of blood from her nose and found the psychotic eyes of Mia Kwon advancing toward her.

Elizabeth ducked a side kick, the force shattering another window behind her.

She countered, chain punching her fists into Mia, rapidly connecting with her face and midsection.

Elizabeth's eyes shot open when Mia somehow diffused the flurry, slapping away her hands and screaming wildly with rage.

She grabbed onto Elizabeth's clothing, lifted her off the ground and drove her back across the passenger car.

Mia smiled as she drove Elizabeth's body into a window, grabbing fistfuls of her hair and repeatedly hammering the back of her skull into the glass, filling it with cracks with every new head slam.

Elizabeth desperately countered, using her darting fingertips to stab the eye sockets of Mia Kwon.

Mia screamed in agony as she stumbled backwards, cradling the right side of her face.

Elizabeth took advantage of the opening and attacked, her eyes sharp and lethal.

She started chain punching the living shit out of Mia Kwon, delivering fist after fist while Mia clumsily attempted to diffuse the attack, hands waving wildly in front of her body.

Elizabeth felt tears leak into the corners of her eyes when she observed the blinded state of Mia Kwon. In the midst of the chaos, she thought about the final moments and unnecessary suffering of Sifu, how scared he must have been, powerless against his attackers, unable to defend himself—a harrowing feeling that crushed her insides and filled her with sorrow.

Elizabeth unleashed stabbing kicks into Mia's knees, driving uppercuts into her chin, filling her face full of blood, utilising fighting tools that were outside the fighting realm of Wing Chun, her unrelenting striking power fuelled purely by vengeful rage.

Elizabeth grabbed onto a pole grip and swung on it.

She felt her fly kick penetrate the insides of Mia Kwon, the force lifting her from the floor and driving her through the shattered glass of the passenger window.

Elizabeth balked as an oncoming pair of headlights lit up Mia Kwon's body as she floated through the air. A charging locomotive blew its horn in the tunnel, applied its emergency breaks, but obliterated her body on impact.

CHAPTER 51
MR. KILE vs. KAIDEN CHAN

K aiden felt like he was doing battle with a snake, bitten by the sharpened edges of Mr. Kile's blades every time he threw out his hands.

He went for his Glock, but found nothing but an empty holster, the romantic fantasy of blowing out Mr. Kile's brains hijacking the inspector's memory, the feel of an empty holster reminding him that the Glock was on the ground back at Central Station.

Kaiden screamed under his breath when Mr. Kile delivered another slice across his gun hand, opening the flesh across his knuckles.

Kaiden took a deep breath as Mr. Kile drifted behind a pole grip, half of his face concealed behind his dark curtain of hair, taunting Kaiden with his visible eye. He slid one of his blades away and clenched a fist.

Kaiden rubbed the knife slit in his forearm and decided he'd had enough of Mr. Kile and his family of knives. He threw out a right-hand punch, and Mr. Kile caught it, bending his wrist inward and locking up his arm.

Kaiden saw the knife coming for his neck and positioned his free hand over his throat, using it as a blockade to protect his jugular.

Kaiden squeezed his eyes shut and screamed out loud when Mr. Kile ran the blade across the bridge of his knuckles, neatly separating the flesh like it had been opened by a zipper.

Kaiden jerked his body, tore his hand free from the grip of Mr. Kile, and went to ground.

He scrambled to his feet, choking on the blood inside his

throat when he found a blurred Mr. Kile advancing again, slicing at the air with one of his blades, threatening to slash the inspector to ribbons.

Kaiden threw a right hook, and again, Mr. Kile caught it.

He held out the limb and drove the knife through his armpit, driving the blade through the roof of Kaiden's shoulder. In a fit of desperation, Kaiden drew one of Mr. Kile's blades from his knife belt and ran it through the floor of Mr. Kile's mouth.

Kaiden made a face as Mr. Kile convulsed wildly in shock, the blade glimmering in the artificial light of the passenger car when he opened his mouth.

Kaiden found Mr. Kile reaching for backup, his fingertips wandering around his knife belt to find a friend. The inspector grabbed a hold of the blade handle under his jaw and viciously twisted it left and right, as though he was turning a key in a door.

Kaiden placed both hands on the sides of Mr. Kile's head, preparing to snap his neck, when he found Mr. Kile's eyes rolling up into the back of his demented skull.

Heaving in breath, Kaiden threw Mr. Kile toward the floor. He screamed in agony as he hauled the blade from his armpit and tossed it at his opponent's dead body, relieved beyond words that he had expired.

CHAPTER 52

General Myong-Su closed up the silver buttons on his jacket as he ventured out onto the deck of the moving cargo vessel.

He wandered through a small maze of shipping containers, looking up through the drifting cloud work of the South China Sea, waiting for its layers to reveal the three-quarter moon resting high in the sky.

The general made his way to the starboard side of the vessel, placed his hands inside a pair of leather gloves, and pulled a tiny set of binoculars from his jacket.

Thinking about the many laws he had broken, he scanned the surrounding ocean, eager to rule out the possibility of incoming customs boats, military ships, or army helicopters buzzing overhead in pursuit of the mammoth cargo vessel.

The general took the lenses from his eyes and smiled when he found nothing but ocean water.

He thought about his fat little idiotic friend standing inside the guts of Kim Il-Sung Square, waving back at his meaningless army and military parade, wondering if the dazzling smile had faded from his chubby cheeks when he noticed that his inventory was a little light on tanks, submachine guns, and soldiers housed in green paint and Kevlar.

A commotion disturbed these pleasing thoughts. Shouting voices came from the stern of the super freighter. Intrigued, the general decided to mosey on down.

He looked over the railing and found a small group of deckhands standing on a platform of timber planks that looked like a skyscraper-washing trolly, suspended by a gang of pulleys anchored to the guard rail of the ship.

General Myong-Su listened while the men argued back and forth in Korean, shaking their fists and spouting swear words at each another in anger.

"Excuse me, General Myong-Su."

A junior lieutenant knocked his feet together behind his general and saluted.

Saying nothing, the general placed his binoculars in the soldier's free hand, peeled off his leather gloves, and hauled his slimline cigarette case from his jacket pocket.

"What is it?" he asked as he lit his smoke.

"I'm pleased to report, General, that we are right on path. We have officially entered Hong Kong's waters and should arrive at the Kwai Tsing Container Terminal at approximately 0700 hours."

The general blew cigarette smoke past his lips, looked at his Rolex, and nodded.

"Three hours. Very well. Have the bridge contact Mr. Zhang and ensure he is on site for our arrival. Inform him that his requested inventory will arrive in its entirety."

"Yes, sir." The junior lieutenant slapped his feet together, saluted his general, and walked away.

Myong-Su turned back toward the stern and found one of the deckhands positioning a premade stencil of words against the butt of the ship, barking at his disgruntled companions throughout.

"What's the name of this rust bucket?" he shouted over the droning hum of the engine room.

The general grunted at the workers to get their attention.

They all looked up at him and stared in silence, waiting from him to speak. He did.

"Jasper's Dream."

CHAPTER 53

"You have arrived at Tung Chung Station," announced a computerised voice as the doors opened with a ping, separating a picture of the Ngong Ping Cable Car that was plastered on the glass doors.

"Grab an arm," yelled Brandon as he hauled Kaiden to his feet.

They carried the inspector from the passenger car, toes scraping along the station floor, blood trailing in devastating streams from his right side.

"Wait, rest him here," demanded Elizabeth. "Set him down."

Brandon fell to the bench seat with Kaiden, crash-landing on arrival.

"Kaiden, where does it hurt?" he said.

"Armpit." Kaiden grabbed at his shoulder, wincing. "It went straight through."

Brandon looked up to find Elizabeth pulling an *"I love Hong Kong"* t-shirt from a coat hanger, one she had just swiped from a nearby tourist stand.

"Quickly, peel off his coat."

She started tearing the cotton apart with her bare hands, using her teeth to hack the shirt at its seams.

"What are you doing?"

"Making a tourniquet," she said. "We have to stop him from bleeding out. Quickly, take off his coat, and stretch out that arm."

Brandon did as instructed. He pulled Kaiden forward and peeled off his trench coat while the inspector swayed back and forth on the bench seat.

Brandon went to work, following Elizabeth's lead, stretching out his ravaged arm, blood filling his hands as Elizabeth tied the tourniquet around his shoulder, concealing the devastating wound in his armpit. The pair looked at each other for answers when the sound of wailing sirens poured into the belly of the train station.

"Now what?" asked Brandon.

"We keep moving. Come on," said Elizabeth. "We have to get out of here."

Outside the train station, Brandon flinched at flashes of soundless lightning in the distance. The black winter sky had come calling for Hong Kong Island, bringing with it promises of booming thunder and typhoon-like rain.

He scanned the Tung Chung shopping village, studying the paved roads that were lined with shops on both sides.

"Come on," he said when the sound of rumbling motorbikes met his ears.

He peered around the brickwork and read the banner hoisted overhead, flapping in the Hong Kong wind: *"First Annual Tung Chung Bike Show."* Behind the sign was a sea of revhead motor-bike enthusiasts, frothing over every bike imaginable, from vintage Harley-Davidsons to the modern classics of Ducati.

Brandon guided Kaiden and Elizabeth through the outer limits of the show, eager to maintain distance between them and the sea of bike junkies. He scanned a nearby collection of vintage bikes and picked one out like he was in a showroom, eager to make a moneyless purchase.

"Get in," Brandon whispered as he hoisted his leg over the bike.

The grey-coloured motorcycle was a World War II BMW R12, complete with a side car bolted to the frame.

Elizabeth followed Brandon's lead, guiding a woozy Kaiden into the side car and sitting behind him.

"Do you even know how to start this fossil?" asked Elizabeth as she watched Brandon explore the switches on the bike.

"I'm Australian. We learn to ride dirt bikes before push bikes."

He flicked the kickstand and jumped on the kick-starter,

forcing the ancient engine to sputter alive, black smoke jetting from its tail pipe.

"Hey, get off that!" a man roared from the crowd. He sprinted toward the trio, waving his hands wildly in protest.

Brandon peered over his shoulder and found a man housed in a German officer's uniform hurling abuse, desperate to rescue his pride and joy.

Brandon smiled wide at the Nazi officer and flipped his middle finger before squeezing the throttle and exiting the minute showground, bringing the Inglorious Wannabe-Bastard to his knees, watching the bike speed from his life and onto the paved road of Tung Chung Shopping Village.

Brandon tweaked the circular rear-view mirror on the handle bars when an engine growled at them from behind.

His eyes grew wide when he saw the busted grill of Zhang's Fleetwood exploding through a popcorn carnival cart, hurling starbursts of popcorn through the shopping village.

Brandon frowned in the rear-view when he saw Shibisaki's head hovering above the dashboard, his filthy hands clutching at the steering wheel, his one good eye huge and filled with hate.

"What is it?" cried Elizabeth, unable to turn around, observing the concern in Brandon's eyes.

He glanced at her quickly, matching frowns. "It's him!"

Brandon twisted the throttle, making the World War II relic work overtime, weaving through courtyard planter boxes that were loaded with Chinese bamboo, separating tourists left and right as Shibisaki obliterated those planter boxes, eating them up like a rogue tsunami, hurling soil and bamboo through the shopping village as the boxes exploded on impact.

Brandon took the BMW wide as the village road branched out to the right, steering the bike under a long corridor of storefront awnings, hoping its thickly rounded timber posts were enough to deter Shibisaki, prying him from their tail, forcing the Fleetwood to take a new route in the deadly pursuit.

Brandon bought his shoulders up around his ears, flinching at what sounded like an explosion of sorts behind them when the plan did not work.

With little regard for the Fleetwood, Shibisaki ploughed through the awning supports, effortlessly mowing them down like picketed fence posts, blasting them apart with the mammoth grill of Cadillac, forcing the awning to collapse behind him, bringing it to the ground as though Tung Chung was enduring an earthquake.

Brandon took a peek in the rear-view, holding his breath as the trail of destruction unfolded in the glass. He found the grill of the Fleetwood probing through swirling mushroom clouds of white dust, as if it were trying to evade the demolition of an exploding building.

Brandon set his eyes back on the road and found the tunnel of awnings coming to an end, along with the village road itself, the only fast-approaching option to exit the awnings and tackle a sharp right that would offer them a place on the regular roads of Tung Chung.

Brandon's eyes travelled right as the Fleetwood abruptly left the tunnel, bursting through its supporting posts, revving hard and pulling alongside the bike like an opponent in a race.

Shibisaki guided the Fleetwood closer, forcing Brandon to steer the handlebars closer to the storefronts as he exited the tunnel of awnings. Shibisaki was boxing them in, ensuring that there would be no escape.

"Make room!" yelled Brandon. He hoisted his leg over the bike and placed both his feet in the side car as the left side of the bike connected with the storefronts, skimming past walls of glass and brick, hurling sparks like bursting fireworks, stripping the grey paint finish from the bike.

"Hold on to your lunch," yelled Brandon as he eyed the road ahead.

Elizabeth turned to see the end of the shopping village road approaching fast. Beyond that lay a steeply inclined staircase, the kind that could be used as a launch pad.

"Oh my god, we're gonna die," cried Elizabeth as she clutched at her father and buried her terrified eyes in his shoulder.

"Nah, we're gonna live. And we're gonna launch off that staircase to do it."

CHAPTER 54

The trio hunkered down as Brandon ordered the bike to make a beeline for the staircase, every muscle in his body tightly clenched as the stairs grew imposingly large with every passing second.

Engine revving out, panels and casings of the side car threatening to break apart, nearly redlining, the bike took to the stairs, losing speed with every step as the tyres kicked and jumped, as though they had suddenly made contact with a long line of speed bumps.

The trio yelled as one, their jolting screams vibrating in time with the concrete stairs as they prepared to launch off the stairwell.

The war machine failed, however, colliding with a guard rail suddenly, stopping the bike dead in its tracks like it had collided with a stop block, flinging Brandon over the handlebars and hurling him through the air.

"Holy shit!" screamed Brandon. "Little help?"

He looked up, eyes wide as saucers, clinging to the railing with his fingertips, hanging on for dear life while Kaiden leaned over and reached for his hand.

"Have a nice trip?"

Brandon locked onto Kaiden's hand, and he hauled him back over the railing. Brandon crash-landed on his back, smacking into the concrete staircase with a thud.

He sat up, smiling at the shredded motorbike, observing smoke curling from the spent engine, coughing in fits from its fumes. "They don't make 'em like that anymore!"

Brandon studied Kaiden, spotting the healthier shade of

colour that had decided to revisit his face when an alarming sight arrived behind him.

He stood, scrambling to his feet, his eyes locked on the staircase as a threatening clap of thunder boomed.

Shibisaki took his time, walking slowly up the staircase, appearing like a menacing lion content with stalking weakened prey.

"Come on. We're not done yet," urged Kaiden.

Kaiden helped Elizabeth from the side car as Brandon approached the top of the stairs, standing his ground, eyeing Shibisaki, the thought of running again suddenly not so appealing. He was sick of it—sick of the fear; sick of the fright and endless panic.

"Come on, Brandon," yelled Kaiden.

"Remember what Sifu said? We need to take him together." Brandon sharpened his eyes and clenched his fists. "Let's take him now."

"No," said Kaiden. "We need to lure him in. Come on. I have a plan."

Brandon reluctantly retreated before taking to the concrete staircase, ascending higher as he peered over his shoulder, waiting for Shibisaki to appear with ninjato drawn, slashing at the air.

"Great. Now what?" said Elizabeth as they reached the top of the stairs to find a closed tourist attraction blocking their way, stopping them dead in their tracks.

Brandon eyed the motionless cable cars of Ngong Ping 360, neatly huddled together, stabled until daybreak, when flocks of tourists would bring them to life.

Brandon cupped his ears, flinching at the sound of broken glass behind him.

He turned, following Kaiden with his eyes as he tossed a chrome-plated barrier post to the ground and reached through the windowless frame of a door, working the handle.

Brandon followed Kaiden as he limped inside, flicking at switches and slapping the buttons of a blinking control panel until something happened.

Something finally did, the cable cars humming to life as Brandon stepped out of the control booth, looking up as they moved one by one, like contraptions on an assembly line, departing the terminal and heading into the lightning-filled skies of Hong Kong Island.

"Quick! Get your asses inside. You're gonna love this. Best ride in the park," said Kaiden. His hands firmly pressed into Elizabeth and Brandon's backs, guiding them forward.

They took to the interior of the cable car as the line hooked onto the crown, towing them from the platform and hoisting them up into the night.

They moved toward the glass panels of the cable car, eyes peeled, hands firmly pressed on the glass, following a number of empty cars as they each took their turn on the line, their tiny ceiling lights lit as they departed the terminal, showering down into the bellies of the cabins.

Brandon turned, eyeing a map inside the cabin, looking to where the cable car ride ended: *"Ngong Ping Cable Car Terminal."*

"You know this is a dead end, right? We're just postponing the inevitable."

He found a picture of a towering Buddha that reminded him of Jabba the Hut drawn into the map, the image resting quietly, perched upon a disc-shaped platform at the top of the longest, steepest set of stairs created by man.

"Don't worry," said Kaiden. "He'll never reach the terminal. I have a plan."

Brandon peered through the glass-bottomed floor of cable car and found hundreds of red and blue lights making the concrete stairwell and Zhang's busted Fleetwood swirl in crazy patterns— patterns that were growing smaller by the second as the cable car ascended into the sky.

"Look," pointed Elizabeth. She pressed her fingertips on the glass and held her breath.

They each took a turn, silently observing Shibisaki as he cruised onto the terminal platform and looked back at the three of them, floating off into the sky.

CHAPTER 55

For Hong Kong Police, the cable cars of Ngong Ping 360 looked like a row of dimly lit lanterns. Lanterns that were now violently swinging back and forth on their towline from the incoming thunderstorm, swaying under attack from its howling winds and the pelting rain that dove into the glass-walled cabins like bullets.

Emotions within the three-strong cable car were on tilt, the equivalent of how some would've felt if they were stuck in a broken-down elevator: one pondered rescue, one anxiously wondered if the cables were about to snap, and one thought about whether or not they'd explode on impact if gravity hurled them toward the bottom of the shaft.

Brandon looked at the blackened waters of Tung Chung Bay through the glass bottom of the car and felt his stomach turn. He felt as though he were standing on top of a tornado, observing the leaves and rain as they raced in circles of madness, the wind howling all around them. He pictured the glass breaking suddenly, then a fall, descending into darkness, his arms and legs flapping wildly before he hit the waters of Tung Chung Bay that would feel like concrete.

"He just entered a cable car."

Brandon blinked away the image of his death and shifted his eyes, catching a glimpse of Shibisaki's ninjato handle winking on the terminal platform before the cable car gobbled him up, hoisting him into the stormy sky, eight or ten cable cars off the pace.

The trio stood as one, mute, monitoring Shibisaki through the drifting panels of floating glass, delighted by the distance between them as cracks of lightning crawled across the sky.

"What's he doing?" Brandon frowned as Shibisaki sat on the glass bottom of his car, neatly crossing his legs as though he was about to meditate.

Shibisaki raised his left hand, positioned it in front of his face, and curled his fingers into a fist.

His right followed, slowly covering the fist of his left like a blanket.

Shibisaki started to tremble as he closed his eyes and bowed his head, quaking in his tattered robes until he shook erratically, as if he were about to explode.

"He has taken on a new form." Sifu's final words at White Crane returned to pay Brandon a visit. *"He has separated himself from nature, branching out to defy the laws of mortality. Laws that would take the life of an ordinary man, parts of him that died long ago."*

"What's happening?" cried Elizabeth as she grabbed onto Kaiden's arm.

"Holy shit, look." Brandon gripped the handle bar and screamed at the glass.

The body of Shibisaki started to fade, disappearing within the walls of the glass cable car, as if he were vaporizing.

"Where'd he'd go?" panicked Elizabeth.

Together, they watched and waited, their eyes bulging, glued to the empty cars trailing behind them.

Shibisaki reappeared suddenly, jumping the queue, advancing forward by one cable car, hands still bolted together.

Brandon stood at the glass panel, wide-eyed in disbelief.

"We are so fucked."

Brandon spotted the twinkling lights of the Ngong Ping Terminal at the peak of the mountain, while Shibisaki kick-started the process again from scratch, covering the curled fist in front of his face, making the cable cars dance on the wire, vanishing and reappearing, drifting from car to car, advancing, now only three cars from becoming an uninvited guest intent on filling their cable car with buckets of blood.

"Three more to go," yelled Brandon as he turned again to eye the terminal, watching it receive the empty cable cars on autopilot, towing them onto the platform one by one. "Two more!"

Shibisaki reappeared again, hot on their tail, close enough now for the frightened trio to see the shade of his milk-white eye.

"Get ready to move," yelled Brandon as their car arrived at the platform, the cable motors waning to steady the car, enabling them to disembark.

They brushed past the car doors as they opened with a hiss, jolting the frames, almost tearing them from their tracks as if their cable car had suddenly caught fire.

Kaiden ran ahead and went to work on the junction box, trying to manipulate the cable car controls, eager to execute his plan and stop the cars dead in their tracks before Shibisaki reached the peak.

"Leave that," screamed Brandon as he leaped over the boundary fence, tugging Kaiden away from the junction box. "We haven't got time for that. It's too late."

Brandon glanced over his shoulder as they sprinted through the Ngong Ping Village, eyeing the cable car terminal, expecting to find Shibisaki pursuing them on foot.

"Where is he? I can't see him!" he said

"You can't see him," Kaiden replied. "But rest assured, he can see us."

The words rang true.

Unbeknownst to the trio, Shibisaki had already begun his pursuit, hidden from their frightened eyes.

The masked assassin leapt from rooftop to rooftop, monitoring the trio's movements from above like a golden eagle, gliding across the rows of tiles, waiting for the opportune moment to strike.

They caught a breath at a crossroad of options, deciding which way to head.

"What's that place?" pointed Brandon as he found what he assumed to be a temple in the distance.

"That's the Po Lin Monastery. It's a Buddhist monastery," answered Elizabeth. "They can't help us."

"Look out!" Kaiden pushed Elizabeth and Brandon aside as a shadow flipped overhead, landing in front of them.

Shibisaki drew his ninjato and sliced Brandon across the chest, forcing his legs to give way beneath him. He fell back onto a towering set of stairs that disappeared into the dark, stormy skies above.

"Come on," yelled Kaiden as he dragged Brandon up the stairs, scurrying away from the tip of Shibisaki's ninjato.

The trio stepped backwards, clumsily tripping up the staircase as Brandon went for his chest, feeling inside the slit of his rain-soaked shirt, searching for spilled blood and guts. Thankfully, he found none.

Kaiden looked over his shoulder and studied the towering set of stairs.

He found a gigantic silhouette in the sky before the lightning returned, revealing a mammoth bronzed statue of Buddha Shakyamuni at the top of the staircase, his hand positioned in greeting, even while being bombarded by wind and rain.

Shibisaki calmly took to the steps and ran the tip of his ninjato along the concrete barrier, unfazed by the wind and rain that tore at his tattered ninja-yoroi.

He calmly ushered the panicked trio toward Buddha Shakyamuni, driving them backward into the stormy skies—toward a place he knew to be a dead end.

CHAPTER 56

Z hang's van was leader of the pack.

He rode up front in the passenger seat, while one of his newly obtained warehouse sheep drove.

Zhang held a large stack of bills in his hands and shuffled, spreading apart the faces of Benjamin Franklin until the bills formed a large fan.

He put Benjamin's face under the van's interior light, using the soft orange glow to check for defects and imperfections on his face.

Satisfied there were none, he slid the bills back into a pile, sent down his passenger window, and jerked the revision mirror.

Inside the glass, he found his money vans trailing in convoy, a neat half-dozen jet-black SUVs gliding over Stonecutters Bridge, following Zhang's every move until he rolled into the heart of Kwai Tsing Container Terminal.

"It's about time," he said suddenly as a satellite phone rang by his side.

He put up his window, mashed the glowing panel with his thumb, and put the receiver to his ear.

"Speak!"

"Mr. Zhang, just wishing to advise that your requested inventory will shortly be in stock. We expect the delivery boy to arrive soon. Would 0700 hours meet your satisfaction?"

With little thought, Zhang smiled at the words, knowing all too well what lines of stock the voice referred to.

"Very well," he said.

Zhang hung up the call and opened his alligator-skin cigar box to celebrate.

He tossed the bills inside, picked out a torpedo-shaped

beauty, and performed his customary sliding of the cigar under his snout. He savoured the fumes of rum and wine for a moment, then lit the tip.

Peering through the drifting smoke in front of his eyes, he observed a cluster of apartment buildings in the distance. He closed his eyes and set the buildings alight in his mind, envisioning orange flames shooting out every window, fire ravaging the homes of many.

He fantasised about the sounds of gunfire, echoing throughout the Hong Kong city streets while men, women, and children cried, desperately running and screaming for their lives.

He opened his eyes with a soothing smile and glanced at his warehouse goon behind the wheel.

"Little music, driver," said Zhang. He clicked his fingers in the air, then took a big puff of the stogie.

The driver looked at Zhang awkwardly for a handful of seconds, then stabbed the radio button with his finger.

When the sounds of mixing turntables and scratching vinyl came over the airways, Zhang found himself nodding in time with the beat, found himself unexpectedly grooving to the infectious sounds of Hip Hop.

He starting mouthing a chorus that was on repeat.

"Fight the power," he said over and over again, agreeing with the lyrics, shaking his closed fists at the windshield as if he was on a stage.

The driver held his eyes on the road and hit the indicator with a disgruntled look.

Choking on Zhang's cigar fumes, he steered the van toward an exit ramp and flew past a sign that read: *"Kwai Tsing Container Terminal."*

CHAPTER 57

Kaiden Chan broke down like a spent race horse when he reached the top of the staircase, stumbling awkwardly, drifting sideways, threatening to crash-land to ground. He fell to his knees, stabbing the palms of his hands into the puddles of rain beneath Buddha Shakyamuni, as if in prayer.

Cringing, he went for Mr. Kile's knife wound near his armpit, his fingertips finding the blood-soaked tourniquet. Blood had started to flow freely again, the escape from the cable car and unwanted stair workout less than ideal in his condition.

"Leave me here," wheezed Kaiden as he tipped over, crashing onto his side in the water, his face returning to shades of vampire white.

"Get up!" yelled Elizabeth. Wet hair webbed across her face as she tugged at her father's lifeless body.

Brandon arrived, skidding on his knees in the rain. "Quick, grab an arm."

They reused their Tung Chung Station tactic, performing a soldier's carry, holding on to an arm each as they hauled Kaiden's lifeless legs across the statue's platform, his shoe tips scraping across the ground, blood dripping from his body to mix with the patches of rain.

"Enough," said Kaiden, grimacing in agony. "Set me down here."

Elizabeth and Brandon peeled Kaiden from their shoulders, positioning him upright on his butt against a barrier gate that surrounded a row of brass lotuses.

"No more. I can't go on. I need to rest."

Elizabeth snarled at Kaiden. "Stop your whining." She

grabbed fistfuls of his bloodied trench coat and attempted to haul the spent inspector to his feet.

"Goddamn it, Elizabeth. No more!" he screamed in protest, slapping away her determined grasp.

"Brandon, get her out of here. Prepare to defend yourselves."

"No, I won't leave you," screamed Elizabeth. "We need to stand together."

Brandon glanced back at the staircase, anticipating Shibisaki's arrival, when Kaiden used his final ounces of strength, grabbing fistfuls of Brandon's clothes to haul him close.

"Get Elizabeth out of here," he screamed in his face. "Keep my daughter safe. That's your job now. Do it!"

Kaiden pushed Brandon away, heaving in breath, sitting in an unmistakable pool of blood and rain.

Elizabeth screamed in protest as Brandon tore her away, kicking wildly, grabbing handfuls of air in her attempt to hold on to her father.

"I love you, Elizabeth," Kaiden whispered, his eyes aimed at his pooling blood.

Despite the pain and scent of death, Kaiden Chan felt a small smile rise in the corner of his mouth, the words filling his insides with both joy and sadness, words he should've had on repeat, words Elizabeth needed to hear.

Kaiden heard feet walking through puddles, then felt the tip of Shibisaki's ninjato connect with his chin, prying him from his dream-like state. The Japanese steel caressed his dampened skin like a chilled, unused razor that was about to get dirty.

Kaiden lifted his weary eyes, squinting at the rain, staring at the blackened silhouette that was Shibisaki.

"Why don't you stop hiding behind that rag and reveal that wondrous beauty of a scar I etched into your face," said Kaiden.

Shibisaki stood on mute for a moment, considering the taunt.

Then he started to do just that, unveiling his face in the dimly lit surroundings, unravelling the fukumen like an Egyptian mummy. Kaiden cringed, studying the scarred flesh as a flash of lightning lit up the sky, illuminating the obliterated half of Shibisaki's face, his expression both hungry and insane.

"I want to kill you so badly I can taste it," hissed Shibisaki, offering Kaiden the courtesy of conversing in Cantonese. "But first, you can watch while I separate your daughter's head from her body. Then, you will have my permission to die."

"And Brandon? Aren't you still Zhang's bitch?"

"I have sworn no allegiance to that Cantonese pig. I've returned to Hong Kong Island for honour, for your life. Like the one I took from your father."

Kaiden kicked at Shibisaki's legs—the only attack he could muster.

"Fuck you. You don't have the honour to speak of my father."

Shibisaki positioned his ninjato, placing the tip beneath Kaiden's right eye.

"Call to Elizabeth," he said.

Kaiden held his breath and stared back, refusing to offer up his fear. "Never!"

Shibisaki's fingers crawled like a spider up the handle of his sword, until his hand butted up against the square cross guard. He made a controlled lunge, threatening to puncture Kaiden's cheek.

"Call to Elizabeth, now."

Kaiden roared under his breath, teeth clenched, heels jumping in the puddle of rain as he felt the Japanese steel nudge at his cheekbone.

"Fuck you!"

Shibisaki pushed on the cross guard, puncturing Kaiden's cheek, neatly slipping the sword tip into the skin.

"Call to Elizabeth, *now*," he repeated as he twisted the handle of his ninjato ever so slightly.

Kaiden clutched at his pants to mask the pain, his vision hazy and on the brink of going dark.

Shibisaki pulled the sword out suddenly, smirking at Kaiden's misery.

Kaiden spat blood from his mouth in reply, intentionally showering Shibisaki's tabi boot. He glanced up at Shibisaki, smiling, blood crying from his cheek, pretending to beg for more.

Shibisaki accommodated. He positioned the sword tip on the other side of Kaiden's face and pressed forward on the square cross guard, puncturing the cheek.

"Call for Elizbeth, or I'll twist this blade and open the roof of your skull."

"You want me?" a voice rasped suddenly.

Elizabeth Chan emerged from the shadows, standing in a puddle of rain.

"You got me," she said.

Shibisaki stole the blade from Kaiden's face and sheathed the ninjato behind his head, looking down at Kaiden as he rolled onto his side, passing out from the pain.

"And your friend?" asked Shibisaki. "I only heard one set of footsteps."

"I'm here," yelled Brandon. He drifted out from the eaves of the platform and stood next to Elizabeth.

Together, they watched Shibisaki turn as lightning crawled across the sky, highlighting the horrid scarring on his face and his ghostly white eye.

The three of them locked eyes, individually obsessing over the scores they had to settle and how willing they were to die for them.

Brandon grunted as he lunged forward to deliver a straight right hand. Shibisaki countered, responding with the speed of the possessed, executing a lightning-fast hook kick to his face, knocking at his jaw with the heel of his boot, sending him spinning to the ground.

Elizabeth arrived quickly with her shuffling Wing Chun fists, intending to chain punch Shibisaki's midsection and face, but he countered before the moment of impact.

The ninja bent over backwards, planted his hands in the rain puddles, and brought over his tabi boots in a gymnastics-style kick-over, viciously connecting with Elizabeth's chin like she had been tagged by an uppercut.

It was almost like tag-team wrestling: every time one went to ground, their counterpart was waiting in the wings, ready to run in screaming, intent on inflicting as much pain on Shibisaki as possible.

Brandon returned for his second attempt.

Catching Shibisaki from behind, he pinned the ninja's arm behind his back and drove him forward, directing him toward a wall of brick and stone, picking out the spot where he planned to smash the front of Shibisaki's ruined face into the wall.

Shibisaki twisted out of the arm-lock, though, running up the wall before the moment of impact. He backflipped overhead, returned to earth behind Brandon, and kicked his legs out from underneath him.

Elizabeth arrived then, catching the ninja off guard. She found the face of Shibisaki with her fists, driving shuffling Wing Chun knuckles toward his face. She could feel the temperature of her blood rising with every strike, despising the very sight of Shibisaki, her heart filled with hatred form his callous nature and unspeakable cruelty.

She pictured Sifu during her barrage of punches, helplessly sprawled out in a pool of his own blood at White Crane, moaning in agony as he slipped away.

Shibisaki blocked the onslaught of punches and grabbed Elizabeth by the throat.

She gabbed at his hands, choking against his vice grip, clawing at his fingers as Shibisaki dug in with unnatural strength. She tried to stab kick him in the groin, but found only air when the ninja twisted away from the attack.

Shibisaki turned, his attention diverted to the kamikaze screams of Brandon Willis.

He released Elizabeth from his Ninjitsu death grip and kicked her in the face, sending her to ground. The oncoming youngster acted as though he were once again back within the walls of Trinity. He drove his shoulder into Shibisaki's hip, cuddled his legs, lifted him off the ground, and spear-tackled him head first into the concrete.

He made a closed fist and started pulverising Shibisaki's face with a series of devastating right hooks, as if he was connecting with the fat face of Johnathan Zhang instead, making him pay for all the pain he'd endured, for the life of his mother, for Sifu, and now, for Kaiden.

Shibisaki tweaked his wrist during the onslaught, calling his escrima stick to his hand. He put it to work, stabbing the butt into Brandon's ribs with a *crack*, the pain forcing Brandon to clench his teeth and point his eyes at the sky.

Shibisaki wheeled the club in his hand and slapped Brandon's forehead with it, the result as if he'd been clocked by a hammer.

Shibisaki tossed a groggy Brandon aside and performed a lightning-fast kip up, returning to his feet. He calmly slid his escrima stick away and wiped both blood and rain from his face.

The ninja drew his ninjato and held it by his side, the sword-face catching a flash of lightning as thumber boomed.

He stared at Brandon and Elizabeth as they rolled around in the rain, fighting to return to their feet. Excited, he gripped the handle of his ninjato, eager to open their insides and soak the entire platform in blood.

He stepped forward, but braked suddenly when a rapid clicking sound met his ears. He glanced down to find Kaiden's enthralled eyes smiling in the rain, his ankle bound to the wrist of the bloodied inspector by his police-issued cuffs.

CHAPTER 58

K aiden rested an open hand by the side of his mouth and hollered at Brandon and Elizabeth.

"When you two amateurs are done napping down there, maybe you could get off your asses and kill this guy?"

Elizabeth and Brandon looked at the cuffs, finding Shibisaki anchored to Kaiden's arm. They took to their feet in an instant, bolting toward Shibisaki as he weaved his sword through the air, showcasing skills that would have intimidated a lightsaber-wielding Jedi.

Shibisaki swung his sword at Kaiden's wrist, trying to cut the chain and free himself when Kaiden tugged at the cuffs, hauling his leg out from underneath him, throwing him off balance.

Brandon and Elizabeth strategically worked together to begin their dismantling of Shibisaki.

Brandon kicked the ninjato from his hand and stabbed a side kick to his face, the force viciously knocking back his head as Elizabeth stabbed a short kick into the side of his knee, obliterating the cartridge with a *snap*.

In a fit of desperation, Shibisaki tweaked his wrist as he dropped to his knee, forcing his escrima stick to arrive in hand.

He wheeled the baton, forcing its lines to blur like a spinning windmill before striking Brandon in the knee with it, bringing him down to his level with a moan. He drove the stick under his chin, clapping his jaws together in a sickening chatter of teeth, forcing an explosion of blood from his mouth.

Elizabeth kicked the stick from Shibisaki's hand and took a knee, wildly trading shots with him, the lightning-fast hand techniques of Ninjitsu and Wing Chun going head-to-head in a flurry of fists and forearms blurring into one.

Elizabeth roared wildly, the speed and power of her Wing Chun punches too powerful for Shibisaki to sustain. She finished with a stabbing finger jab to his one and only working eye, sending him drifting backward, madly clutching at his face as he crash-landed on his back in the rain.

She scooped up his escrima stick and cracked him in the skull, the blow instantly rendering him unconscious.

Brandon sat up and watched from afar, rubbing at his aching jaw.

"Let's get out of those cuffs, huh?" said Elizabeth. She tossed the stick away and arrived by Kaiden's side.

She took the key from his trembling hand and jigged the lock, unhooking his wrist.

Brandon sighed with relief when Kaiden sat up as best he could, sending out signals that he was going to make it, a tiny smile arriving in the corner of his mouth as he opened his arms for Elizabeth.

They bolted themselves together, squeezing each other tight, making up for lost time.

Brandon winked when she looked at him, peacefully resting her head on her father's shoulder.

She smiled back, exhaling, at peace now that she had her father back, gripping him so tightly it was as if she was never going to let him go.

Brandon looked at Shibisaki and observed the rain falling on his motionless form, hopeful that there would be no movie-like scenario where the villain would magically return from the grave, screaming wildly to deliver one final scare for the audience.

Satisfied that reality wouldn't mimic fiction, he flopped onto his back and opened his mouth, letting the Hong Kong rain tap on the surface of his tongue. He took in the majestic sight of the towering Buddha, ascending toward the sky as the blackened storm clouds hovered overhead.

Brandon frowned when a high-polished plaque attached to the brickwork picked up a flicker of movement, as if someone was directing a reflection of light.

Curious, he sat up, his eyes loaded with concern. Elizabeth was still smiling as she pulled away from Kaiden, her eyes locked on his. She didn't see Shibisaki drifting upright, didn't see him grab his sword from the ground, didn't witness him driving the sword tip through the air, sending it straight toward Elizabeth's back.

"Look out!" Brandon screamed.

Elizabeth gasped as the sword pierced her, Shibisaki's hand slipping the blade between her ribs with expert ease, effortlessly forcing the Japanese steel to arrive through her front.

She gripped onto Kaiden's clothing, trying to mask the pain, her eyes wide with shock and fear.

Brandon scrambled to his feet as Shibisaki twisted the blade left, then right, forcing a pocket of blood to explode from her mouth.

CHAPTER 59

O blivious to the madness unfolding beneath the statue in the sky, Jing Xiu shuffled inside his meditation chamber at the Po Lin Monastery and slowly went to ground.

The Buddhist monk rested in a seated lotus pose as he always did, a cup of sage burning at his side.

He used his consciousness of breath to calm his mind and drown out the frightening sound of wailing wind and bulleting rain bombarding the monastery.

Jing found himself frowning as an unknown presence suddenly disturbed him.

He hesitantly reached for his chest when he felt something cold arrive inside—something hard; something sharp.

He squeezed his eyes closed and breathed deeply, trying to shake off the uncomfortable sensation, working to settle himself when a stranger's voice demanded attention, a voice eager to occupy the spaces of his mind.

Jing turned his head when he felt the presence of a former being within.

The spirit of a man, he thought. An elderly man who was eager to commune, a man willing to go mind to mind.

"Elizabeth," the spirit whispered suddenly.

Jing repeated the words silently, then found himself wandering through pathways of strangeness and mystery, drifting through the alleyways of his mind.

Jing walked through stabbing beams of warm sunlight until he found himself at the gates of what appeared to be a school.

He walked up the stairs and pushed on the timber doors, curious as to what might lie on the other side.

Inside, he found sunlight showering the frail frame of an

elderly man who swept dried autumn leaves with a straw broom. Behind him, hoisted high up under the eaves of a building, was a sign.

Jing studied the oblong-shaped sign filled with Cantonese characters and found a circular drawing of a defending crane doing battle with an attacking snake.

"White Crane Wing Chun," he whispered to himself.

The unknown man smiled lovingly at his words. He slowly raised his hand and pointed toward the sky.

Jing gulped as the building and courtyard fell away behind the tip of the old man's finger, his eyes open wide, bearing witness to a distant place, somewhere far from the school walls of White Crane Wing Chun.

The sunlight disappeared with the buildings, and the sky transformed into a threatening mass of black, bringing with it the sound of racing winds and pouring rain.

Jing frowned when a young girl arrived in his eyes.

She was hurt, hunched over, with wet hair webbed across her face, her bloodied hands clutching at the tip of a ninjato sword protruding through her chest.

Jing grabbed at his chest as the cold, sharp pain he had felt earlier returned.

He shielded his eyes with his hands when a flicker of lightning illuminated a statue under the blackened sky. It was a god, his god: the mammoth, bronzed statue of Buddha Shakyamuni that was positioned a few hundred feet away from his beloved Po Lin Monastery.

The spirit of the elderly man effortlessly floated forward, as though on wheels, the wind and rain tearing at his clothing. He smiled at Jing as he approached. He slowed to a stop an arm's length short of Jing and whispered a name: "Elizabeth."

The vision finished just as quickly as it had arrived.

Jing rushed his eyes open and looked around his meditation chamber, taking a moment to gather his thoughts, staring at the flicking flame and burning sage at his side as the mammoth Buddha arrived behind his eyes.

Jing rose to his feet and shuffled across the chamber floor on autopilot, allowing deep feelings of hurt, love, and loss be his guiding light.

He slid open the chamber door and let the sounds of the storm come inside.

He closed his orange robe across his chest and stared through the ill-lit sky at the mammoth, bronzed statue of Buddha Shakyamuni.

He recalled the name spoken by the old man and whispered it softly to himself.

"Elizabeth."

CHAPTER 60

B randon charged across the statue platform, eyes bulging in their sockets as Shibisaki hauled the blade of his ninjato from Elizabeth's back.

He scooped up the ninja's escrima stick from where it had been discarded on the ground and brought it down on the ninja's forearm, shattering the bones on impact, forcing the blade to fall from his hand.

Brandon swapped the club for the ninjato and kicked Shibisaki in the chest, sending him onto his back.

He stepped over him, lifting his sword above his head, hands both clenched tight on the handle.

"Do it," said Kaiden. "Kill him."

Brandon hesitated for a moment, then brought down the ninjato down like a spear, driving the tip of blade into the Ghost Ninja's chest until the sword met with the concrete platform beneath him.

He took a breath and stood back, eyes transfixed in horror as Shibisaki clutched at the steel lodged in his chest, blood spouting from his mouth.

He stared back at Brandon and delivered a ghoulish smile as he started to fade, seeping into the atmosphere along with the departing storm in the sky.

Shibisaki was gone, leaving behind his weapon of death, the Japanese steel standing as still as a statue in the concrete beneath Buddha Shakyamuni.

Brandon looked up into the clearing skies, then turned to find Kaiden cradling a motionless Elizabeth in his arms.

"Elizabeth," Kaiden whispered. "Can you hear me?"

Her eyes flickered open. She was alive, but barely. "Elizabeth?"

She looked at the inspector and smiled. "I'm here."

Brandon moved in, placing his arm around Kaiden as he looked down at her broken form.

"Dad," she whispered. "Make sure Sifu is buried right—you know the place. Don't stick him in one of those godforsaken cemeteries. He'll come back and beat you."

Kaiden chuckled under his breath, forcing a smile as he desperately tried to hold back tears. He wiped a trickle of blood from his daughter's chin and caressed the side of her face.

"Dad," she whispered again, her eyes growing wide and distant, as if she was looking right through him, gazing into a realm beyond Lantau Island. She held out her hand and positioned her palm on Kaiden's chest, her eyes focusing on him one last time. "I forgive you."

Kaiden closed his eyes and squeezed her hand, nodding as he wept.

Brandon watched as Elizabeth gasped for air in short bursts, her eyes wide and still. He gently squeezed her shoulder and whispered.

"Elizabeth . . . everything is going to be okay. We'll be fine. You can rest easy now. We did it. We're safe."

Elizabeth reached out with her other hand and took Brandon's. He felt his lip tremble as she towed his hand into her chest.

Kaiden brushed back the hairs on his daughter's head and hauled her close as her eyes closed for the final time, looking like a child that had suddenly drifted off to sleep, calm, peaceful, and safe in her father's arms.

Brandon looked to the top of the staircase when a group of people arrived out of the blue. An army of monks stood on the platform, housed in orange robes, slowly stepping toward them, their hands held together in prayer.

"Kaiden, look."

Kaiden observed the arrival of the Buddhist monks from the

Po Lin Monastery as they formed a circle around the trio. They looked at Elizabeth, smiling peacefully.

Jing Xiu reached in and gently took her lifeless body from Kaiden's arms. The assisting monks pitched in, banding together to hoist Elizabeth overhead.

A child ran up the legs of his elders, balancing on their shoulder as he respectfully crossed Elizabeth's arms across her chest and positioned her legs neatly side by side.

Brandon helped Kaiden to his feet as the monks shuffled back toward the statue's staircase, carrying Elizabeth away on a bed of hands.

"Where are they taking her?" asked Brandon.

"To say goodbye in their own way," said Kaiden. "They'll take her to the Po Lin Monastery, where they'll shower her in prayer, cover her body in flowers, and say goodbye to her spirit."

Jing Xiu arrived to attend to Kaiden's arm. He removed the spent tourniquet. He peeled a fresh robe from a child's shoulder and took to the wound, providing a new bandage. He tied a new knot, then placed his hands together and bowed.

Kaiden and Brandon followed Jing until they arrived at the top of the staircase. There, they stood side by side, watching the stream of monks head for Po Lin Monastery as the morning sun showered Elizabeth's body in light, offering her one final sunrise.

"It's over," said Brandon.

Kaiden moved away from the staircase, watching the sun roll over the horizon of the South China Sea.

There, he found a cargo vessel in a wide space of ocean. He studied the bulk carrier as Chow's voice randomly arrived inside his head:

"*I keep the force off his back, and allow him to complete his deal.*"

"Wait a minute," Kaiden said suddenly. He wiped the tears form his eyes and took out the folded piece of paper from Zhang's warehouse.

"Jasper's Dream, February fifth," he said as he studied the deck of the vessel. "Brandon, what's the date?"

"Uh, the fifth. Why?"

Kaiden revisited the words in his head and closed his eyes.

"A code, a parade, a racehorse, a whore, a street name, a ship . . . holy shit," he said suddenly. Kaiden folded the paper and stuffed it back into his pocket. "We're not done yet. Shake it off. We've got one more. Come on."

Kaiden and Brandon stopped as a stream of Hong Kong Police officers took to the right side of the staircase, mountaineering in droves, guns drawn, eyes locked on their targets beneath Buddha Shakyamuni.

"Quickly, this way," said Kaiden.

Brandon went with Kaiden without arguing. As the pair turned their backs on Hong Kong Police, he wondered how they'd manage to evade their clutches in the dead end of Lantau Island.

CHAPTER 61

"Wong, Jackman," said Brandon as he plucked the taxi driver's ID from the dashboard and examined his thin black moustache. "I think Mr. Man is gonna be pissed when he returns to find Mr. Taxi long gone. Nice going, Inspector."

"Knock it off. We needed a ride."

They had been driving their new set of wheels for quite a while.

Just two hours earlier, they had made their descent off the back of the Tin Tian Buddha, taking to the Nei Lak Shan Country trail, using a canopy of trees as cover while police helicopters hovered overhead, unaware that they were below, backtracking to Tung Chung Station, where they commandeered Mr. Man's taxi.

"I can't believe you talked me into jumping off that ledge." Brandon examined the criss-cross of scratches down the right side of his face in the sun visor's mirror, feeling like he'd been ravaged by the claws of a bear. "Thought I would have learned my lesson after surviving that swan dive you talked me into taking back at White Crane."

"What did I tell you, hm?" answered Kaiden with a rise of the eyebrows. He lit a much-needed Chesterfield behind the wheel and clapped his lighter closed. "Grab onto a branch when you fall through the canopy—*not* bounce off every one of them like a marble in a pinball machine."

"Is that it?" pointed Brandon as Kaiden steered the taxi onto Stonecutters Bridge.

"Yeah. Kwai Tsing Container Terminal." Kaiden flipped down his visor and squinted at the morning sun.

"It looks busy," said Brandon as he watched a row of towering cranes pluck shipping containers from a berthed freight vessel.

"It's the eighth busiest container port in the world. Well over a thousand employees. Countless trucks, cranes, incoming and outgoing vessels—it's chaos. There are a multitude of diversions Zhang will be counting on to use as cover."

"Zhang's down there?" Brandon sharpened his eyes at the terminal.

"If my hunch is right, he is."

Kaiden blew out cigarette smoke, eyeing the rear-view mirror as he changed lanes.

Brandon shifted in his seat, his voice creeping up a notch as it all fell into place for him. "You think Zhang completed production of the money, don't you?"

"That's what I'm thinking, and if Zhang is down there on the docks, we can be almost certain that the money is, too, along with whatever cargo it is he's going to buy."

He handed Brandon the piece of paper he'd kept stuffed in pocket and waited while he unfolded it.

"Jasper's Dream, February fifth. What does it mean?"

"I think it's the name of a ship," said Kaiden.

"And I assume you've got some brilliant plan to sneak us inside? We can't exactly roll up to the front gate with our pictures plastered all over the news, now can we?"

Kaiden smirked at Brandon as he hit the indictor, drifting toward the exit lane for Kwai Tsing Container Terminal.

"Trust me."

CHAPTER 62

"This is your plan? Kaiden, can we talk for a second?"

Brandon followed Kaiden as he headed for the driver's side door, looking at the tyre iron in his hand.

"It's Fort Knox in there. Look!"

The entrance to Kwai Tsing Container Terminal looked more like a jail than a shipping hub. Its mammoth entrance was sealed by double fifteen-foot wire gates and viewpoint boxes that looked like gun towers positioned on either side, each housing armed security personnel who were scanning the entrance like motion detectors.

"Have you lost your mind? I mean, sending Wong Jackman's taxi on a driverless kamikaze mission is a touch much, don't you think?"

Kaiden replied with a wink as he proceeded to open the driver's side door.

"I guess not," Brandon said to himself. "*If* this even works, how the hell are we going to find Zhang once we're inside? It's gonna be like looking for a needle in a haystack."

Kaiden wedged the tyre iron handle between the driver's seat and the gas pedal of the taxi, sending its four-cylinder engine roaring into overdrive, like a standing car in pole position at a race track.

"Better back up over there, Brandon. The wheels will tear your legs clean off."

Brandon exhaled, anxiously eyeing the front gate as Kaiden reached through the driver's side window and placed his hand on the column shift. "Fire in the hole."

Click.

Kaiden tapped the column shift and set the needle hovering

over D for "drive" before jumping back out of the way. The driverless taxi was off, speeding on autopilot, barrelling down the entrance corridor to the terminal's gate.

"Halt! Stop your vehicle," a security guard hollered over a megaphone.

Brandon frowned when he observed the security guards from afar, their eyes growing wide, uniformed men and women parting like the sea, running for dear life as the taxi roared toward them.

The taxi must have been redlining when it barged through the gates of Kwai Tsing Container Terminal, tearing its fifteen-foot wire gates from their hinges, its rounded aluminium framework smashing into the viewing towers, forcing the armed occupants to jump for their lives.

"Quickly. This way," Kaiden slapped at Brandon's stomach and started to move, sticking close to the fence line, headed toward the now unmanned and obliterated entrance.

Brandon braked suddenly when he found a maritime security vehicle near the entrance. Inside, draped over the driver and passenger seats were matching security personnel jackets, each with their very own Kwai Tsing Container Terminal patch sewn onto their sleeves.

Brandon smashed the window with his elbow, shattering the glass in time with the explosion of the rogue taxi. Kaiden turned to find the taxi's front end buried in the belly of a shipping container, consumed by flames.

"One for you. One for me," said Brandon as he handed out the jackets. They fed their arms inside and continued toward the entrance, shielding their eyes from the flames.

"Inspector Tequila Yuen, Maritime Police," yelled Kaiden Chan as he arrived through the obliterated gates, shouting orders at the stunned security personnel, confidently waving his inspector's badge.

He dished out orders to wide-eyed security guards who, until today, hadn't ever dealt with anything more sinister than late container arrivals or malfunctioning entrance gates—much like the one Kaiden Chan had just destroyed.

"You, look at me," pointed Kaiden, singling out one of the guards. "All right, I want two groups. Group one will work with Fire Services. Highest priority: contain the blaze. I'm going to get very upset if I'm blown to pieces an hour from now because that fire spreads to our dangerous goods Terminal." The confused guard nodded, looking around for the rest of his designated group.

"Group two," Kaiden continued, pointing to another random guard. "Work on resealing our entrance gate. For God's sake, we can't have just anyone waltzing through the front door like they own the place. Move like you've got a purpose. Now, people!"

Brandon cringed as the taxi exploded again, its red-and-white paint now a thing of the past as flames ravaged the exterior, instantly turning the iconic Hong Kong taxi a dark charcoal black.

"You," pointed Kaiden, his eyes sharp and intimidating as he turned on yet another victim.

"Me?" answered the pimpled teen who looked as if this was his first day on the job.

"Yeah, you. Come with me. You're going to lead us to the operations tower."

CHAPTER 63

K aiden front-kicked the door to the operations tower and charged in, quickly flashing his inspector's badge, too fast for anyone who wanted to read it.

"That's a wrap, ladies and germs. We'll take it from here."

He gave the operations staff a verbal spray, filling their ears with a barrage of maritime and nautical terms—things of which he knew nothing about.

"Now, everybody out. Get your asses downstairs and secure that cluster fuck on the ground. I want the name of that taxi driver, even if we have to get a dentist on site to identify the body. Nobody messes with Kwai Tsing Container Terminal and gets away with it. No sir, not on my watch."

Kaiden shifted gears suddenly.

"You," he pointed. "Sit!" Kaiden arrived at one of the larger computer desks that housed the brains of the outfit, lowering the startled tech with his hand as the man rose in his chair.

"I need you to bring up the vessel schedule for the terminal. I want all arrivals and departures set for today."

The IT operator stared blankly at his computer for a second, then went to work, his hands still a little shaky from the exploding taxi outside.

"Here, take these." Kaiden held out a pair of binoculars. Brandon took them, eyeing the inspector with curiosity. "Look for anything that seems out of the ordinary, anything unusual."

"What the hell do I know about freight terminals?" Brandon asked.

"Learn."

Brandon looked out at the terminal, bringing the lenses to his eyes, scanning the outer limits of a container terminal that

LUKAS KRUEGER

appeared to be operating as normal, unrestricted by the explosion below.

Kaiden scanned the vessels on the monitor, trying to make sense of it all, following the miniature bulk carriers as they cruised across the screen like a video game.

"Let's narrow it down," he said. "Concentrate on ships coming from other parts of Asia. Exclude European vessels and arrivals from Australia."

"This could go a little quicker if you could tell me exactly what you're looking for?" said the operator.

"I'm not sure yet. Just do it." Kaiden glanced up to find Brandon at the operations window, scanning the terminal like a captain on a ship, peering through a mass pane of glass that looked like the windshield of a cruise liner. "How's that terminal looking, Brandon?"

Brandon shrugged in reply, still gripping the binoculars. "I don't know. I see trucks, boats, cranes . . . I don't know what I'm looking for."

"Just keep looking. I'll let you know if—"

Kaiden stopped mid-sentence when a picture on the front page of the South China Morning Telegraph caught his eye on the operator's desk. The border took up the entire page. Inside was a picture of a jet-black Carbine MP4 assault rifle, resting on a torn North Korean flag.

He lifted the folded newspaper, flicking away pens and notepads while the operator crunched his data. Kaiden read the article quietly, whispering the headline himself: "North Korean arms bunker gutted . . . hundreds of assault rifles, thousands of rounds of ammunition and explosives expected to hit the black market . . ."

"Okay, got all the names for the incoming arrivals," said the Operator. "Thirteen in total. Want me to prattle them off?"

"Yes, do that," said Kaiden, his eyes still glued to the newspaper.

250

"Albion Princess, Venetian Tiger, Silk Cobra, Parklee Island, Bozen Yokohama, Jasper's Dream, Sea Success—"

Kaiden lifted his eyes from the paper when a vessel name struck a chord. "Back up. What was that last one?"

"Sea Success?"

"No, the one before that?"

"Oh, Jasper's Dream."

"Jasper's Dream, Jasper's Dream . . . that's it." Kaiden repeated the name as he searched his pockets, pulling out the tiny piece of torn paper. "Jasper's Dream, February fifth."

Kaiden retrieved the newspaper from the desk and married the piece of paper with the news, reading the front-page title aloud, "North Korean arms bunker gutted . . ."

"Hey, Kaiden," yelled Brandon. "I'm seeing a dozen or so G.I. Joe lookalikes in the far corner of the terminal. Looks like they're unloading a heap of crates."

"G.I. Joe?"

"Yeah, you know, G.I. Joe—army-looking guys."

"Let me see that," said Kaiden as he stole the binoculars from Brandon's eyes, bringing them to his own to have a little look-see.

Inside the circular lenses, Kaiden found military personnel, infantry soldiers housed in camouflaged uniforms standing in a human chain, passing an endless line of crates from the belly of a berthed vessel onto a row of courier trucks.

"What's the origin of Jasper's Dream?" he asked the operator without turning.

The operator pecked at his keyboard and pressed on the bridge of his glasses. "Vessel arrived this morning. Cleared by our shipping agent, no issues. Vessel origin: Nampo, North Korea."

Kaiden frowned when a truck rolled past the rear of the vessel, revealing its name: Jasper's Dream.

"Could it really be that simple?" said Kaiden. He pulled the lenses from his eyes.

He handed the binoculars to Brandon and looked to where he'd set the newspaper article, the note from Zhang's warehouse lying on top. "What berth number is that vessel sitting at?"

"Berth Forty-Nine," answered the operator. "They have a planned departure window in ninety minutes."

Kaiden lifted his eyes form the newspaper and looked at the operator.

"Yeah, well, that plan's gonna change. Brandon, here," said Kaiden. He took a walkie-talkie from the operations comms desk and made it beep, flicking through the channels until he found one he liked.

"What are you doing?" asked Brandon.

"Setting the radio to a discreet channel, that way no one can listen to our comms."

He tossed the walkie-talkie into Brandon's hands and paired a Bluetooth earbud-style mic with the other, shoving it in his ear.

"You got me?" asked Brandon as he mashed his thumb into the button of the walkie-talkie.

Kaiden replied with a thumbs-up and turned to the operator.

"What's the range on these things?"

"Uh, about half a mile, I think?"

"Good," said Kaiden. "Pick up the phone and ask for Superintendent Yeung at the Kowloon Police Precinct." The operator took notes like a journalist, scribbling lines, armed with pad and pen. "Tell him you have a confirmed sighting of an Inspector Kaiden Chan that's been in the news: Berth Forty-Nine. Do it now. Brandon, let's go."

"Okay," Brandon replied immediately, walkie-talkie and binoculars in hand as he followed Kaiden out the door.

"You know there's gotta be like thirty guys on the ground out there, right?" said Brandon as the pair arrived outside. They started weaving through a cluster of terminal staff who were flagging down the incoming fire trucks, sirens wailing as they headed for Wong Jackman's burning taxi.

"Yeah. That's why you're gonna be my eyes," said Kaiden.

"How do you figure?"

"I want you up there," Kaiden said, pointing. Brandon gulped when he spotted the size of the container crane running high toward the clouds like a skyscraper, its long, straight arm reaching out to the waters of the terminal.

"Nah-uh," objected Brandon, shaking his head. "I'm going with you."

"Forget it. We didn't come all this way to let Zhang put a bullet in your skull."

The very mention of the name made Brandon's stomach turn. He thought of Lena and how he wanted revenge so badly, he could taste it.

CHAPTER 64

B randon's heart hammered in his chest as he climbed the endless ladder of the crane, moving toward a sky filled with bright whites and blues.

"Don't look down. Don't look down," he rambled on repeat, climbing through the rows of the ladder. Feeling a mile from the earth, he pulled himself onto the steel-grated platform and held on like he was bolted to it.

"I made it," he said with a sigh.

He pulled open the crane's cabin door and slipped inside, collapsing into the controller's chair, heaving in breath.

After a moment to recover, Brandon immediately went to work, scanning the terminal below, binoculars in one hand, walkie-talkie in the other, fishing for Kaiden through the lenses.

"Kaiden, you there?" he asked, mashing the button with his thumb. "I can't see you."

He ran the lenses over hundreds of shipping containers that were now the size of small cars.

"Over here," answered Kaiden, his voice arriving through the walkie-talkie. "Near a row of red shipping containers. Look to the west."

Brandon groaned in complaint. "I'm a tourist, moron. Which way is west?"

"Just look down and to the right."

"Then why not just say that to begin with!"

Brandon scanned the terminal, shifting the lenses to the right.

"Got ya," he said when he found Kaiden flattened against one of the containers, pressing on the earpiece against the right side of his face. "Now what?" asked Brandon.

"I'll need a boarding pass to get on the container ship."

Brandon thought for a handful of seconds, then pulled the lenses away from his eyes. "Guess a soldier's uniform will have to do."

He scanned the terminal again, in close proximity to Kaiden, searching for his ticket.

"There," he said suddenly, raising his eyebrows at the lenses. "Kaiden, behind you to the left, around twenty feet or so. There's a soldier, alone, on a cigarette break. There's your ticket."

"Okay," said Kaiden.

Brandon watched as Kaiden went to work, skimming through the rows of shipping containers until he found the lone soldier leaning against a container, repositioning the strap of his AK-47 as he blew out clouds of cancer toward the sky.

Brandon held his breath and rose in his chair as Kaiden arrived around the corner suddenly, elbowing the G.I. Joe looka-like in the face, knocking him out cold.

"Took ya long enough," laughed Brandon as he spoke into the walkie-talkie. "I would have kicked his face"

A few moments later, Kaiden emerged from the side of the container, housed in the soldier's North Korean uniform, AK-47 slung over his shoulder.

"That uniform suits you," joked Brandon.

Kaiden adjusted his earpiece and stabbed his eyes up at the crane. "It reeks of menthols and kimchi."

Brandon turned his face upside down, recalling the foul stench of fermented cabbage.

"Yuck. I hate that stuff."

"I'm going aboard," said Kaiden. "How's the entrance look?"

"Uh . . ." Brandon broke transmission when he spotted a cluster of armed soldiers crowding the ramp to Jasper's Dream. "Make sure that gun is fully loaded."

Brandon frowned as Kaiden approached the arrival ramp, watching him pluck the earpiece from the side of his head and tuck it into his camouflaged jacket. He nodded at the gathered soldiers as he headed for the ramp, keeping his eyes low, playing it cool.

The smirk faded from Brandon's face when one of the soldiers pulled on Kaiden's jacket and tossed him a nasty glance, one that stopped Kaiden Chan dead in his tracks.

Brandon held his breath as Kaiden turned to the soldier making a smoker's action with his fingertips. Kaiden smiled and fished for his Chesterfields. He looked in the pack and found he was down to his last one. "Keep the pack," he said with a friendly smile, his Korean a little rusty, but fair enough to get him over the line. Then he trudged up the ramp and disappeared into the belly of Jasper's Dream.

CHAPTER 65

K aiden made his way down a tight passageway, nodding at passing North Korean infantry headed in the opposite direction, clutching at their weapons, their cold, driven eyes hard as nails.

He panted as he moved, gasping for breath, trying to play it cool, worried that if any of the soldiers saw past his camouflaged costume, he'd be found floating face-down in the South China Sea.

The passageway through which he was navigating was long and straight, barely wide enough for his shoulders. It had grey steel walls studded with rivets—the kind one would find on a military vessel, only this wasn't.

Kaiden braked suddenly when he heard a loud commotion coming from a holding bay to his left. He spun the fly wheel and opened the hatch to take a peek.

Inside, Kaiden Chan acquainted his wide eyes with a large force of men and women a few thousand strong, armed to the teeth, gearing up in an armory as though preparing for World War III.

"Holy shit," he whispered as he scanned the mammoth-sized space the size of an auditorium, gulping while vast quantities of hands slapped magazines into submachine guns, holstered small arms by their hips, pulled on camouflaged Kevlar, laced up army-issued boots, and streaked army-green paint on their faces.

Kaiden pondered the news report he'd read and realised that the media outlet had been a little light on the details, neglecting to mention the fact that along with an endless supply of weapons, the person responsible for gutting the arms bunkers in North Korea had also swiped howitzer tanks, armed assault gunship helicopters, and dozens of missile trucks with rocket launcher pads bolted to their trays, neatly aligned in rows like they were about to partake in a military parade.

Kaiden leaned over the railing and listened as two North Korean soldiers shared a cigarette, marvelling at the arsenal, amused by the fact they were about to play their part in something very dark and sinister.

Kaiden felt the earpiece vibrating against his chest, like a phone receiving an incoming call on silent. He pinched the earpiece under his jacket and stuck it in his ear.

"Kaiden!" Brandon screeched. "Get up here. I've got eyes on Zhang!"

Saying nothing, Kaiden retreated back into the long, narrow hallway and closed the hatch, like he was concealing a dark secret. A million anxious thoughts raced through his mind as he headed back down the tight passageway: Hong Kong was about to be brutally invaded by an army of submachine guns, orange and yellow fire jumping from their gun barrels to tear holes in innocent citizens, while darting rockets and attack helicopters buzzed high overhead.

He plucked the door handle that would release him to the outside and squinted up at the sun, trying to gauge what section of the ship he had emerged from. He shimmied through a maze of shipping containers and tilted his head, shielding his eyes from the sunlight, searching for Brandon's crane up in the sky.

"He's on the bridge," said Brandon in Kaiden's ear. "And he's not alone."

Kaiden peeked around a corner and ran his eyes up a narrow staircase. He eyed the closed steel hatch that led to the bridge, worried about how many guns were inside.

"How many?" he whispered, shifting his eyes back to the crane as he pressed on his earpiece.

"Six in total. Four armed G.I. Joes, Zhang, and some older

dude in a military suit. Looks like he's in charge. His jacket is plastered in military ribbons."

Kaiden's eyes wandered as he thought, trying to piece it all together. He thought of Benny's counterfeiting plate, wondering if he could spoil the party by shedding some light on the North Koreans' newly obtained bills, which he was sure they'd now have.

"I'm going in," said Kaiden as he flicked off the safety of his AK-47 and took to the stairs.

"Get near the door," said Brandon. "I'll guide you from ther—" Kaiden pressed on his ear, stopping in his tracks when Brandon abruptly cut off.

He aimed his eyes back up at the crane. "Brandon, are you there?"

Kaiden's words died on his tongue as he felt a tiny gun barrel poke into his bum cheek, like a child was pressing the muzzle of a water pistol into his Kevlar.

He turned on the staircase and lowered his eyes to find Dozer's black-and-blue face smiling back at him, his stub-nosed pistol clenched tightly in his hand.

CHAPTER 66

K aiden inconspicuously unplugged his earpiece, then offered his open hands in submission.

"Gun," demanded Dozer with a flick of his stub-nosed pistol.

Kaiden did as instructed. He slowly unslung the AK-47 from his shoulder, hooked the strap onto the stair rail, and waited.

"Mr. Zhang will want to see you now," said Dozer, as a minute smirk arrived in the corner of his mouth. "Move."

Kaiden trudged up the narrow staircase, headed for the bridge, his fingers interlocked behind his head as he glanced up at Brandon's crane, realising what had caused his abrupt radio silence.

Upon the opening of the bridge door, Kaiden was granted a superb view of Stonecutters Bridge, along with the departure channel of Kwai Chung Container Terminal.

Jasper's Dream must be next in line, he thought. The clock was undoubtably ticking.

He eyed the container deck outside and took a peek at Brandon's crane, realising he now had a clear view of the bridge and everyone in it. He fantasised about a bolt-action Remington sniper rifle clutched in Brandon's hands, positioned high in the sky, winking at the enemy in the cross-hairs of the rifle scope, picking them off one by one so he could take control of the ship.

"Hoy," Dozer grunted in a bid for Zhang's attention.

Zhang turned away from the money cases, looking up in sync with General Myong-Su.

"Well, well, well, what do we have here?"

He repositioned the fur coat on his shoulders and walked toward Kaiden, his eyes narrowed to crinkled slits.

Kaiden felt his stomach turn when Zhang positioned the burning tip of his cigar about an inch from his frightened eyes, the glowing cherry close enough to sear the tender flesh on his face, the heat burning the wounds left by Shibisaki's ninjato.

Zhang plucked the torpedo-shaped beauty from his mouth and deliberately blew out a cloud of smoke, forcing the inspector to cough in fits.

"Kaiden Chan, I presume," said General Myong-Su as he arrived by Zhang's side, hands neatly pinned behind his back.

"That's Inspector Chan to you."

Zhang lifted his hand and slashed his knuckles across Kaiden's face in a backhand, splitting open his lip.

"I'm sorry?" smiled the general as Kaiden wiped blood from his mouth. "I didn't catch that."

He repositioned his head as one of his soldiers arrived to whisper an update in his ear. "Twelve minutes, General, and all infantry personnel will be armed and ready for Phase One."

The general flipped the Rolex on his wrist and nodded.

"Excellent," he said. "Three minutes ahead of schedule."

He turned his back on Kaiden and set his eyes on the cases of money, drooling over the rows of bills, smiling at the face of Benjamin Franklin. "Have the money taken below and seal it inside the foxhole. We depart this terminal at 1000 hours, sharp."

Kaiden watched as the soldiers swooped down on the cases, closing the hatches and locking the clips in place.

General Myong-Su turned to Kaiden and appraised him with his eyes. "How do we know he's alone?"

"He's alone," smiled Zhang. "Right now, Hong Kong Police are tearing the city apart to find him. Last I heard, our inspector here —the great Kaiden Chan—is a cop killer." Zhang took the cigar from his mouth and circled Kaiden like a shark.

"The news report said one Inspector Lindsey Chow was slain inside a Zhang Industries warehouse, but the slug in his chest matched our dear inspector's pistol, the one they found discarded on a platform at Central Station." Zhang stopped in time to meet Kaiden face to face. He raised his eyebrows and smiled.

"Am I right, Inspector?"

Kaiden sharpened his eyes at Zhang and lunged forward in attack.

"Arrrhh," he screamed when Dozer thundered his tiny fist into Kaiden's crotch, the tremendous crunch of testicles bringing him to his knees.

Zhang laughed out loud as Kaiden cradled his package.

"I have good news, Kaiden. Your miserable life is about to be over." He approached the wraparound windows of the bridge and stretched out his arms, eyeing Hong Kong in wonder.

"You shall have a front row seat to the revolution. In precisely ten minutes, Hong Kong as you know it will cease to exist and will be reborn by my design." He flashed Dozer a subtle grin and eyed the harbour in a daze. "We will take back the power from our cutthroat politicians, cutting them off at the knees, reverse their trends of corruption and self-serving greed."

"You won't get away with it," said Kaiden as he struggled to his feet.

"No?" Zhang turned away from the glass and flicked on a tiny TV monitor, showcasing the auditorium-sized armory in the belly of the container vessel, a sight already witnessed by Kaiden's eyes.

"As you can see, we have enough fire power to crush any possible defence scenario. It's already over. Beneath you, I have over four-thousand armed men and women ready to die for our cause."

Zhang turned his back on the monitor and raised a closed fist at Kaiden.

"My howitzer tanks will reduce skyscrapers to rubble. Our rockets will obliterate bridges, while our gunships will turn highway vehicles into scrap metal, and when the citizens of Hong Kong are sent running from the spine-tingling sound of gun chatter, echoing throughout the city, they too will know that within that final moment of breath, they were part of something greater than themselves. A revolution."

Kaiden took his eyes from Zhang's evil gaze and found Dozer analysing the earpiece poking out of his jacket. Kaiden watched him as he silently put two and two together, his tiny mind ticking in overtime as he turned toward the wraparound windows, searching for Kaiden's backup.

"That arsenal of yours must have cost a pretty penny," said Kaiden. "How exactly did you afford such a purch—"

Zhang hauled out his Heckler pistol and whipped Kaiden's face with the barrel, preventing him from letting the cat out of the bag. Kaiden fell to his knees, his mouth turning into a water-fall of blood.

"I'd love to stand around and watch you play executioner, Mr. Zhang, but I'm afraid some of us have places to be," said the general.

Zhang stuffed his Heckler away and pinned back the strings of hair on his head.

"Very good, General. I wish you a safe voyage."

They shook hands as Dozer scanned the container terminal with his tiny eyes, appearing confused as to where Kaiden's backup might be, unsure perhaps if he indeed had any at all.

That all changed when the sound of wailing police sirens floated over the bridge.

Kaiden sighed with relief and glanced at Zhang's worried face. He flashed him a "*gotcha*" smile.

"Quickly," ordered General Myong-Su, barking orders at his men. "Cut the lines! We are nothing but a memory inside of sixty seconds."

Zhang took his cigar from his mouth and marched out the

door, spouting words of reminder over his shoulder as he went. "Not until my merchandise and troops hit the docks, General."

Kaiden dropped to the floor and threw out his leg, sweeping Zhang to ground. He jumped to his feet and raced out of the bridge, closing the door behind him to the sound of AK-47 gunfire.

CHAPTER 67

B randon smiled through the lenses of his binoculars when he found Stonecutters Bridge overrun by a wave of red-and-blue sirens. The police vehicles sped in convoy, undoubtably headed for Kwai Tsing Container Terminal, responding to the operations tower employee who had dropped the name: Inspector Kaiden Chan.

He guided the lenses back to Jasper's Dream when the vessel's engines rumbled to life, the ass end of the ship churning seawater and vibrating in its entirety.

"Kaiden, they're making a break for it!" yelled Brandon as he thumbed the walkie-talkie, watching the North Korean troops run from the dock to board the ship in droves.

He found Kaiden sitting against the bridge door, feet firmly planted on the railing, fixing himself into a human barricade. "Tell me something I don't know!" groused Kaiden as he pressed the earpiece to the side of his face, jolting continuously as the North Korean soldiers trapped inside the bridge hammered at the door with the butts of their AK-47s.

The inspector tore a small section of pipe from the staircase railing, wedged it under the door lever and pulled, tearing the handle from the door to buy some more time, ensuring that Zhang and company would be confined to the bridge—at least for now.

"That'll hold 'em for a bit," said Brandon. "But we'll hav—"

Brandon unintentionally cut short his broadcast when he found Dozer standing on the bridge console, staring back at him with his very own set of binoculars, his tiny eyebrows moulded into a V.

Brandon felt his stomach turn as Zhang shouted voiceless

words at the glass, aggressively pointing at the crane. The general ushered his soldiers into an attack formation at the wraparound windows. They lifted the barrels of their AK-47s and winked at their target in the sky: Brandon Willis.

Brandon dove to the floor of the crane's cabin, heart stumbling over its own rhythm as the chatter of the AK-47s began, roaring wildly inside the bridge.

Scared out of his mind, Brandon curled himself tightly into a ball, screaming in time with the gunfire, his arms pinned overhead, reeling his head toward his chest.

He was terrified, but he needn't have been.

Confused by the lack of bullets that should have sprayed the crane cab in its entirety, Brandon gazed around, inspecting the unmarked panels of glass with wide eyes.

How could they have missed? he thought. He crawled across the cabin floor to a window, sneaking a peek at the ship to find widespread cracks in the wraparound windows that ran all the way to the edges of their fames.

Brandon blew out a breath when he found Zhang and General Myong-Su cursing at the soldiers and their insufficient assault rifles, their bullets unable to penetrate the glass panels of Jasper's Dream, unaware that the bridge was heavily fortified and had been provided with bulletproof glass to thwart pirate attacks and the ferocious strength of rogue waves.

Brandon scooped the binoculars and walk-talky from the cabin floor and returned to his feet, rushing the lenses to his eyes, eager to get eyes back on Kaiden. He flinched when the barking AK-47s started up again inside the ship. He dropped his gaze to the bridge door and found the gunfire was obliterating the door hinges.

"Kaiden, the door. They're about to escape."

Kaiden reached the bottom of the staircase and retrieved his surrendered AK.

He turned back to the staircase, yanked on the barrel, and

took aim at the door, showering the doorway with bullets as it fell from its hinges, forcing Zhang and company back inside the bridge.

"Kaiden, the ship's moving!" yelled Brandon as Jasper's Dream tore its stable lines from the docks.

He shifted the binoculars from stow line to stow line, watching the concrete anchor points crumble under the departing force of the ship.

Kaiden screamed into the headset as he and the soldiers exchanged fire, barrels spouting orange flames in a collision of bullets that rained down the narrow staircase, narrowly missing one another, bullets whizzing by overhead as rounds clunked into nearby shipping containers and steel stairs.

Brandon gulped, realising they were only seconds from disappearing as the ship pulled away from its berth. Zhang's plan had gone up in smoke. His army of troops and their vehicles were trapped on board, headed back out to sea. But that also meant Zhang and his crew would get away.

Looking around for options, Brandon spotted the arm of his crane hanging stationary over the departure channel. His eyes went back and forth, his mind ticking into overdrive as he looked from the departing ship to the crane arm.

"Fuck it," he said out loud. He dumped his binoculars on the ground and jumped into the driver's seat, anxiously scratching his head at the blinking control panel. He started flicking switches and jerked at the control sticks, forcing the sound of winding and grinding from the mechanics of the crane, like someone who was learning to drive a stick for the first time.

"Shit!" he shouted into the walkie-talkie. "Kaiden! Help me move this stupid crane." he looked down and found Kaiden prying his eyes away from his AK-47. He lifted the barrel toward the crane's cockpit and winked into the sights.

"Get down," Kaiden roared into his headset. Brandon ducked as gunfire raced toward him, showering the arm of the crane, obliterating its supports, the breaking metal dull, but loud, like hammer hits.

The crane arm slid down its runners and stopped in midair with a thud, its welded framework hovering, hanging on by just the obliterated wires, swaying directly into the oncoming path of Jasper's Dream.

Brandon scooped up the binoculars and watched as the bridge of the ship erupted in panic.

Zhang drew his Heckler and roared wildly at the shattered glass, popping off shots into the wraparound windows of the bridge as Jasper's Dream headed for collision.

With only seconds remaining until impact, Zhang pocketed his Heckler and tossed Dozer into the shattered glass, using his rounded concrete frame as a human wrecking ball.

Brandon followed Dozer through the lenses as he broke through the glass and bounced from container to container like a medicine ball before landing in the waters of Kwai Tsing Container Terminal.

"Zhang is gonna make it," yelled Brandon as he watched him haul his fat frame though the Dozer-sized hole in the glass. He dropped onto the roof of a shipping container and jumped for his life.

General Myong-Su and his soldiers went down fighting, emptying their remaining magazines into the windows as the crane arm shaved off the top of Jasper's Dream, causing the bridge to erupt in an explosive fireball, burning them all alive.

Brandon exited the crane cab and shielded his face with his shirt, coughing uncontrollably at the blackened fumes that looked as though they were pluming from the mouth of an erupting volcano.

He looked down in search of Kaiden, frowning at the drifting swirls of smoke.

"Hey," said Kaiden through the walkie-talkie.

Brandon smiled when he found the inspector out and on his

feet, trudging along the docks like a three-legged dog, the AK-47 still gripped tightly in his hands.

Brandon gave him a thumbs-up.

He moved into position and was preparing to climb down the ladder when he saw Zhang's balding head arrive at the base of the runners. Hauling his Heckler pistol from his drenched fur coat, using the smoke as cover, he took aim at Kaiden and fired.

Brandon froze on the ladder as the scene unfolded in black-and-white, the same paralysing fear he'd experienced in Yuen's store returning with the force of a blast wave, seeping into his bones as the unmistakable sound of Johnathan Zhang's firearm spent a single round. He closed his eyes, depriving himself of the starburst of blood he feared was about to exit the crown of Kaiden Chan's head.

CHAPTER 68

B randon clutched tightly at the ladder, crippled by the intoxicating fear that froze every muscle in his body. Squeezing his eyes shut, he flinched as the echo of Zhang's shot ricocheted throughout the terminal.

Finally, he steeled himself and summoned the courage to peer down over his shoulder, searching through the blanketed haze of drifting smoke, fearing that the man he'd grown to respect was now dead, lying flat on his back on in a pool of his own blood.

The wandering smoke revealed a motionless Kaiden Chan, Brandon's greatest fear now realised. The inspector lay sprawled out on his back, the loaded AK-47 resting by his side.

Brandon frowned at the sight and turned away, resting his head on one of the ladder rungs, heaving in breath.

Standing still as a statue on the ladder, Brandon felt his anger boil inside him. He squeezed the rails of the ladder, his knuckles cracking loudly from the uncontrollable force in his hands as rage consumed him.

Ready to take control of the chaos, Brandon positioned his feet on both sides of the ladder and released the tension in his hands. He raced towards the earth, sliding down the rails at the speed of a missile.

Arriving at the base of the ladder, Brandon stabbed both his feet into the crown of Zhang's head, sending his fat frame to ground, forcing the pistol to jump from his hands.

Brandon stared at the nickel-plated gun as he jumped to the ground. It lay alone in the drifting smoke, just aching to be held. He took hold of the blackened grip, scraping the barrel across the concrete.

Growling at Zhang with wild eyes, Brandon considered how

fitting it would be for the Cantonese mob boss to be finished by his adored gun, a gun that suddenly felt at home in his hands.

He thought about the unnecessary loss of life, the hearts and minds of loved ones and strangers swelling inside his head like a storm, arriving in sporadic frames like a series of post-mortem photographs: Benny, Lena, Inspector Chow, Sifu, Elizabeth—people who were all gone due to this vile, self-serving parasite of a man, to this the individual lying before him. Johnathan Zhang.

Brandon flinched in shock when Zhang groaned in complaint, sitting up, clutching at his aching head.

He muted his groan and smirked at Brandon's seething eyes when he found his Tacargi executioner wobbling in his hand.

"You like that gun, Brandon?" he hissed. "It suits you."

Brandon lifted the muzzle of the Heckler and guided the sights to the middle of Zhang's forehead.

Zhang went to work, using his narcissistic toolkit in an attempt to bend Brandon's youthful mind.

"You ever shoot someone, Brandon? Hmm?" He hauled a cigar from his fur coat and lit it. "It takes a real man to pull that trigger."

Zhang blew out a puff of smoke and smiled at the barrel as the wailing sirens in the background grew louder.

"Better hurry," he said. "Once those boys in blue arrive, you'll have missed the opportunity, and I'll be back on the streets within a week."

Fearing the inside of a cage, Zhang decided to tighten the screws, hoping to go out in style.

"Do it, Brandon. Make your mother proud. You owe her that." He took a sideways glance at the arriving police cars, knowing that time was running out.

"I wish she had survived," he said, suddenly in a panic, poking at the one wound he figured would get Brandon to take the shot. "Just knowing she would have spent the rest of her days rotting away like a vegetable in some rock garden would have filled my insides with joy."

Brandon sharpened his eyes and compressed the trigger, preparing to punch Zhang's brains out the back of his skull, when a familiar voice arrived from behind.

"Don't do it, Brandon," ached the voice. "He's not worth it."

Brandon glanced his over shoulder with his bloodshot eyes and found a battered Kaiden Chan, barely alive, barely able to stand, clutching at his right shoulder, the one Zhang had just put a bullet in.

He held out his hand and locked eyes with Brandon, pleading.

"Give me the gun, Brandon."

Brandon glanced down at Kaiden's blood-soaked hand, then studied the grave concern in his eyes. "Come on. Give me the gun," he repeated.

Wrestling with his hate, Brandon hesitantly raised the Heckler in a bid to relinquish it.

Zhang snickered at him. "Coward."

Brandon's eyes grew huge. Drifting on autopilot, he guided the muzzle of the Heckler back towards Zhang's forehead, enraged by the taunt. Again, he found himself compressing the trigger, this time gripping the handle tightly with both hands, winking at the sights, jaw tightly clenched.

"Brandon . . ."

The plea was nothing more than a breath, but it was enough. Brandon moved the pistol, guided the sights down onto Zhang's knee and fired, forcing a bullet to punch through the cartilage and out through the back of his leg.

"Oops," laughed Brandon as Zhang let out a torturous scream that echoed throughout the container terminal. Brandon looked at Kaiden and shrugged, giving the inspector a smile. "Sights must be off."

Kaiden shook his head in reply and tried to hide the tiny smirk that grew in the corner of his mouth.

Turning, Brandon peered out into the waters of Kwai Tsing Container Terminal, breathing deeply, glad for the brief reprieve, watching while Jasper's Dream was swarmed by a barrage of fire boats spouting long arcs of seawater at the burning vessel.

Maritime Police pitched in, rounding up Zhang's rent-a-army that were abandoning ship by the dozens, jumping for their lives into the ocean below.

"Wow, hey," said Brandon as Kaiden fell to the ground, stabling the barrel of his AK-47 into the dock, using it as a crutch to keep him from colliding face first with the concrete.

"I got you," he said as he caught the torn inspector in his arms. "I got you, partner."

Brandon watched Kaiden's eyes roll into the back of his head, his face turning as white as paper. "Help," he screamed.

He reached for Kaiden's blood-splattered neck, desperately searching for a pulse that wasn't there.

"Help me!" he screamed again.

He lowered Kaiden to the ground, talking to him throughout, holding him tightly in his arms while clusters of police and EMTs bolted toward his cries for help, arriving through the wandering smoke of Jasper's Dream like they were running through a brush fire, their guns and badges drawn, ambulance kits bolted to their hands.

"Let me go," yelled Brandon as Hong Kong Police tore him away from Kaiden, viciously rolling the inspector onto his belly with blatant disregard for his injuries, treating him like a piece of trash, like the low-life, cop-killing scumbag they thought he was.

Brandon fought against the tide, struggling to fend off four uniformed cops that worked as one to subdue him, clenching his teeth nearly hard enough to crack them, every muscle aching with anger as he roared against their grip.

"Let him go! He's been shot," he pleaded, trying to place one of the armed officers in a wrist lock.

"It's okay, Brandon. Calm down," assured Ethan as Brandon went to ground.

"Ethan?" said Brandon when he saw the uniformed ambulance officer who'd helped his mum. "Ethan! Kaiden's not breathing. I felt for a pulse, but there wasn't one. He's been shot."

"That man is injured," screamed Anna Lee as she swooped in on Kaiden, ambulance kit in hand, peeling the uniformed cops from his breathless body. "Back off. Let him go."

Brandon watched as the cops relinquished their hold, allowing Anna Lee to roll the inspector's lifeless body onto his back. She quickly checked for vital signs, ordering the officers to remove the cuffs.

Brandon watched as Anna Lee placed an open ear on his chest, listening for anything that went boom.

"Ethan, there's no heartbeat," she yelled, requiring assistance. "We're gonna need to begin CPR."

"Okay," he said, peeling a stethoscope from around his neck.

He took up a position opposite Anna Lee, and together, they went to work on Kaiden Chan. Ethan interlocked his fingers across Kaiden's sternum, counting out loud as he shifted up and down with chest compressions.

CHAPTER 69

B randon was running on fumes, exhausted by emotion, spent from the torturous, marathon-like pursuit that must have covered most of Hong Kong. He flattened himself against the wall of the moving ambulance, his face smeared by the blackened smoke of Jasper's Dream, his defeated, bloodshot eyes aching from a concoction of diesel fumes and tears.

He stared at the empty spaces inside Anna Lee's ambulance and went back in time, remembering where Lena had been parked while in transit to the Harbour Grand Hotel, watching Anna Lee haul Mr. Kile's deadly dagger from Kaiden Chan's forearm.

He rubbed at his grief-stricken face, smudging the diesel fumes across his skin, bowing his head toward the floor, accepting that everyone had now left him, accepting that he was now all alone.

Turning his head in his hands, Brandon peered through the windshield, watching as the ambulance probed through the congested Hong Kong traffic, Anna Lee riding shotgun, Ethan clutching at the wheel, tooting the horn and pleading for a clear path.

"I thought we were going to the hospital?" asked Brandon as he cleared the toxic diesel fumes in his throat. He watched the hospital sign whisk by and decided that Ethan had missed the turn.

Saying nothing, Anna Lee and Ethan smiled at one another before turning their eyes back to the road.

For Brandon, it felt like déjà vu as the ambulance suddenly veered off the main road and pulled into a downhill drive. He watched a roller door rise, revealing a garage of fluorescent lights and parked ambulances. It felt like the ambulance was arriving in the belly of yet another Harbour Grand all over again, sneaking underground, rolling in quietly on arrival, hidden away from public eye.

Ethan guided the ambulance between two white lines, put it in park, and killed the engine.

Brandon gulped as Anna Lee and Ethan turned back, smiling at him, saying nothing.

"What's going on?" he asked. "What is this?"

Ethan and Anna Lee looked at one another, then back at Brandon.

"I think it'll be easier if we just show you," said Ethan.

Brandon found himself holding his breath as Ethan and Anna Lee got out of the ambulance, their behaviour odd to his weary eyes.

He faced the rear double doors of the ambulance as they opened, watching the expressionless faces of Ethan and Anna Lee standing side by side, staring back at him.

"This way," said Anna Lee.

The ambulance officers parted at the seams, offering Brandon a clear path out of the ambulance.

He placed himself on mute as he followed Ethan and Anna Lee, a million thoughts running through his mind: *it's another trap. Ethan and Anna Lee aren't who they said they were. Another twisted extension of Johnathan Zhang, spies on his payroll, just another version of the phony airport marshal.* The one that helped Dozer, Mia and Mr. Kile storm the Medical Services flight at Hong Kong International.

Nevertheless, he followed, acting purely on instinct, accepting the idea that a gun might be put to the wall of his brain, realising he now had nothing and no one to live for.

Anna Lee and Ethan arrived at door and stopped, looking

back at him. Brandon frowned at the plaque screwed the the door panel: "*Storage Room.*"

Anna Lee watched him, smiling with tear-filled eyes as she opened the door.

Brandon quickly found his face in his hands when the storage room interior revealed a sight for sore eyes.

Unable to make eye contact, he shuffled across the floor, his eyes gooey with tears.

He arrived beside a bed and held out his hand, holding it in midair, hesitant to touch, fearful that it was just a cruel dream, one designed by the wicked and callous mind of Johnathan Zhang, or the twisted, dark magic of the Ghost Ninja.

Slowly, unable to watch, he lowered his hand and felt the warm skin on Lena's hand, resting peacefully by her side.

He opened his eyes and found her chest rising up and down, unassisted from the transport ventilator that had been retired. He looked at her closed eyes and observed the warm colour in her cheeks.

Anna Lee floated forward and whispered in Brandon's ear.

"When we heard the news about the death of Inspector Chow, we decided we had no choice but to move Lena. Though the Hong Kong Police's first search of the Harbour Grand turned up empty, we feared the rat in the force would learn of her location, so we staged her death, acting it out with Kenneth for any spying eyes that could have been wandering around the hotel looking for her."

Brandon wiped a rogue tear from his check and squeezed Lena's hand.

"We knew that if we pretended to kill her, Zhang and his men would abandon their search for her."

Ethan arrived by Brandon's side, squeezing his shoulder with a warm smile, a smile that said everything was gonna be all right.

Brandon touched the corners of his eyes in turn, unwilling to let go of Lena's hand as he wiped away the rows of tears on his cheeks.

He faced Anna Lee and Ethan and muttered two small, inadequate-feeling words: "Thank you."

B randon made his way through the honeycomb alleyways of Hong Kong Island, using memory to light the way. The maze of walkways made him think of Kaiden Chan, of the night he guided him from shadow to shadow, using what remained of the night to sneak through the streets undetected.

He arrived at a stream of red-and-white taxis and looked at the oblong-shaped sign filled with Cantonese characters across the road. He studied the circular drawing of a defending crane doing battle with an attacking snake and knew he was back at White Crane.

When the traffic broke, he jogged across the road, intending to knock on the closed school gates, eager to start his Wing Chun journey with the teacher who had been rumoured to take over the school, carrying forth the torch of White Crane Wing Chun, passing down its teachings to the next generation of practitioners.

He held off knocking when the sounds of training arrived in his ears. Instead, he stood at the gates, smiling as bellowing yells came from inside the walls of White Crane.

He looked at the neighbouring bamboo scaffold and smiled.

A handful of seconds later, Brandon found himself climbing through the rows of bamboo, mountaineering toward the sky. He took position on a timber platform and looked inside the belly of White Crane, watching men, women, boys, and girls moving through the fixed positions of White Crane, punching and kicking the air, moving in sync to the commands of a man teaching the class.

Brandon smiled, preparing to climb down when a folded

newspaper resting beside a construction worker's lunchbox caught his eye:

BONE MARROW TRANSPLANT
SAVES YOUNG BOYS LIFE

In exchange for smoking privileges during his life sentence, former mob boss Johnathan Zhang donates bone marrow, saving the life of fallen police inspector, Lindsey Chow's son.

Brandon ran his finger across the page as he whispered the report to himself. He looked down at the black-and-white photo and found a picture Lei Chow sitting up in his hospital bed, smiling for the reporter's camera in his gown, his tiny thumb pointed up toward the ceiling.

Another photograph showed Lei's late father, Inspector Lindsey Chow, saluting the camera in uniform, back when he was a young Hong Kong Policeman fresh out of the academy.

Brandon turned the page with a smile and read a new title.

CHARGES DROPPED AGAINST
POLICE INSPECTOR KAIDEN CHAN

An independent panel of Hong Kong Police yesterday dropped all charges against Police Inspector Kaiden Chan, after the testimony of an unknown murder witness who helped to foil the terrorist plot of criminal mastermind, Johnathan Zhang, helping to seize thousands of illegally imported weapons, along with millions in counterfeit bills that were seized at Kwai Tsing Container Terminal last month.

Brandon lifted his eyes from the page as the White Crane students shuffled their feet and neatly fell into long rows, like they were standing at attention for a commanding officer in the military.

From under the eaves of White Crane Wing Chun, Kaiden Chan emerged, hobbling across the quadrangle with Sifu's cane, his right arm still in a sling from Zhang's bullet.

Brandon set the newspaper aside and observed the freshly shaven skin and glowing complexion of Kaiden Chan. He looked a picture of health, shining with every week of sobriety he now held under his belt.

He turned to his newly obtained students and happily smiled.

Then he turned his back to the class and eyed a vase of burning incense set beneath two glass-framed photos evenly positioned side by side on the wall: Sifu and Elizabeth Chan.

Brandon stood, rising to his feet on the timbered platform, and joined the class from afar, slapping his hands by his sides to bow respectfully in time with Kaiden Chan and the students of White Crane.

CHAPTER 71

T he sun was halfway down the horizon as the waters of Stanley Bay glimmered in time with a gentle twilight breeze. Brandon sat on a bench seat with his toes in the sand, flicking at the obliterated remains of sea shells that were scattered throughout the beach.

He looked out at the calm ocean and sighed with relief, the horrific ordeal of his arrival now in his rear-view mirror.

He breathed in through his nose, taking in the fresh, salty air of Stanley Bay, feeling a hundred million miles from any kind of self-doubt, like at last, he was where he belonged. He felt at peace, a feeling he'd once taken a needle to his arm for.

He opened his mouth and emptied his lungs, smiling at the speckles of sunlight that bounced off the ocean.

"What the hell?" Brandon said suddenly as a screeching sound arrived in his ears. He glanced up into a crooked Indian almond tree that was running overhead.

He rose and moved around the thick trunk of the tree, trying to pinpoint the screech.

He smiled when a long-tailed macaque emerged from a bushy branch, its beady eyes wild and frightened.

"Franco," he whispered. "Come on." He held out his hands, like he was coaxing a small child.

Franco looked at him for a moment, then bolted down the tree and leapt into Brandon's hands. "Hi, buddy," he said as Franco ran up his arm and took position on his shoulder.

"I was wondering where you had got off to."

He pulled a tiny banana from his pocket and sent it north, placing it in Franco's tiny hands. His eyes wild with hunger,

Franco eagerly nabbed the banana with a screech and started to peel.

"Come on, buddy. Time to go home."

Brandon and Franco took to the corridor of Stanley Market, navigating their way through a wave of bustling tourists, headed for a particular market stall, one that specialised in calligraphy scrolls and works of art.

He read the sign overhead as they approached: *"Yuen's Engravings."* He frowned as he noticed the market janitor climbing a ladder to take it down.

"Whoa, wow. What are you doing?" Brandon asked.

He let a couple of shopping tourists through and approached the ladder.

"I thought you'd want the sign taken down," replied the janitor.

Brandon looked at the sign again and shook his head. "The sign stays, understood?"

He looked at the janitor with serious eyes and waited for a nod of approval.

The man shrugged. "Hey, you're the boss."

He climbed back down the ladder and fetched a clipboard from his tool bag.

"Market manager said I'm supposed to get you to sign this, so here you go."

Brandon took the clipboard from the janitor's hand and read the heading at the top of the page: *"Store Lease – Stanley Market."*

Brandon slid the pen out of the board holder and drove the ball point to the paper.

"Are you sure you want to do this?" urged the janitor. "I hear you have some pretty big shoes to fill."

Brandon smiled at the janitor and scribbled his signature, locking himself into a twelve-month lease.

"Absolutely," he said confidently, with a wide smile.

He slapped the pen onto the clipboard and passed it back to the janitor.

"Cute monkey," the man said. "What's his name?"

"His name is Franco, and I am Brandon."

"Oscar," he said. "Is that a New Zealand accent?"

Brandon fixed his lips to reply when the roller door to Yuen's Engravings rolled up suddenly.

"Brandon, where do you want me to set up these tables?" asked Anna Lee, almost unrecognisable outside of her ambulance uniform.

"Um, up in the back," he said. He smiled at the janitor and then ducked inside to help. He weaved past a handful of tradesmen who were busy plastering the walls in fresh coats of paint, and arrived at Yuen's timber desk, finding it just as he had left it weeks ago: littered with jars of used brushes and streaks of paint. Only this time, it housed a different artist in the making: Lena Willis.

"Brandon, I can't do this," laughed Lena. "I'm a history professor, not an artist."

Brandon pulled a blank canvas from a drawer and slid it onto the desk's face, covering Lena's butchered attempt.

"Come on. Trust me, there's nothing to it," said Brandon as Anna Lee and Ethan arrived at the desk.

"Clear your head," he said.

Brandon followed the lines of a Chinese character on the wall with his finger, repeating the tutelage of Yuen Lau.

"Study and memorise the character, feel its shapes and curvature, notice the beauty in its lines. So simple, yet so perfect. You see?"

Lena doubtfully shrugged. "Yeah, I guess so."

"Now, close your eyes."

Lena did as directed and waited for Brandon's instruction. He leaned in toward her ear and whispered, "Now, draw."

"Are you serious?" joked Lena, her eyes still closed. "I'll paint all over this beautiful desk if my eyes are closed."

Brandon spoke softly. He moved from side to side behind Lena, using a calm tone to help ease all doubt.

"The mind must be calm and tranquil, like a still pool, for creativity to unconsciously emerge. Be calm and still like tranquil pool."

"Okay . . ."

"Breathe in, and out," Brandon repeated softly. "Calm your mind. Consciousness of breath is everything." He paused and turned to the canvas.

Lena slowly reached out and pulled a brush from one of the jars, her eyes still closed. She dipped its bushy head into a cartridge of black paint and gently wiped its edges.

Brandon shared a smile with Ethan and Anna Lee as Lena effortlessly guided the brush to the canvas unassisted. She drew the lines perfectly, running the brush tip sideways, then up and down on the canvas. She made the final stroke and flicked the tip of the brush head on the edge of the canvas as if she had done it a thousand times before.

Brandon stared at a framed photograph of Yuen on the wall. He smiled as the words of Yuen Lau came running back to him:

"Remember, if the mind is calm, clear, and relaxed, it can be free to accomplish whatever it desires."

Brandon winked at the photo, then turned to greet a group of tourists who'd entered the store.

Epilogue

B raving the never-ending Hokkaido blizzard, Sujin Yamamoto stepped out into the bitter cold, hauling his hooded rags overhead as he stood on the steps of Kinjo Temple.

He crunched his way through the knee-deep snow, battle axe in hand as he made his way to an enormous woodpile.

Once there, he brought the threatening steel axe down from overhead, separating timber blocks in half on the chopping block, cringing against the hellish winds until an unknown presence disturbed him.

He turned suddenly, heaving in breath, shielding his eyes from the racing snow, gripping the axe tightly in his frozen hands.

He inventoried his surroundings, scanning the open spaces of white and snow, driving his good ear toward the howling winds, trying to detect sounds and movements that weren't his own.

Failing to discover anything, he delivered the axe head into the chopping block and knelt in the snow, stacking the timber logs in his arms like a tiny earth mover.

Sujin made it back to the stairs of Kinjo Temple and started stepping through the rows of racing rats, tackling the stairs one by one, when the sound of crunching footsteps arrived behind him.

Sujin stood still as a statue for a handful of seconds, as if he, the caretaker, had been startled by a ghost.

He turned at the sound and pulled down the frayed rag that was concealing his face.

Sujin Yamamoto smiled.

About Author

Lukas Krueger was born and raised in the state of New South Wales, Australia.
In addition to writing novels, Lukas is also passionate about cinema, dabbling in both film direction and screenwriting.
He prides himself as someone who is an honest story teller, someone who only considers the art of fiction during the process of creation, a story teller who prefers on leaving the rules of society at the door when he writes.
For Lukas books and cinema have, and will always be about escapism, art and emotion.

Influences include: Neo-noir, punk rock, cinema, family, nonlinear, love, film score, and heavily distorted guitars.

Printed in Great Britain
by Amazon

72813254R00180